SHATTERED LIVES

Orphaned as children, sisters Hannah and Julie were either ill-treated or left to their own devices. Hannah was always the more sensible of the two and now, happily married with a steady job, her determination to succeed has paid off. The same cannot be said for Julie. Easily led by the wrong crowd, she drifted apart from Hannah when she fell pregnant at fifteen and the sisters eventually lost contact. Now, with three children from three different men and surviving on benefits, Julie is living a life of misery and drug addiction. She needs help and it's up to her sister to step in, but in doing so Hannah discovers to her horror that her own life might not be so perfect after all . . .

Books by Bernardine Kennedy
Published by The House of Ulverscroft:

MY SISTERS' KEEPER
OLD SCORES
PAST CHANCES

SPECIAL MESSAGE TO READERS

This book is published under the auspices of

THE ULVERSCROFT FOUNDATION

(registered charity No. 264873 UK)

Established in 1972 to provide funds for research, diagnosis and treatment of eye diseases. Examples of contributions made are: —

A Children's Assessment Unit at Moorfield's Hospital, London.

•

Twin operating theatres at the Western Ophthalmic Hospital, London.

•

A Chair of Ophthalmology at the Royal Australian College of Ophthalmologists.

•

The Ulverscroft Children's Eye Unit at the Great Ormond Street Hospital For Sick Children, London.

You can help further the work of the Foundation by making a donation or leaving a legacy. Every contribution, no matter how small, is received with gratitude. Please write for details to:

**THE ULVERSCROFT FOUNDATION,
The Green, Bradgate Road, Anstey,
Leicester LE7 7FU, England.
Telephone: (0116) 236 4325**

**In Australia write to:
THE ULVERSCROFT FOUNDATION,
c/o The Royal Australian and New Zealand
College of Ophthalmologists,
94-98 Chalmers Street, Surry Hills,
N.S.W. 2010, Australia**

Bernardine Kennedy was born in London but spent most of her childhood in Singapore and Nigeria before settling in Essex, where she still lives with her husband Ian. She also has a son, Stephen, and daughter, Kate. Her varied working life has included careers as an air hostess, a swimming instructor and a social worker. She has been a freelance writer for many years, specialising in popular travel features for magazines.

BERNARDINE KENNEDY

SHATTERED LIVES

Complete and Unabridged

CHARNWOOD
Leicester

First published in Great Britain in 2008 by
Headline Publishing Group
An Hachette Livre UK Company
London

First Charnwood Edition
published 2009
by arrangement with
Headline Publishing Group
An Hachette Livre UK Company
London

British Library CIP Data

Kennedy, Bernadine.
Shattered lives
1. Sisters- -Fiction. 2. Unmarried mothers- -Fiction.
3. Women drug addicts- -Fiction. 4. Large type books.
I. Title
823.9′2–dc22

ISBN 978–1–84782–730–2

Published by
F. A. Thorpe (Publishing)
Anstey, Leicestershire

Set by Words & Graphics Ltd.
Anstey, Leicestershire
Printed and bound in Great Britain by
T. J. International Ltd., Padstow, Cornwall

This book is printed on acid-free paper

For my family, as always

1

'It's on days like these that I get really pissed off with this job,' Hannah Durman muttered as she slammed the phone back on to its base before pushing her chair back and standing up. 'I've got all these files to write up before I can leave, and there's the inevitable end-of-day emergency and I really don't want to tackle any of that crap right now. I hate social work! I want a job with no stress.'

'Tell me about it!' Her colleague Barry laughed and patted the teetering pile of files on his own desk. 'Every day in every way the queue gets longer, the staff get fewer, and the file mountain gets higher . . . but at least you can never say it's boring here.'

Hannah snatched up a bulging diary and a notebook from her desk. 'Actually boring would be nice sometimes. Especially today when I shouldn't even be here. We're leaving for the airport at five tomorrow morning and I haven't packed yet . . . ' She paused and flashed a pleading smile in Barry's direction. 'I don't suppose you want to go out and have a chat with young Cleo Riley, do you? She's in reception. It's the usual problem — her mother's thrown her out yet again. I'm sure she can go to the emergency foster carers, they always take her when they've got the space, it's just a couple of phone calls . . . '

'Not a chance.' Her colleague shook his head emphatically. 'No, no, no. I've still got three home visits to do this afternoon as it is. Go on, get it over with, and then you can take off on your hols and forget all about the rest of us, slogging away here like the busy, busy worker ants we are!'

Hannah shrugged her shoulders and laughed in easy acceptance.

'How did I know you'd say that? Still, it was worth a try!'

She walked quickly out of the cramped office that she shared with Barry and several tall filing cabinets, and into a long corridor, which led along to the dingy reception office where the clerks were protected by a toughened glass screen from the public waiting area. The front line.

The grey building that housed East London Social Services office was a characterless four-storey concrete-and-glass box that would have been seen as cutting edge and ultra-modern when it was built in the sixties. Now it looked dated and tired with graffiti covering almost every solid external surface, cigarette ends and dried chewing gum littering the entrance and car-park, and a palpable air of neglect hanging permanently over all the public areas, both inside and out.

Hannah was constantly relieved that she no longer lived in the area of East London where she had grown up, but when she had been offered a job there a few months ago had made the decision to go back. It had meant a promotion, a large pay rise and the opportunity to work flexi-hours, so three days a week she drove in from the quiet village in Essex where she and her husband had lived for over ten years. The other two days she worked from the comfort of her own home. It suited her perfectly.

Screwing up her eyes, she scanned the waiting area that looked just as crowded and noisy as she'd expected. Friday afternoons and Monday mornings were always hectic at the High Street office, and that particular Friday afternoon was certainly no exception. There were not enough chairs for the number of waiting clients so they just milled around aimlessly, spilling out into the corridor and growing angrier by the minute at having to wait so long. Children of all ages, bored with their surroundings and uninterested in the few battered books and torn magazines strewn on the table, ran around unchecked, bickering and shouting and creating mayhem.

Above the general hum of boredom and irritation, Hannah had to shout through a gap in the glass screen to make herself heard.

'Cleo? Cleo! Go along to interview room two, I'll meet you there in just a moment . . . '

As the teenage girl jumped up and pushed her way out into the corridor, another female voice rose above all the others, loud and strident.

'Oi! That is so not fair! I was here long before her. I've been waiting for over two fucking hours and I want someone out here to see me now. *Now!* Or else I'm really going to lose it. We're not pigs in a pen out here, you know, we're human beings, all of us . . . '

Hannah had already turned away but something familiar in that voice and intonation made her stop in her tracks. She thought she recognised it. She was sure she did. But rather than turn back to look, instinct made her move to the far end of the desk and position herself to one side of a cupboard, where she could see the people in the waiting room but hardly anyone there could see her.

The waiting throng, some wary of a confrontation and others relishing the thought of it, had quietened and parted slightly, leaving the woman who had spoken out standing in an aggressive pose in the middle of the room, hands on hips, glaring venomously through the glass.

She was tiny, probably only just touching the five foot mark, and skeletally thin, with a straw-coloured pony-tail pulled through the back of her baseball cap and several gold ear-rings in each ear. There was also one in her left eyebrow, and a huge stud just under her bottom lip. Over-tight faded jeans skimmed her bony hips and there was the statutory band of pale bare flesh around her midriff. Her whole persona was one of youthful arrogance coupled with a blatant defiance of authority.

At first glance she looked like a stroppy teenager mid-tantrum, but when Hannah screwed up her eyes and looked more carefully she saw that the fine-featured angular face half concealed by the peak of the cap was pale and lined in contradiction to the youthful body stance. Her face showed she was a good twenty years older than she first appeared.

Angrily, she looked around the room for support, and Hannah could feel the woman's rage and frustration seething in her just under the surface. She was teetering at the limit of her self-control, and at any second could lose it and attack someone; anyone. Hannah knew all too well that that level of anger and frustration could be very infectious.

'I think you need to call security, Pat, just as visible backup, and so there's someone on the spot if it all kicks off.' From her obscured vantage point, Hannah spoke quietly to the desk clerk. 'That woman out there, winding everyone up and making all the noise . . . what's her name? Is she known to us?'

'Oh, heavens, yes, she's known to us all right. Her name's Julie Grayson. She's not one of the real regulars to the office, but when she is here she likes to stamp and shout and generally make her presence felt. It's lucky she's on her own today. Makes it easier for us.'

'Why's that?' Hannah tried to keep her voice professionally calm.

'Well, she has a lot of problems to deal with, I admit, but when she has her kids with her, especially the boy, it's instant chaos. Though, to be fair, she's right about today. She has been waiting reasonably quietly for ages for someone to see her.' The middle-aged woman smiled at Hannah hopefully. 'Everyone is so busy today and two duty workers are out on calls . . . maybe you could see her after young Cleo? I know you're not on duty but I'm sure it won't take long. It'll be to do with her son, I'm sure . . . '

'I'm sorry, Pat, I really can't, I'm well into overload already, but if you try and catch Barry he might just help out if he's still in the building. He was in our office a few minutes ago. Explain the situation to him.'

Shrugging apologetically, Hannah turned away and only then did the smile slide from her face. She forced herself to take shallow breaths to stop herself from hyperventilating at the shock of seeing Julie Grayson.

Julie *Grayson?*

Hannah didn't recognise the surname but she knew the Christian name and she certainly recognised the voice, the tone, and the basic facial features. As well, of course, as the obvious raging fury bubbling away inside.

She knew without doubt that the woman called Julie Grayson, who was still shouting, swearing and making threatening gestures in reception, was Julie, her own younger sister, the runaway she hadn't had any contact with for around twenty years.

The interview with Cleo passed in a haze as Hannah went through the process of making the usual arrangements for her on auto-pilot. Normally she had a soft spot for this pretty young girl who was part of one of the most dysfunctional families on her caseload, but this time Hannah just wanted to get away from the interview room and back to her own office.

As she walked past the reception area she glanced in sideways. Julie was no longer there and Hannah wasn't sure whether she had been sent packing or was being seen by someone else.

She also didn't know if she was relieved or disappointed. Suddenly it was imperative that she should get back to her desk and computer so that she could surreptitiously look up the records and address of the woman she knew only as her little sister, Julie Beecham.

* * *

The next morning, after a long and sleepless night, Hannah stared out of a window in the plane at the clouds below and carried on pondering the unexpected events of the day before.

The initial shock of seeing her long-estranged sister had quickly been replaced by a resurgence of the buried sadness of her childhood. As soon as she had got back to her office, Hannah had pulled up the Grayson records, read the potted family profile, and slowly digested the information that flashed up on the screen. Scanning her way through the details, she couldn't believe that this troubled and angry-sounding person with such a fearsome reputation was actually her sister Julie, her own flesh and blood.

It had made uncomfortable and guilt-inducing reading for Hannah.

Despite its being strictly against all the rules, she had printed out as much of the file as she could and quickly tucked the pages away in her briefcase before leaving the office for her holiday. Once home, she'd surreptitiously transferred the pages to the inside pocket of the suitcase now stored away in the hold of the aircraft. She was hoping for some time to herself while she was away so that she could study the information properly.

'Are you with me or is your head still in that shit-hole of an office of yours?' Her husband nudged her sharply with his elbow and turned his head to look at her. 'You're very distracted for someone just off on a fabulous holiday. I mean, come on, *I've* managed to switch off and my job is far harder to leave behind than yours. Now you have to do likewise.'

The sound of his irritated voice brought Hannah back to the present and she forced a smile before leaning her head against his shoulder. 'Sorry. Yesterday was so chaotic it's taking longer than usual for me to forget about it. I'll be okay by the time we get there. But it's no bad thing, you know, sweetheart — it's the horrendous stuff like that that makes me realise how lucky I am in my own life. With you.'

Ben kissed the top of her head. 'Good! That's what I like to hear, a bit of appreciation from the missus! Now I'm going to close my eyes and relax, and so should you. I want us both to be fresh and ready to hit that beautiful reef. I've been in scuba withdrawal for six long months.'

Straightening himself away from her dismissively, he reclined his seat as far as it would go then, leaning back with an exaggerated stretch and a deep sigh, linked his hands across his rounded stomach and closed his eyes. Hannah obediently followed suit but she only feigned sleep; her nerves were wired and she wanted to try to get her thoughts clear before they arrived in Egypt. She knew Ben would be angry if she was distracted on the holiday.

Her husband knew nothing about the disturbing events of yesterday; she had decided, after some thought, that it wouldn't be fair on him to have the spectre of a dysfunctional sister-in-law he had never met, and knew very little about, overshadowing his much-needed break. After all, she and Julie hadn't even spoken and there was no certainty that they ever would so it really wasn't worth upsetting him over something that might never happen.

Shifting carefully in her seat so as not to disturb him, Hannah peered through her lowered eyelids and studied her sleeping husband.

Benjamin Durman was dynamic and fiercely ambitious, and these combined qualities somehow implied a physical stature he didn't actually have. He was only five foot nine, a similar height to his wife in her bare feet, with thinning light brown hair and a slightly paunchy body; but he was always well-groomed, snappily dressed, and supremely confident in himself. His strong Estuary accent and over-loud voice could often intimidate, even scare her, but he was the only man Hannah had ever been with and she loved him totally, admired him absolutely, and always deferred to him.

Spending her working life with so many unfortunate and dispossessed people of all ages made Hannah appreciate her own good fortune in having a motivated husband who worked hard and wanted the best for them both. Even when he was being mean-spirited and self-centred, as he sometimes was, she still felt lucky to have a successful marriage to someone who cherished and protected her. Because of her own shattered childhood, she desperately wanted her marriage to last for ever and for it to be a success. The thought of it ever failing, for any reason, was just unbearable. Trying to relax, Hannah let her mind continue to roam.

It had been such a shock just seeing Julie again after so many years. But after having gone back to her office and skimmed the available information about her sister and her family, a great weight of guilt had pressed down on Hannah, forcing a surge of panic-stricken adrenalin through her whole body. A day later she could still feel it as she thought about her sister strutting angrily around the waiting room. In that respect Julie hadn't changed a bit.

Hannah hadn't ever forgotten about her, of course she hadn't; over the intervening years, on certain dates and at certain events, she had occasionally wondered how her sister was doing, whether she was married, had children, where she was living.

If she was happy.

Hannah knew that Julie could always have contacted her in the early years, if she had really wanted to. The fact that she hadn't meant, of course, that she didn't, and Hannah had never tried to find her because she had known it would upset Ben. Despite being the younger sister, Julie had always been the more forceful and determined of the two. It had simply never occurred to Hannah that her sister's life would have turned out to be so dysfunctional and tragic, so completely the opposite of Hannah's own.

For not even considering that, she suddenly felt very selfish.

Despite the sisters being close during the pre-pubescent years of their disrupted and unhappy childhood, the onset of adolescence had sent the two disparate personalities in completely different directions. The day that eighteen-year-old Hannah, full of high expectations for her future, had set off for University had been the day their sibling relationship had ended.

Looking back, Hannah was ashamed to realise how little insight she had had at that moment. Fifteen-year-old Julie had made a big thing about bouncing around and looking overly happy as she stood at the edge of the kerb and waved her elder sister off with a wide grin and a V-sign.

But the next day, while their aunt was out, Julie had quietly packed up her own sparse belongings, written two angry notes, one to her aunt and one to her sister, and had disappeared. With the benefit of hindsight, Hannah couldn't believe she hadn't taken more notice of Julie's air of bravado on that last day; the same display of devil-may-care high spirits had always preceded her doing something out of the ordinary.

From that moment on, Hannah had known nothing of her sister's life until she had spotted her in the office.

2

'I don't know what's up with you but you're starting to really piss me off,' Ben snapped. 'This is the first time this year I've had the chance to chill out and *you're* moping around with a face like a smacked arse and spoiling it all for me.'

Without making eye contact, he rubbed angrily at his hair with a beach towel while at the same time slipping his sandy feet into flip-flops. 'And, of course, being you, you won't tell me why. I just don't understand you.' He carried on ranting sarcastically as he flicked his wet hair into position. 'Most wives would be thrilled to have the opportunity to spend a week scuba diving in the Red Sea plus staying in a five-star hotel. But, oh, no, not you . . . '

He flung the towel down on the sand right next to where she was leaning back on a padded wooden sun-lounger, sending spirals of grainy sand flying all over her oiled body. 'You're one ungrateful bitch lately!'

'I'm not ungrateful, darling, really I'm not and you know that, but I am sorry if I've upset you.' Hannah smiled apologetically and reached out to touch his leg affectionately, aware of the attentive ears of others on the beach who were staying at the same hotel.

'Really, I am sorry, Ben, but I just didn't have the energy for snorkelling this morning. I guess I'm still a bit under the weather after my surgery.

They say it can take up to a year to recover fully and get back to normal . . . '

'Well, I wish they'd explained that properly beforehand. I'd never have agreed to you having it done if I'd known the disruption it would cause to our personal life. It's ridiculous! It's like being on holiday with an ageing granny.'

Hannah was both embarrassed and hurt; she always felt bad when her husband was being unfairly angry with her. Nonetheless she bit her tongue and smiled. She knew he had a big problem with feelings and emotions so, telling herself that he didn't mean to be unkind, she rarely ever confronted him.

Jumping up, she looped her arm into his. 'It's nearly lunchtime. Shall we eat at the hotel or in town? How about that little restaurant we found last time we were here? The one with the gorgeous honey desserts.'

'Not a chance. I'm not in the mood for an over-priced glorified beach café. We'll eat here,' he stated dismissively. 'I'm going out on the dive boat this evening so I'm going to have a rest this afternoon . . . '

'That sounds good to me. It's what being on holiday is all about: sun, sea and long siestas!'

'I said *I* need a rest. I wasn't including you. You've been lolling around all morning doing bugger all, the last thing you need is a siesta . . . '

Her husband pulled his arm away and marched up the beach to the hotel, leaving Hannah to trudge through the sand behind him like a pack horse carrying everything, including his snorkelling gear. But she didn't mind, not really; not if it kept the peace. And of course he was right, the holiday was expensive and she had been distracted.

No matter how hard she tried to enjoy herself, thoughts of Julie were never far from her mind, even during the night; Hannah tossed and turned constantly, and the resulting lack of sleep meant she was over-tired and emotional the rest of the time.

Although she wouldn't have dreamed of telling him so, she was pleased that Ben was going out on the night boat; it would give her time to sit and relax on her own, and also to study carefully the paperwork she had brought with her.

That evening Hannah stood under the illuminated entrance to the sumptuous five-star hotel and waved as Ben climbed aboard the trolley bus that would take him and several others round to the local dive centre. His earlier bad mood had dissipated and he waved happily back to her as the trolley chugged off up the drive.

Relieved that he was happy again, she went through to the air-conditioned lounge and settled herself into a wide leather armchair that was tucked away in a quiet corner. After ordering a pot of coffee, she pulled a magazine out of her bag and opened it carefully. At the centre she had hidden the printout that gave her the potted life history of her sister Julie Grayson.

First, she skimmed quickly through all the pages and then she flipped back to the beginning to re-read them. Slowly and carefully, Hannah read and digested every word of the case history and notes that covered the bare facts of her sister's tangled life. When she had finished she signalled for another pot of coffee and, after carefully closing the magazine with the reports still inside, sighed deeply and tried to understand how so much could have happened without her knowing about any of it.

As she pondered what she now knew, events that she had promised herself she would never think about again, events that she had long since consigned to history, gradually came back to her . . . along with the heaviest sense of guilt imaginable.

Hannah knew without a doubt that she had let her sister down.

Thirteen-year-old Hannah lifted the sash window just far enough to be able to slide her head underneath once she'd turned it to one side. The autumn air was damp and misty, and it took a few moments for her eyes and ears to adjust to the sights and sounds of the unusually dark, moon-free night.

But the sound that she was listening for wasn't one of the normal night-time sounds, it was the all too familiar angry sobbing of her younger sister.

'Julie,' she whispered loudly. 'Julie, can you hear me? Call her and tell her you're sorry . . . please say you're sorry and then she'll let you back indoors . . . I'll go and tell her you're ready to say sorry. It's so cold tonight, you can't stay out there . . . '

'I'll stay here as long as it takes. Why should I

say sorry?' Julie shouted back angrily. 'I didn't do anything.'

'You did, you defied her and answered her back. You know she hates that. Please tell her you're sorry.'

'I'm not saying sorry to that old witch!' Julie's tearful but nonetheless defiant voice floated up to her. 'I don't care if I freeze to death out here, I won't say sorry to her. Ever. I haven't done anything.'

'Please, Julie, do it for me? I hate it when you're out there.'

'Oh, just fuck off, Miss Goody Two Shoes. Go on . . . get your head back in the window and shove it up that bitch's arse! Like you always do. You never even try to stick up for me.'

Hannah sighed and pulled her head back in but wedged the window up just far enough so she could keep an ear on what was going on; she wanted to be able to hear when her aunt went back out to release her sister.

It had all started at supper when Julie had refused to eat the sodden greens that swam in liquid like pond water on her plate and invariably made her gag. It ended up, as it had done so many times before, with their aunt slapping her several times around the head and face, dragging her forcibly into the garden by her pony-tail, and bolting her in the outside toilet as punishment.

These confrontations happened regularly and Hannah could never understand why her sister couldn't just be submissive, at least on the surface, and let Aunt Marian, their guardian, have her own way.

All they had to do was behave exactly as they were told; as long as they were totally obedient and submissive, she would leave them alone. But Julie would always argue, and invariably ended up suffering one of the cruel punishments that their aunt loved to come up with for her.

Hannah snuggled down in her bed, intending to wait for Julie to be allowed back in, but it was cold and dark in the bedroom. She dropped off. It was dawn before she woke and realised the bed next to hers was still empty.

Grabbing her dressing gown, she ran downstairs and straight out by the back door. She pulled back the heavy bolt that Aunt Marian had pushed across to bar the toilet door and tried to push it open, but it wouldn't budge.

'Julie, it's me! Let me open the door.' She pushed harder and, when it wouldn't shift more than a few inches, kneeled down and peered under the gap at the bottom. She could just make out an unresponsive Julie lying on the concrete floor, her body curled around the pedestal of the toilet.

'Aunt Marian,' she shouted, 'Julie is unconscious on the floor! I can't move her. She might be dead . . . you've got to do something! Aunt Marian, Aunt Marian . . . '

After a good five minutes, during which time Hannah became increasingly hysterical, a half-asleep Marian Beecham appeared at the back door, pulling the belt tight around her quilted dressing gown.

The woman was tall and broad-shouldered with thick wiry hair that constant dyeing had turned orange; she always wore it the same way, piled on top of her head and secured with a wide tortoiseshell comb, adding to her height. Borderline obese, she knew exactly how to use her bulk to intimidate. Tiny Julie would often win a battle of words but never stood a chance when a confrontation became physical. Which it usually did.

Marian paused on the back step long enough to light a cigarette and take a couple of deep drags before marching the few paces to the toilet door where Hannah was crying and hopping from foot to foot in a panic.

'She's just acting up', the Aunt sighed, pulling Hannah aside by the arm, 'same as always. Now you get yourself indoors and leave that little primadonna to me.'

The woman kicked the door once, and then kicked it even harder.

'Don't!' Hannah screamed. 'She isn't acting up. I looked under the door, she's really sick. What if she's dead? Oh, my God, she's dead . . . you've killed her, you've killed her!' She started screaming hysterically and pushing her shoulder against the door.

'Stop it! Just stop all that nonsense right now, you silly child, and go indoors before you break her legs. I'll deal with Julie and her histrionics . . . '

As she angrily pushed Hannah aside, a worried face appeared over the high wooden fence that divided the two small semi-detached houses.

'Hannah love, is everything okay? I heard you

screaming. What's going on?'

Marian Beecham's whole persona changed in an instant. Her tense shoulders loosened and the deep frown lines that criss-crossed her angry face faded into a smile. 'Oh! Good morning, Gerald. I'm sorry if the noise disturbed you, it's just Hannah getting herself into a state again. Julie must have gone out to the toilet during the night and got herself locked in. Heaven knows why the girl gets herself into these situations . . . '

'Oh, my Lord,' the man exclaimed loudly as he shook his head from side to side. 'The poor baby must be frozen if she's been out there all night. Hannah, you go and unbolt the side gate and I'll come round and see what I can do.'

By the time Gerald Kelly made it through the gate, Marian Beecham had nipped indoors, tidied her hair and flicked cold water over her face. Then she pinched Hannah sharply in the bony area of her ribs as a warning.

'I think I'm going to have to take the door off its hinges if we're to get her out. Then we can see how she is, she may need to go to casualty,' Gerald said cautiously. 'I hope she's not got hypothermia . . . '

'Oh, she'll be fine. Let's just get her indoors in the warm, she's only cold. Honestly, sometimes I despair of that girl's stupidity! I swear she's got mental problems, that one.'

As Gerald pulled the door away, Hannah pushed past him and her aunt and tried to pull her sister's head forward, away from the lavatory bowl. Almost immediately Julie sighed and fluttered her eyes. Her naturally pale skin looked almost translucent from the cold that had seeped right into her body.

'See?' Marian smiled triumphantly as she peered over Hannah's shoulder. 'She's fine. Let's help her indoors and sit her by the fire in the sitting room. Hannah, you turn it on. She'll be right as rain in a few minutes, then you can both get ready for school. I could do without this, you know.'

Gerald swept the little girl up in his arms and carried her into the house.

'How did you get stuck in there, Julie?' he asked once he had put her in an armchair and she had fully come round.

'She locked me in there . . . she locked me in and left me there all night just 'cos I wouldn't eat her rotting, rancid greens for supper!'

Shaking her head in disbelief, Marian laughed out loud and looked at Hannah. 'Oh, dear. There she goes again, head in cloud cuckoo land . . . that wasn't what happened, was it, Hannah? You were there. It's Julie's own fault she got stuck in there, isn't it, Hannah?'

The emphasis on her name brought Hannah out in a sweat. She knew what would happen if she sided with her sister; the bamboo cane that should have been supporting runner beans but which stood concealed behind the kitchen door would be brought out . . . She paused for a moment. She could practically hear the swishing sound, feel the vicious cane cutting into the palms of her hands or her buttocks, depending on her aunt's mood. It had only happened to her once but the unspoken threat of another dose was enough to make her feel faint from fear, especially as she had seen Julie on the receiving end of it so many times.

Hannah Beecham was ashamed to find she was nowhere near as strong as her younger sister; she simply couldn't face it.

'Yes, that's right. I think Julie's got a bit muddled 'cos she's so cold. She went out to the toilet and just got stuck in there. The door's a bit dodgy when it's damp, and because I was asleep I didn't notice she was missing'.

Her aunt smiled. 'Come on, Gerald, come through to the morning room and I'll make you a nice cuppa as a thank you. And I've got some shortbread. Honestly, those girls . . . I gave up everything to look after them and this is the thanks I get. Lies and lies. All the time it's lies . . . '

'My pleasure, Marian, my dear, but then you must let me fix the door safely back on. We don't want this happening to anyone again, do we?'

'Thank you so much, Gerald.' Their aunt folded her arms under her enormous bosom and twittered girlishly, 'You really are a wonderful friend and neighbour! Whatever would I do without you?'

Hannah looked at her aunt and wondered at her ability to pull the wool over everyone's eyes; she despised this woman, hated her, but more than that she despised herself for not standing up to her, especially when she glanced at her younger sister and saw the venomous anger in Julie's eyes.

But although she felt guilty for not supporting her sister, she was also furious with Julie for not complying and making life easier for them both. Marian Beecham wanted to be in control. She could so easily be appeased if Julie would just not fight against every little thing.

'Well, it was your own fault!' Hannah told her later, when they were on their own. 'Why couldn't you have just eaten your dinner like I did? It might be vile but it won't kill you like being out in the cold all night nearly did. You are so stupid sometimes.'

'What? Eat that shite she keeps bringing out every mealtime because she knows I hate it? Every dinnertime it's scraggy greens sloshing around in toilet water or else it's boiled cabbage. I can't eat it without gagging and she knows that. So do you.'

Julie's teeth were chattering loudly as she shivered non-stop, despite being as close to the gas fire as she could get.

'Yes, that shite. If you'd just eaten it in the very first place without moaning, we wouldn't get it almost every day now. I hate it too, but I have to eat it because of you! Why do you have to do this all the time? I'm sick of it. You make everything into a war and then drag me into it. Now I'm going to get ready for school. Are you coming?'

Julie shook her head. 'You've got a nerve, Hannah. Just piss off and leave me alone. I hate you! And Mum and Dad would have hated you as well, for being such a coward.'

The words cut right through Hannah because she knew her sister was right.

3

The moment they reached the baggage hall at the airport, Ben Durman pulled his mobile phone out of his pocket and switched it on. Instantly it started beeping madly. While Hannah grabbed a trolley and went over to the carousel to look for their suitcases, Ben sauntered over to the line of seats at the opposite end of the hall with the phone clamped to his ear and sat down. Although Hannah was used to it, she was once again disappointed that he couldn't wait another couple of hours until they actually got home before dealing with his messages.

The luggage carousel, piled high with bags of all shapes, sizes and colours, lumbered around noisily and she tried to watch both ways at once, checking for their own familiar cases while also watching Ben. She knew she shouldn't feel so resentful, especially as it was the same routine every time they returned from a holiday, but she did. The moment the wheels of the plane touched the runway Ben would start shifting his feet and fidgeting with the phone in his pocket, the holiday already gone from his mind.

As she looked back and forth from her husband to the carousel, a man standing beside her caught Hannah's eye and smiled.

'This is the worst part, isn't it? Everyone hanging around, playing spot the bag. It's like trying to find your coat at the end of a party. You just want to grab it as quickly as possible and get away.'

In her job Hannah was used to making quick evaluations of people and it was a hard habit to break. Ben called them snap judgements and instantly she made one. This man was in his thirties, blond and tanned with an easy grin; tall and lithe; wearing slightly scruffy surfer-boy clothes.

Her instant thumbnail assessment was Idle Beach Bum. She had met so many like him over the years on their scuba-diving holidays. Their lives revolved around the next dive and the pretty girls in bikinis who flocked around them adoringly. It was the same in every resort they went to.

'Yes, it's the depressing proof that the holiday is over and we're back in the real world.' Hannah smiled at him politely.

'How did you like the über-exotic Blue Gulf Hotel?' He paused for a second and then laughed as she frowned in surprise. 'Oh, it's okay, I'm not a stalker! I only know where you were staying because your husband and I are both scuba junkies. We went out on the same night dives and I spotted you both together on the plane. Great guy, Ben.'

Hannah smiled with relief. 'Yes, he is, and yes, we both love that hotel. We've been there before — twice, in fact. It's not as expensive as it looks actually, and we love the peace and quiet of being slightly away from the crowds. And the scuba, of course, but I haven't done any this time. Just some minor snorkelling off the reef.'

She broke off as she recognised one of their cases, but as she leaned forward and grabbed the handle, so did he.

'Here. Let me get that.'

He dragged it from the moving carousel and lifted it effortlessly on to her trolley before reaching forward again and snatching up a battered canvas holdall that he dumped on the floor in front of his feet.

'Where were you staying?' Hannah asked.

He smiled widely. 'I was in the centre of town at the no-star, no air-con Riviera Club. Contradiction in terms calling it that — it wasn't a club and was nowhere near any Riviera — but it was fine for me. I just wanted to dive so all I needed was a bed and a bar. And of course we had a few good parties. But now it's over and I'm back to saving up for the next trip. Scuba is an exorbitantly expensive hobby, as I'm sure you know!'

Hannah smiled again but kept one eye on her husband. Ben had flipped the phone closed but still stayed where he was. She tried to catch his eye to beckon him over but he was too busy looking at himself in the glass doors and finger-combing his gelled hair to notice.

'A bit of a high flyer, your old man. He told us all about his job and how he travels constantly around the country. Not my choice of stress level but he seems to love it . . . '

Hannah reached for the second case and again the man took it.

'Yes, he does, that's why he's over there on the

phone already. He's a complete workaholic. At it twenty-four/seven.'

'And you?' he asked, looking at her curiously. 'Are you a twenty-four/seven workaholic?'

'No,' she laughed. 'I like my job, of course, but as Ben says, it's just a job.'

She turned the trolley sharply and pushed it away from the throng. 'Anyway, nice meeting you . . . er, sorry, I don't know your name. I'm Hannah, by the way.'

'Hi, Hannah. I'm Declan. Declan Taylor. But I'll be seeing you again, I'm sure. Ben and I are going to keep in touch. Maybe go diving in Dorset in the summer.'

'Oh, great. That'll be fun for you both. I'm a fairweather diver, I only do the warm seas.'

Hannah smiled widely and held out her hand. She knew it would never happen. Holidays were one thing, but at home Ben only socialised with useful people and she couldn't see Declan Taylor, with his bleached khaki shorts, faded sweat-shirt and raggedy holdall, coming under that heading.

Declan smiled back, his eyes holding hers. Suddenly Hannah felt over-dressed and a little prissy in her flat patent pumps, non-crease navy slacks and pristine white jumper, the clothes that had hung in the hotel wardrobe while they were away, waiting for the trip home. For the flight she had pushed her collar-length bob back with an alice band and suddenly wanted to rip it off and shake her hair loose; prove she wasn't frumpy at all.

Just as Declan reached out to shake her hand

Ben sauntered over, a wide grin on his face. 'Ah, you've already collected the cases — I was just going to do that. You shouldn't be so impatient, you know, they keep going round, that's why they call it a carousel . . . ' His smile faded and he raised his eyebrows curiously as he looked from his wife to Declan and back again. 'I didn't know you two had met . . . '

'Only just, we met over the suitcases.' Hannah's tone came across slightly cooler than she'd intended but she was tired and upset at the way Ben had once again left her to do everything. 'Declan here very kindly dragged them off the belt on to the trolley for me.'

Ben turned down the corners of his mouth, rolled his eyes and made a big display of looking sheepish. 'Ooops! Looks like I'm in the doggy-doo-doo again, Dec my man! The joys of being married, eh? I told you, I can never do anything right.'

'I wouldn't know, I've never got into that myself.' His tone non-committal, Declan shrugged and picked up his bag. 'Must go or I'll miss my train. Call me when you want to give the Dorset dive a go — it's so cool!' 'Bye, Ben. 'Bye, Hannah. Nice to meet you both.'

With a casual wave he disappeared off through the 'nothing to declare' channel.

'Good bloke that — and such good company on the boat. A really cool guy . . . and a great dive buddy. Appearances can be so deceptive, you know? He looks like he's a real loser, doesn't he?'

Ben took the trolley from Hannah and headed

in the same direction as Declan. 'Right, let's go and find the driver, he should be waiting at the exit. Look for the board, will you?'

'You know, I wish you could have waited until we got home to deal with those calls,' said Hannah, failing to hide her irritation. 'Another couple of hours wouldn't have hurt. I felt silly having that Declan bloke I didn't even know help me with the bags while you were just sitting there on the phone.'

Ben stopped in his tracks and looked at her reproachfully. 'Well, pardon me for trying to keep my career on track and money in the bank for us to live on! Time is money in my business and there were things to be done as soon as poss. You should know how it works by now. As soon as I set foot in the country, I'm back to work with a week's worth of calls to deal with. We don't all have the luxury of 'work when you want' hours!'

His voice was loud and his tone sarcastic. Hannah cringed, aware that everyone nearby could hear; she also noticed Declan, who was striding ahead of them, slow his step slightly. She prayed he wouldn't turn round and compound her embarrassment. Hannah looked down at the ground and didn't respond to her husband. She wanted to retaliate by saying that, despite his promising not to work while they were away, she had seen him getting his phone out of the hotel safe several times before disappearing off on some pretext or other. But she didn't. Instead she told herself again that he was working for both of them, and of course she herself had been distracted.

'Hannah? Are you listening to me?'

'Yes, I am listening. You're right, of course, and I'm sorry. I'm just so tired after the flight. I really didn't mean to be critical, I know how hard you work and I appreciate it.'

He smiled and put an arm around her waist. 'And I know you didn't mean it, so apology accepted. Come on then, let's hit the road home and see what's been going on while we've been away. I'm anticipating hundreds of emails and a mountain of post. I hope the old bat next-door remembered to check the house every day.'

'I'm sure she did, Fliss is . . . ' Hannah stopped mid-sentence. She didn't want to get into another argument.

* * *

'How was the hol? You look all fit and healthy and sickeningly tanned.' Barry grinned as Hannah dumped her briefcase on the desk. 'Fancy a cuppa and a catch-up before you look at your in-tray? The two agency staff have upped and gone to earn their pennies in a better catchment area and there's no one to replace them yet. Basically you and me are stuffed. Again.'

'Lovely. Just what I wanted to hear after a week off,' Hannah laughed. She was actually pleased to be back at work in the office where she was both valued and needed. Much as she loved Ben, she hated the way that he constantly put her down and made her feel inadequate and irrelevant.

The same way Aunt Marian had done all those years before.

As quickly as the thought had popped into her mind she dismissed it again. Ben loved her; Aunt Marian didn't.

'A large strong coffee would be good,' she continued quickly, 'a bit of a caffeine hit before I get back into the swing of things. No milk, though, and certainly no chocolate digestive. I have to lose all this weight I've put on on my hips. Ben says I was lucky not to have been harpooned when I was out in the sea. He kept on joking about whaling factory ships heading my way.'

Hannah laughed along with her workmate the way she always did, but she was inwardly distracted. All she really wanted to do was fire up her computer and see what, if anything, her sister had been up to during the week Hannah had been away, but she had to wait until Barry was out of the office.

It was against all the confidentiality rules to look up a family member's files and the last thing Hannah wanted was to lose the job she loved, the one part of her life that was all hers.

Barry put the mug down beside her and smiled gently. 'So, Hannah, is everything okay with you? I mean really okay with you, you . . . '

'Of course, whatever makes you think it isn't?' She shook her head and laughed. 'Well, okay, apart from the fact I've just come back from a glorious holiday on the shores of the shimmeringly gorgeous Red Sea to an office in total chaos with no staff!'

'I just wondered, thought you looked a bit down,' he said. 'But, you know, if you do ever want to talk, I'm a damned good listener. I've learned well after so many years living in a female-dominated house, with a wife and three assorted daughters, not to mention the nearby mother and mother-in-law. I mean, I couldn't get a word in even if I wanted to. I'm an elective mute at home.'

Hannah looked at him and hesitated for a few seconds. Barry was a good man and workmate, he was also very perceptive, but even so she decided against confiding in him right away. It would be unfair to put a colleague on the spot like that, especially as, if she kept quiet, she could keep an eye on her sister from a distance without actually getting involved.

'I'm fine, Barry, really, but thank you for asking. I appreciate it. I'm just a bit deflated . . . post-holiday blues . . . you know what that can be like. Suddenly you feel as if you've never even been away, and the next holiday is so far in the future it's not even worth thinking about.'

'Okay. It's your shout. But if you do ever want to talk, about anything, my door is always open. Well, it would be, wouldn't it? It's your door as well!' Barry laughed and swung round on his chair. 'But now I suppose we're going to have to talk about all these cases . . . we've got to figure something out staff-wise, there's no way we can manage this lot on our own. We'll have to contact the agency . . . '

Before he could finish talking his phone starting ringing and the ensuing conversation gave Hannah a few moments to gather herself together. When he'd been looking at her quizzically she had been worried for a moment that he had found out about her relationship to Julie; that he knew about her printing out confidential files that weren't connected to anyone on her caseload, and taking them out of the office. She knew it was probably just her own guilty conscience in overdrive, but still she was concerned.

Barry Ryman was a huge bear of a man who at first glance looked quite intimidating, though he was actually one of the gentlest men Hannah had ever met. His perfectly round, shaven head gleamed like ebony under the fluorescent lights of the office, and when he walked into a room he filled the doorway with his six-foot-six, twenty-stone bulk that was a combination of healthy muscle and lots of rich Caribbean home cooking.

Hannah was tall and naturally big-boned with wide shoulders and hips and large hands and feet, but when she stood alongside Barry she felt small and feminine, the way she had longed to feel all her life.

The way her sister had always been.

Even when they were very young, Hannah had always been aware of being the big sister in every sense of the word. Julie was the dainty doll-like child while Hannah had always felt large and ungainly by comparison. Even when she had been asserting herself in the reception area, Hannah had aware that her sister was still tiny and flat-stomached. Despite having had three children.

As she flicked through her overflowing in-tray, Hannah's thoughts kept drifting back to Julie's current situation and her own dilemma. Although her job involved solving everyone else's problems, she didn't have a clue what she was going to do about her own.

4

'Just give me a break, Seb. If you shut your fat mouth for five minutes then I can think about what I'm going to do.'

With her arms clamped tightly around her skinny midriff, Julie Grayson paced the kitchen floor; or rather she tried to, but the debris spread everywhere made it seem more like crossing an assault course.

'Can't you make yourself useful and clear some of this crap up off the floor? Or at least take your daughter out somewhere so that I can do it?' she continued aggressively. 'I have to get this sorted today. There are no bed-clothes for Jethro — he drenched two lots of sheets last night and the others are trapped in this fucking useless machine.'

Toys lay scattered everywhere and a pile of urine-soaked bed linen was stacked in front of the broken washing machine that was slowly oozing grey scum from underneath. The spreading pool had nearly reached the rubbish bin that had recently been knocked over by the dog, spilling cans and fast-food wrappers from the night before all over the backdoor mat.

The young man sitting at the kitchen table, idly fiddling with his iPod earphones, sighed loudly and shook his head in exasperation.

'Oh, stop the whingeing, Julie! Just for once stop stamping your feet and shouting the odds and try and think logically. The washer is screwed, broken, dead, and no amount of effing and blinding is going to make it better so we have to think of something else. Shouting about it over and over doesn't . . . '

'Shut up.' She leaned forward and put her face right up against his, poking her forefinger hard into his chest and screeching while he was still in mid-sentence. 'Just shut the fuck up!'

Slamming his mug down on the table with such force the dregs slopped over the side, Seb glared back at her.

'I told you the machine was fucked and I told you not to turn it on until I got it fixed. Why didn't you wait until I sorted it or else ask for a new one at the Social? You're entitled, what with Jethro and everything.'

'No, I'm not entitled, Seb.' She kept her face close to his as she replied to his question. 'Their take on it is: why doesn't the fit and healthy layabout toyboy get a job and at least support his own daughter? They think you're a no-good scrounger, hanging about here when it suits and taking advantage of me.' She paused and stared dismissively at him. 'And they're right, of course. You sit there telling me how stupid I am for putting the machine on, but what else was I supposed to do? I've got no money. You've given me nothing!'

Seb's face darkened visibly. 'You're kidding me, right? I've put food on the table and money in the meter *and* I've got you plenty of stuff to smoke and powder your nose with. *You're* the one with the expensive habits, not me. I don't do drugs, remember?' He spoke slowly and sarcastically to her. 'You're a hypocrite, Julie. You want me here to help with Katya, and then you complain about it! Toyboy? What you want is a sodding houseboy, a nanny, a slave to be at your beck and call, with a wad of cash in his back pocket to top up the Social. Well, that's not me any more. I'm done here!'

Angrily he stared her down for several seconds before jumping up from his chair and kicking it away fiercely. He was a chunky young man with a strong, compact body and long muscular legs.

'I'm off.'

'Not without Katya you're not. I've got all this shit to deal with. You take your daughter with you.'

'Not a chance. I'm not your babysitter.'

'Too right! You're not a babysitter, you're Katya's father. You're her *father*. I let you be her father, allowed you into her life, how dare you . . . '

Julie screamed at him in desperation, but instead of responding he just turned his back on her and in one fluid movement snatched up his denim jacket, took two long steps across the room and, without another word, disappeared out of the back door.

Julie's shoulders slumped as the door slammed behind him. She wanted to call him back and say she was sorry, wanted to plead with him to help her get the washing sorted before Jethro got back, but as always her pride wouldn't let her.

Instead she simply pushed the dirty washing

closer to the front of the machine with her foot so that it absorbed the scummy leaking water. Then she leaned back against the sink and tried to figure out what to do about the sodden mess that was inside the machine as well as outside it on the floor, before the school bus delivered her middle child home.

Jethro James Grayson was her beautiful, happy, twelve-year-old son who, because of an accident of nature, would forever have the mental and physical capacity of a toddler. A toddler who was already taller than his own mother and much heavier, with wide clumsy feet that flattened anything in his path. A toddler with absolutely no idea of his own strength.

Jethro was a lovable wide-eyed innocent in the body of an increasingly pubescent young man. Julie knew that it was only a matter of time before she would no longer be able to cope with him at home, but she tried not to think about that.

'Where's Daddy gone? I want to go to the park.'

Absorbed in her anger with Seb, Julie jumped as the little girl appeared in the doorway that linked the kitchen to the lounge. Tiny and dark, she had her father's thick hair and perfect features but her build resembled her mother's and she was dressed as a miniature version of Julie, right down to the jeans, midriff-baring tee shirt and designer trainers. Katya was Julie's very own MiniMe. The Barbie doll she had never had as a child.

'He's had to go to see someone about the

broken washing machine, sweetie, but he won't be long and then he'll take you to the swings.' Julie reached under the child's arms and swept her up high over her head, making her giggle, and then hugged her tight, savouring the feel and smell of the tiny warm body that clung close against her ribs like a young monkey.

She adored this perfect little girl to the point of obsession and was determined not to lose her, the way she had lost her elder daughter.

It had been careless to get pregnant during a drug-fuelled fumble at a party with a man considerably younger than herself but she had, and after much thought she had decided to go ahead with it, despite this being her third unplanned and unwanted pregnancy.

As she hugged her youngest to her she caught sight of the framed photo of Katya with her father, taken when she was a baby, which hung crookedly on the wall. Julie reached out a hand and straightened it, her anger at Seb suddenly tinged with a certain sadness as she studied his photograph.

Sebastian Rombar was a darkly attractive young man with thick collar-length brown hair, chocolate-coloured eyes, and an appealingly wide smile that he knew how to use. He was a classic flirt but he didn't only flirt with young women. He would automatically flirt with everyone: female, male, young, old. He couldn't help himself, he just had to charm everyone. His Spanish parentage showed through in his looks and mannerisms and, even though he had been born and raised in Hackney, he often used his heritage to his own advantage. He had perfected a Spanish-accented English and could turn it on and off at will. It worked every time.

It had been all those things together that had attracted her to him. That and the fact that she had been completely off her head at the time on puff and pills.

Julie rarely felt really sorry for herself — she knew that if she let that happen then she would fall apart and her whole life would implode — but at this precise moment, as she looked at the photograph, she could feel herself teetering dangerously on the edge of a total meltdown.

Her usual way of dealing with everything bad in her life was with the raging anger that had been her best friend all her life; in fact, it was the only friend she could really rely on, and she couldn't imagine what would happen to her if she did calm down and let go of it.

Anger kept her in control of her other emotions, it stopped the tears, and, most importantly, it scared everyone else when she kicked off. Her rage was her power. She glanced up at the clock on the wall to see there was just twenty minutes to go if the bus was on time.

'Come on, Gorgeous Grayson, your big brother will be home soon and we need to get all this stuff out of the way so he doesn't fall over again like he did yesterday. Will you help Mummy? How about you put your toys in the big pink box and I'll clean up this yukky floor. It's all a great big mess of yuk, yuk, yuk!'

Katya giggled infectiously as her mother pulled a face and jumped up and down. The little girl was still young enough to enjoy the simple task of scooping up her toys so Julie put the plastic crate on the floor for her to fill while she herself emptied the rubbish bin and gathered all the dirty washing up into a rubbish sack. She hoped she might find time to take it to the launderette when Seb came back. He had been known to disappear for weeks on end when he was angry. Seb was certainly not reliable but he always came back eventually because he too loved his daughter.

'Stay there for a minute, Katya. Mummy has to make a phone call. In fact, you go through to the front room and look out of the window. Shout when you see Jethro's school bus outside.'

Somehow she had to get a washing machine, but there was no money in the house and she was so far up to her neck in debt that when some did come in, it went out again immediately.

Julie weighed up her options for getting a washing machine.

One way was to ask Jethro's social worker, but he had only just got her a new bed for the boy so it was unlikely he would be able to help again.

Another was to go back on the streets, just for a couple of nights, but she knew that might bring her back into contact with the past she had tried so hard to bury. It could also bring her back into contact with Jethro's father, her ex-pimp from a time she would sooner forget.

Her third option was to phone her daughter Autumn who was a dancer in an upmarket club in the West End and doing very well for herself despite her dysfunctional upbringing.

But as always Julie wasn't in the mood to be nice to the daughter she deeply resented, and she didn't have the energy to go back on the streets, so she called the social worker.

'Hello, Jacob. It's Julie Grayson here, Jethro's mum. I need a washing machine and I've got no money. My machine has died, I'm knee-deep in slimy water, and Jethro's got no clean sheets. You need to do something or I'm going bring him down the office and leave him there for you to deal with. You have to do something! Get me a loan, I don't know . . . '

She could hear herself starting to gabble and she could feel that tears were just a blink away. She didn't want to cry, she hated that, so she shouted and ranted at Jacob, blaming him for all her ills.

Then, on the spur of the moment, she phoned her daughter and ranted wildly at her answer-phone.

After she'd put the phone down Julie started to laugh hysterically.

Everything was falling apart again. The way her life always did.

5

'I can't keep on like this, I've had enough. I can't do this any more . . . '

Julie Grayson was upstairs in the bathroom muttering the same words over and over again, aware that she was fast reaching the point where she wouldn't be able to cope. She'd been there before so she knew it was time to see her doctor and get some help if she was to be able to continue the struggle. She needed something.

Her day-to-day life had become even harder recently. Seb hadn't been back to see his daughter since the row and she had no idea where he was; Jacob hadn't been able to help with the washing machine; apart from some dusty dregs in the bottom of the tin she had no drugs in the house; and Jethro was off school with a cold.

Although she knew he was under the weather, Julie had crossed her fingers and taken a chance, putting him on the bus as usual, but the school had phoned mid-morning asking her to collect him. Julie had tried to argue but the secretary was adamant that he should not be at school so, with no other way of getting him home, she had taken the car and driven the five miles to his school.

On the way back she had been flashed at ten miles an hour over the limit by a newly sited speed camera so by the time she got home she was steaming mad, knowing her details would be checked and the police would soon discover that she was driving without any tax or insurance while still banned from the last time. She only hoped that the speed-camera had no film in it otherwise it would be a triple whammy and another fine she wouldn't be able to pay. Maybe even jail-time.

With Jethro tucked up in his bed with no sheets after an extra-large dose of sedative mixture and Katya under threat of being sent to hers if she moved from in front of the TV, Julie carried on frantically trying to hand-wash her son's bedding from the night before in the bath. There was far too much in there to wash properly but she knew it had to be done so she swilled it around as best she could, wrung it out and then piled it all into one of Katya's toy buckets to take down to the garden.

Just as she was hooking the dripping sheets over the line it started to drizzle and then the phone and the doorbell rang simultaneously.

'Oh, for fuck's sake, leave me alone, will you?' she shrieked at the top of her voice. 'I can't carry on like this any more. When is all this going to end?'

By the time she got to the phone it had stopped ringing so she ran through and flung back the front door, only to be confronted by the sight of her eldest daughter.

'What is going on in here?' Autumn demanded. 'I could hear you shouting and swearing from the other side of the gate. I even tried phoning from the doorstep . . . '

Julie threw up her hands. 'If you've just come round to be all lady la-di-da, then you can just fuck off back to wherever you came from. I don't need you telling me again what a useless, inadequate apology for a mother I am.'

'Excuse me?' Her daughter crossed her arms and frowned. 'When have I ever said that? And anyway, you called me, remember? You left me a message. Said you had no washing machine and Jethro had no dry sheets, remember? Well, I've got you one and it's being delivered this afternoon along with a tumble dryer. They're second-hand but reconditioned. And don't worry — I know from experience not to expect any thanks.'

'That's lucky then because you won't get any. I shouldn't have to grovel to you. And anyway, you could have just phoned to tell me, you didn't have to put yourself out and come all this way.' Julie shrugged her shoulders awkwardly. '*And* you took your sweet time about it.'

'I was in Dubai . . . '

'Well, how absolutely fucking wonderful for you to be in fucking Dubai while I struggle on here, washing Jethro's sheets in the bath.'

Julie had always resented her eldest child and made no attempt to disguise the fact. Deep down she knew it was illogical and unjustified but still she found it hard to accept that while her own life was one of daily grind, with nothing much to look forward to, the daughter to whom she had given birth at barely sixteen had risen above her background and was already financially secure with a comfortable future ahead of her; a future to which she could actually look forward. To compound Julie's resentment, her eldest child was also stunningly attractive. It all seemed so unfair that, rather than being proud of her daughter for doing well, Julie ignored her most of the time.

Autumn Grayson was tall and statuesque. Even in flat shoes she towered over her mother by nearly a foot. Her gently rounded hips and breasts and long slender legs made her the most sought-after lap dancer in the expensive Soho club where she worked, and she could easily pull in hundreds of pounds a night. Her regular features and long auburn hair meant she could present herself as either sultry or sweet, which was useful for a dancer who earned by getting up close to the punters.

At work her outfits were minimal and glitzy, but outside the club she was always immaculately groomed and looked classy even when she was dressed down as she was today in skinny jeans and baseball boots, a spotless white tee shirt and a distressed leather bomber jacket.

But her daughter's pristine appearance simply irritated Julie even more, making her continue with her diatribe.

'You're Jethro's sister and you can afford it. Why should I have to grovel around you, saying thank you for every little crumb you throw? You should *want* to help him. It's him who needs his sheets washed, not me. I don't piss the bed every night.'

Julie shook her head angrily, turned and walked away down the narrow hallway into the kitchen, leaving Autumn to follow or not.

And the girl did. As always.

'You know I want to help you all, not just Jethro, and I do. So what happened to the old washing machine?' she asked.

'It's completely fucked,' Julie snapped without turning round.

'Do you have to swear and snarl all the time? None of this is my fault, you know.'

'Yep, I do have to swear all the fucking time — so like it or lump it. You'd swear too if you had to live my life. Just walk a mile in my shitty shoes and then tell me not to swear! You swan round with your head up your arse, thinking you're so superior to the rest of us . . . '

'Oh, change the record. I don't need all this verbal, I just asked a question about the machine. I do try to help you but I'm never right, whatever I do.' Autumn looked despairingly at her mother and shook her head. 'I really can't do right for doing wrong, can I? You said you need a washing machine so I've got you one. I kitted Jethro out when he grew out of his last lot of clothes. I got you a car to help you get around with the kids . . . '

'Oh, yeah, great idea that was when I can't afford to run it! I had to get Jeth back from school today because of a stupid sniffy nose and I got flashed again with no tax or insurance.'

Julie knew she was challenging her daughter, trying to push her to the limit, but she couldn't help herself. The girl just wound her up.

'Where's Katya?' Autumn asked instead, changing the subject.

'In the front room watching TV, and Jethro is upstairs in bed with no sheets. I've given him a double dose of sedative. Oh, and Seb has done a runner. Again.'

'He'll be back.'

'What makes you say that? How do you know?' Julie belatedly spun round to face her daughter.

'Actually I don't know, I haven't a clue.' Autumn sighed. 'I was just trying to reassure you. Seb's not such a bad bloke and he loves his child, which is more than my father or Jethro's ever did. Neither of them hung around, did they? Look, I don't want to fight with you so I'm going to say hi to them both and then I'll be off.'

Julie listened from the other side of the door to Autumn talking quietly to her little sister. She wished she could be nice to her eldest, she really did, and when they were apart she promised herself that she would be, but every time they were together something stopped her.

She wondered if it was because of the circumstances of her daughter's conception or simply because Autumn was a clone for her much-hated, estranged sister Hannah. The big sister who had gone off and abandoned her just when Julie had needed her most.

'I can't wait to get to University! Just three more days here. Who'd have believed it, eh? I never thought Aunt Marian would agree to it. Good old Miss Farrell for backing her into a corner . . . and, of course, Uncle Gerald helped. I'd never have persuaded the Aunt on my own. I'll

get a degree and a good job. Never have to live in this time-warp dump again.'

Julie sat on the end of the bed pretending to look enthusiastic as her sister sorted her sparse belongings into two piles, one to pack and one to throw away. She was leaving nothing behind.

Hannah kept making all the right noises about coming back to see her sister in the holidays, but Julie knew that once she'd actually escaped and found another life then she would never return to Aunt Marian's House of Horrors. Julie hated her sister for not being honest enough to admit it, she hated her for going off and leaving Julie herself behind, and she hated her for not realising what was happening and exactly how much it mattered.

And because it mattered so much, Julie knew that when Hannah left she would have to go too — if she was to survive.

'Yeah, well, the old cow doesn't see it like that. She thinks that with a degree you'll be able to keep her in her old age — her and that pervy old creep next-door. You'll end up supporting them both. Senile old bastards! Unless they both die first . . . that'd be good, wouldn't it?'

'Oh, Gerald's not that bad . . . at least when she's twittering around him it keeps her away from us for some of the time!' Hannah laughed and pulled a face. 'Isn't it just too awful to think of the two of them together, you know, doing it? If they do, that is . . . '

Julie didn't join in with her sister's laughter, just shook her head.

'Oh, yes, you can laugh and say he's not that

bad — you're not the one he keeps pulling down on to his lap. 'Come and sit with Uncle Gerald.' Yuk! Disgusting old bastard, wriggling around underneath me when he thinks the old cow isn't looking . . . You've seen him do it, I know you have. Or maybe she does know and just ignores it.' Julie screwed up her face and shuddered.

'Oh, I doubt it,' Hannah laughed. 'But anyway, he didn't actually do anything, did he? He was just being a bit randy. Men are like that. And he didn't touch you . . . not really . . . and he's never tried it with me so you must have let him think it was okay; she replied distractedly as she carried on sorting through her belongings, oblivious to just how angry and upset her younger sister was.

'You know, I wish you were coming as well . . . maybe if you really work hard at school, then when you've done your exams you could get into University as well.'

Julie laughed out loud. 'Yeah, right, like that would ever happen! But don't fret, I can deal with Aunt Marian and the perv once you've gone. If she ever lays another finger on me, I'll smash her right back. A fist between the eyes should keep her safely at bay!'

'Julie!' Shocked, Hannah looked up from her packing.

'Well, The old cow has made our lives a misery for years, just for the fun of it. Now it's my turn . . . ' Julie jumped up and started manically shadow boxing around the room. 'Pow! Pow! And as for him . . . it'll have to be a carving knife straight in the nuts. Instant castration!'

Hannah shook her head. 'Why do you always have to react so violently to everything? I don't understand you. It would be better in the long run if you just keep quiet when I've gone, take the path of least resistance. I had an easier time because I let it wash over me. And she did take us in when we had nowhere else to go. We could have been put in care and split up. No one else was interested, no one else bothered about us . . . ' Suddenly Hannah stopped talking and smiled. 'But I don't want to argue with you now. Not when I'm going away. Look, here's my old ragdoll. I'll leave her to keep you company.'

Julie smiled back at her but inside she was raging with anger at Hannah for thoughtlessly chattering on about going off to her bright new life; at that moment Julie hated her sister nearly as much as she hated the Aunt.

Why couldn't Hannah read between the lines and realise that Julie couldn't say what she wanted to say? Why didn't she understand? They were sisters. Shouldn't there be some deeper connection between them?

Forcing herself to be outwardly calm, Julie reached out and took the battered and worn ragdoll from her sister despite the memories it dredged up for her.

They had each been given one by their parents the Christmas before the accident and those dolls had been more precious to the girls than anything else they owned, but only Hannah's remained.

When she was only seven years old Julie had been judged to have been 'insolent', so Aunt Marian had taken her large dressmaking scissors from the sewing box and carefully cut her doll into several pieces. With a smile she forced the hysterical child to watch every cut, every amputation, and then she made her throw the pieces into the dustbin.

Later that night, when Julie had crept down to retrieve whatever she could, her aunt had been ready and waiting with the cane in her hand and a victorious smirk on her face.

The next morning when Julie sneaked a look in the bin the doll had disappeared completely apart from one foot with an embroidered shoe that was caught up among the tea-leaves. Julie had snatched it up then hidden it behind a loose brick in the outside toilet.

Whenever she was locked in the toilet for punishment, it was that dusty and raggedy doll's foot that made her stand her ground and not give in. From that moment on it was the only time Julie gave way to her emotions. Crouched down on the floor in front of the toilet bowl, she would hold it close to her face with one hand and suck vigorously on the thumb of her other hand while she tried to imagine her mother and father looking down on her from above.

On the actual day of Hannah's departure to the distant Bristol University, Julie watched silently as her sister gathered her final bits and pieces together and stuffed them into her suitcases. A classmate was also going to Bristol and her parents were giving Hannah a lift.

As the car pulled away, Julie had waved until the car was out of sight. Then she had gone up to the bedroom they'd shared and jammed her few clothes and possessions into a backpack.

She knew she had to leave and start afresh all on her own. It was time. She was nearly sixteen and she was also pregnant. Aunt Marian would kill her if she stayed.

Julie shook herself free from her memories and went into the sitting room. Autumn was perched on the outside edge of the battered sofa with her little sister on her lap, watching a cartoon on TV. Her long thick hair fell forward over both of them and it hurt Julie that they looked so perfect together.

Autumn sensed her mother's presence and looked round. 'I went up to see Jethro but he's asleep so tell him I'll see him soon. I hope the machines get here in time for you to sort his bedclothes out for tonight. They should be delivered around four. I do know it's a nightmare for you with everything, really I do . . . '

'We manage. Usually. Thanks for sorting it.' Julie forced the words out but still couldn't look her daughter in the eye.

'No prob, Ma. No prob!' Autumn smiled and gave Katya a hug at the same time. 'I know we don't always agree but I do care about you all. Whatever happens, we're the only family we've all got. It's just us.'

Scared of the sudden intimacy of this conversation, Julie turned away abruptly. 'I can hear Jethro.'

She walked up to the turn in the stairs, sat down and watched surreptitiously as Autumn gave Katya one last hug then slipped quietly out of the front door without saying goodbye to her mother.

As the door closed, Julie went into the bedroom and watched from behind the curtain as Autumn got into a waiting mini-cab and disappeared back to the flat Julie had never seen which she shared with the boyfriend Julie had never met and knew nothing about. Not even his name.

Autumn Grayson had successfully compartmentalised her life.

Julie went back down to the kitchen and dug around at the back of an overfilled drawer until her hand found the battered tobacco tin she had hidden away from Seb. There was not much more than dust in it but she expertly managed to roll a skinny joint and light it then inhaled as deeply as she could.

After a few more inhalations she felt the anger and frustration subside a little. Then she saw the envelope on the table. She ripped it open and counted out the notes.

One hundred pounds.

But still it made no difference. She resented Autumn with a passion and blamed her alone for everything that was wrong in her life.

6

Hannah slammed the lid of her laptop shut, stood up and stretched her arms over her head. It was a work-from-home day but no matter how hard she tried it was impossible to concentrate. Her mind was now constantly straying to her sister and, because of that, she also thought about their half-brother Raymond who was eleven years older than her.

She hadn't given either of them any deep thought over recent years. In her eyes Ray was virtually a stranger who lived in a different country, and Julie had long since chosen her own path.

Hannah's world now revolved around Ben; they had a good life together and loved each other in a comfortable way; they had agreed right from the beginning that neither of them needed anyone else in their lives. No family, no close friends, no one except each other.

And she was secure in her contentment.

Or had been until she had spotted Julie at work and read the circumstances of her baby sister's life. Then everything had flooded back and once it was there in her mind there was no way she could ignore it any longer.

Raymond, Hannah and Julie Beecham . . . How could three siblings be so separate?

* * *

Hannah had no direct memories of the traumatic events of the summer of 1973, when she was four and a half years old and Julie nearly two, but over the years she had found out bits and pieces of what had occurred and had pieced the story together. It had been in the final week of the summer holidays that the three Beecham children's lives had changed irrevocably.

At the end of a long, hot, idyllic family holiday spent camping in Cornwall, the family had been driving home overnight when, without warning, a sleepy drunken driver had pulled alongside and side-swiped their car, forcing it to swerve across the central reservation and into the path of an oncoming lorry.

The three children who had been asleep in the back of the big old Volvo estate, tightly wedged among all the camping gear, had suffered only minor injuries, but their parents, Rowena and Ted Beecham, had been thrown straight through the windscreen and had died of their injuries within twenty-four hours.

Raymond's birth father who lived in America, had flown over immediately and, after the funeral, had taken the teenager back to live with him and his second family in a small town in Nevada. Chuck De Souza had apparently offered to take Hannah and Julie with him as well but Marian Beecham, Ted's elder spinster sister and closest blood relative, had come forward and insisted on taking her two young nieces back to her home in East London.

Because of Marian Beecham's rigid control over every aspect of the girls' lives from then on they had had no further contact with their brother, although Hannah had eventually searched him out once she was safely at university out of her aunt's reach. But by then Raymond was a total stranger, already married and with a family of his own, and Julie had disappeared.

Hannah had done her best to keep in loose contact with Raymond because he was her only link to the first few years of her life. As he was fifteen when the accident happened he could remember their parents and their life as a family. But it was a difficult relationship. At first it had been limited mostly to cards and letters at Christmas and later to an occasional email as well, but even that much contact was problematic because Ben disliked Ray intensely even though he had only met him once.

She wondered sometimes why it was that Aunt Marian had never wanted the girls to have anything to do with Raymond and been glad that Chuck had taken him. Maybe there was something about her brother that Marian could see and she couldn't.

Hannah was so deep in her thoughts of the past that the sudden loud buzz of the doorbell made her physically jump. Looking at her watch, she knew instinctively that it was her friend and next-door neighbour Fliss who didn't seem to want to understand the concept of working from home.

'I saw your car on the drive so I thought, *A-ha!* Young Hannah's off work today and no doubt gasping for a relaxing cuppa with the mad old woman next-door . . . ' The older woman smiled widely as Hannah pulled the door back and raised her eyebrows high.

'I'm not off work today, Fliss, as you well know! I'm working from home like I do every week.' She smiled and shook her head. 'I really do have heaps to do, though a cuppa does sound inviting, I must admit . . . '

'Okay, I know,' the other woman laughed and held her hands up, 'you're working, I understand, but you're entitled to a tea break. Only difference is, it's going to be next-door with me. Come on, keep me company for half an hour. I can see Ben's not here. No car, no Ben!'

Hannah smiled wryly and quickly gave in, knowing that the time it would take to try and explain her workload might just as well be spent in Fliss's cosy kitchen with a mug of something hot and healthy, accompanied by a bit of a gossip.

'Okay. You're right, I need a break, but I'll have to be really rude and bring my phone with me, though, just in case someone from the office calls. I really can't be unavailable.'

'Deal! You and your phone for tea.'

'Then just let me lock the doors and I'll be right with you.'

Although they were next-door neighbours there was an expanse of garden and a tall manicured hedge between the two properties that had previously been two pairs of semi-detached farm cottages, down a quiet lane on the outskirts of the extended village of Endel in Essex. It was close enough to the M11 to be able to get quickly into East London, but still nicely countrified. Clever conversion by an entrepeneur builder some years before had turned the four derelict old cottages into two attractive detached renovations, each with landscaped wrap-around garden and in and out gravel driveway. Hannah and Ben, and Fliss and her husband, had moved in at the same time.

The two women took a short cut through a small gap in the hedge and went in at the back door of Fliss's cottage.

The two properties were identical on the outside, but inside was a different story. Fliss's homely cottage was cluttered and chinzy and welcoming to everyone, from neighbours to overactive grandchildren, whereas Hannah and Ben's cottage next-door was minimal, elegant and very adult. They had carefully chosen every item of furniture and everything was placed strategically to show off its design points. They had no sentimental ornaments or souvenirs, just a couple of framed photographs; Ben had no time for nostalgia of any kind.

'It's so nice to catch up with you at last, it's been ages since we last talked properly,' Fliss said cheerily as Hannah settled herself into one of the pair of battered old pine rocking chairs in the kitchen. 'What with your holiday and my Jen's ongoing wedding planning, it seems ages since we caught up. That's why when I saw your car was there and Ben's wasn't, I thought to myself, Right, Fliss. Catch up time with Hannah, see how she's doing.'

Hannah rocked gently and smiled.

'It's good to catch up with you too. I'm doing

okay, though I do seem to be tired all the time . . . just generally worn out. I even felt like it on holiday which was really unfair on Ben. I think it upset him that I wasn't able to do all the things he wanted . . . '

'Well, you probably still have a bit of recovering to do from your hysterectomy. You went back to work much too soon, my girl.' Fliss wagged a finger at her. 'The body needs time to recover from something like that.'

'Oh, I don't know, Ben said it would be better for me to get back to normal as soon as possible. I'm sure he was right. It wouldn't have been good for me to be slouching around at home all day, putting on even more weight.'

'Phooey! That's not how I see it . . . Now then, what tea would you like?' Fliss expertly changed the subject by holding out a small wicker basket full of different flavoured tea bags individually wrapped.

'Camomile sounds nice and calming, I'll try that.'

Hannah really liked her neighbour and also admired her optimistic attitude to life. Two years previously, Fliss Wellsen had woken up in the early hours of the morning to find her previously healthy, sixty-five-year-old husband dead in bed beside her from a heart attack. Despite her shock and grief, Fliss had stayed in the cottage they had both loved and, with the help of her family and friends, built a different life for herself.

Her outgoing personality and her taste for good-natured gossip meant that she was well-suited to life in a village community where she joined in everything and helped everyone. A regular earth mother, both in appearance and personality, she grew fruit and vegetables in the garden, made her own floaty clothes, and rode a battered old-fashioned bicycle, often with her beloved Yorkshire Terrier Dolly Daydream in the basket on the handle-bars.

Hannah could never figure out why she thought it but there was something about her neighbour that made her wonder if that was what Rowena would have been like if she had lived. Ray had told her that their mother had been a fun-loving wife, an adoring parent, and a free spirit who had loved her children and always put them first. Fliss fitted that description perfectly too.

'Do you want to take some runner beans back with you for dinner? And some rhubarb as well?' she asked. 'I've got plenty of both, and if you're under the weather some fresh fruit and veg will do you the world of good.' She paused for a moment. 'And Ben, of course. What time is he due home today?'

The question was casual enough, but although possibly only related to the beans and rhubarb, Hannah wondered if it had in fact been asked because Fliss wanted to be prepared for him storming round in a temper looking for his wife. Again.

'He's away until tomorrow evening. I know what you're thinking, Fliss, but last time he was just so stressed out after getting caught up in the gridlock of the M25 and then worried because, when he finally got home, I wasn't there but my car was. And of course I'd forgotten to lock the back door. He's not usually like that, you know, really he isn't . . . '

'I understand, Hannah my love, really I do,' Fliss replied softly. 'And you're right — stress can do all sorts of things to people. I imagine he was just letting off steam at you as you were nearest to him at that moment . . . again.'

'That's right.' Hannah smiled in relief. 'And it really was my fault, you know. I wasn't there when he got home, and because I'd left the door unlocked he was worried something had happened to me. But I do feel awful that he ranted at you as well, that was unforgivable of him . . . '

Hannah knew she was going way overboard in her defence of Ben but she hated it when other people misunderstood her husband. She didn't want them to think badly of him.

'It's no problem, Hannah, you know that. I've told you often enough, you really don't have to apologise for him. Now, do you want a cup or a mug? I must admit, I do like a nice big chunky mug though my sniffy young sister Olivia always wants a bone china cup and saucer, preferably Royal Albert. She thinks I'm uncouth even to have mugs in the house, says they're common. No one would ever guess we were sisters but I love her dearly, regardless of her foibles . . . '

Fliss stopped as she saw Hannah's eyes fill up.

'Whatever's the matter, Hannah? Tell me, is it Ben?' Fliss leaned over and touched her arm gently.

'I guess it's you talking about your sister. Did I

ever tell you that I have a sister? A younger sister? A sister I never see?'

Fliss frowned.

'No, I don't think you did. I know you have a brother in America whom you don't see but I don't think you've ever mentioned a sister. Though of course you might have . . . you know how forgetful I can be. What's brought this on all of a sudden?'

Hannah sniffed loudly. 'Julie is my little sister who ran away when she was only fifteen, when I went off to university, and I haven't seen her since. Well, I *have* seen her recently but that's the problem . . . ' As the words flowed so the tears started. 'Can I talk to you in strict confidence? Will you promise me you won't tell anyone? No one? I haven't told a soul about this and I can't tell Ben, not yet. I'm so ashamed of myself . . . '

'Oh, Hannah, you know me. I won't say a word, I promise. I know I love a bit of a natter now and again, but I'm like a priest in the confessional when I have to be!' Fliss put a stacked plate of chocolate biscuits on the small table between them and smiled. 'Have a couple of these first, before you say anything. They'll make you feel so much better. Raise your sugar levels. Camomile tea and chocolate biscuits . . . now there's a mix for you.'

'Oh, God, I daren't have biscuits. Ben says my arse is way too big. He says I ate too much on holiday but the food was wonderful . . . '

'Oh, bugger Ben. What does he know? You've got a fantastically feminine figure, all the curves in the right places, unlike me with my non-existent boobs and droopy old woman's scrawny bum, dragging along the floor behind me . . .'

Hannah managed a watery smile as she wiped her eyes and tried to stop the tears. Without commenting, Fliss pulled a small pack of tissues out of her handbag and passed them over before settling down in the opposite chair and quietly sipping her tea. She didn't force the issue or press Hannah into words, simply sat there and waited.

Hannah's brain was in turmoil. She knew that the moment she confided the situation she was in she would be committed to doing something about it. She would have to go and see Julie.

But she also knew Fliss would be sympathetic and a good adviser. And right at that moment, when everything was closing in on her, Hannah had to talk to someone. She needed a friendly, dispassionate ear more than anything.

'I don't know where to start. Whatever way I put this, I'm going to sound completely uncaring and selfish. Well, I *was* uncaring and selfish. I was so horribly self-centred, so wrapped up in myself and my own life, that I simply dismissed Julie from my mind. Now I've found out that she's had a truly horrendous life with no one to help her out ever.'

She paused and looked at Fliss sadly. 'I know our Aunt Marian was the catalyst for so much of that unhappiness, and that she was the adult, but I should have been stronger. I know that now . . . How could I have been such a bitch? I was her elder sister, I should have looked out for Julie, and yet I did the most selfish thing imaginable.'

'We all do things that with hindsight were a bad idea, but I don't think you could ever have been deliberately malicious, and certainly not at that age. But start at the beginning and between us maybe we can figure out a solution. Something that helps put the past in perspective.'

'I don't see how that can happen now. What I did was so bad . . . '

'There's a solution to everything,' Fliss said. 'It just takes a while to find it sometimes.'

'But, Fliss, I can see it all so clearly now. She must have been pregnant when I went away to university, and I think in the back of my mind I knew it.' Looking down, Hannah slowly ripped the tissue in her hand into tiny pieces as she spoke. 'I knew she was sleeping with that boy, I just didn't want to think about it because then I would have had to do something and maybe lose my own chance to get away. So I went off and left a pregnant fifteen-year-old to fend for herself. No wonder she ran away! Imagine having to tell our aunt that . . . '

'It wasn't your fault, I'm sure. Now start at the beginning, I'm lost already.' Fliss reached across and patted her hand sympathetically.

'Oh, it *is* my fault,' Hannah stated firmly, 'it's definitely my fault. And now I don't know what to do to make amends.'

7

At nearly eighteen, Hannah was eagerly anticipating both her birthday and her new life as she made her way back home from school.

'Going to University' had changed from being a pipe-dream to reality and now she was looking forward to being away from both Aunt Marian and East London for ever. Just one more term to finish at school, one more, exam, one more lot of school holidays, and that would be it. Hannah didn't even contemplate not getting the right grades, she knew without doubt she had worked hard enough.

Already she was spending as much time out of the house as possible, either working in the local bookshop or studying in the library, as she detached herself in anticipation of the change she knew she would have to make, from submissive child to independent adult; she was going to be a person in her own right.

Although over the previous few years, life with Aunt Marian had become a little easier, it was still far from being a normal existence. A part of Hannah was sad about going away and leaving her sister, but the two girls had grown as far apart as it was possible for two siblings who lived together to be, and she doubted that Julie would really miss her.

Although they still shared the same bedroom, they no longer shared secrets. Julie openly despised Hannah for being a doormat to their aunt, and Hannah hated the fact that Julie was forever bunking off school and rebelliously hanging around with the local bad lads. It also seemed to her that every time her sister got in trouble, Hannah too became caught up in it.

She was relieved that over recent years they had found a protector in Gerald Kelly, their next-door neighbour. The elderly man had become quite a fixture in the house although he still kept his own home and went back and forth between the two. When he was around, Aunt Marian was less hard on the girls and Hannah was relieved to think that, once she was on her own, Julie would have a fatherly figure to stick up for her and keep Aunt Marian in check; it made her feel less guilty about going away to university.

Not that Julie had any more time for him than she did for the Aunt, but then she was always on a short fuse and didn't actually seem to have time for anyone.

That particular day Hannah had been let out of school early to study but instead of going straight to the library as she usually did, she headed for home, concerned about her sister who was off school with one of her regular bouts of tonsillitis. She went into the house as quietly as she could and ran up the stairs. When she got to the top she heard an unusual sound and stopped. Their bedroom door was shut tight but still Hannah could hear what sounded to her like the muffled sounds of sex. Suddenly it hit her that Julie had someone in their bedroom!

Hannah immediately guessed it was Josh, the older boy from school with whom Julie was always hanging around and getting into trouble. The pair had both been given detention only the week before after being caught in the girls' toilets together, having a cigarette and a fumble.

As Hannah stood outside the door, silent and petrified with shock, the rattling of the headboard against the wall and the muffled huffing and puffing carried on for a few seconds more until there was a final undisguised grunt and then silence.

Gently she tried the door but it wouldn't move. Hannah could tell instantly that the chest of drawers had been pushed up against it.

For a moment she thought about trying to force her way in there, it was after all her bedroom as well, but instead she rattled the door handle and coughed loudly enough for Julie to hear before running back downstairs. The house was silent and seemed empty but when she looked out of the kitchen window she saw the Aunt in the garden, snipping away at her plants.

Hannah went out and stood beside her, unsure what to do but aware that she had to protect her sister somehow, give Josh time to get out of the house unseen. If they were caught Aunt Marian would certainly throw Julie out and then Hannah's own university future would be in doubt.

The woman glared as Hannah walked towards her. 'What are you doing here? You're supposed to be at school. It's bad enough having the other one home, I can't be doing with two of you here . . . '

'I've only come to get changed and see how Julie is then I'm going to the library. And anyway, it won't be long before I'm gone for good.'

The clicking sounds from the secateurs grew louder as the Aunt snipped faster.

'Well, I wish you'd take that no-good sister of yours with you. Still, she can't stay here much longer anyway. As soon as she leaves school and the money stops, that's it. I can't afford to keep her. She'll have to get a job or you'll have to have her. It'll be down to you then . . . or you could call in the cavalry from America. I bet they're rolling in it now.'

Hannah stood close to the back door, letting the woman rant on while at the same time listening out for the sound of someone moving around inside the house.

It seemed like forever before she heard the stairs creak very quietly and then the sound of a door; she sighed with relief.

'I'm just going to go up and see how Julie is. She was really poorly when I left this morning . . . '

Hannah coughed loudly to cover any other possible sounds from the house then turned and ran up to their room. Julie was tucked up in her bed with the covers pulled high and her face to the wall.

'You stupid, stupid cow!' Hannah whispered fiercely as she leaned over the bed. 'I heard you. You had that bloody useless specimen Josh in here. What are you thinking of? The Aunt is downstairs, she could have caught you . . . '

Julie turned and pulled the sheet tighter round her neck, staring back with eyes full of hatred. 'More like what are you thinking of? There was no one in here. It's just me and my sick tonsils. Definitely no Josh . . . you must have heard me coughing and sneezing. I've got a cold and a sore throat, remember?'

'Oh, give it a rest! I'm not that stupid, I know the difference, it was you and that bloke at it. Did you do it? Did you use a condom or something? God, you're so stupid.'

Julie sat up in bed angrily and as the sheet dropped down Hannah was relieved to see she still had her nightdress on.

'Just you give it a rest, Little Miss Perfect,' Julie snarled nastily. 'You don't have a clue about what you might or might not have heard. You're still a fucking virgin so don't try and be the big I am with me. You know nothing about sex. And, anyway, what I do is none of your business.'

'You're such a bitch!' Hannah was nearly in tears at her sister's unfairness. 'I heard you from the landing and then I went and stood out in the garden with Aunt M so that I could stop her catching you. I wish I hadn't bothered now. Never again am I going to risk my future at university for you. You're on your own now.'

'I always have been, sister dearest.'

Hannah slammed out of the room, furious that Julie had managed to turn it all around again, and went downstairs.

'Hello, Hannah love, you're home early today.'

She glanced round the door and saw Gerald stretched out in the armchair in the corner of the small morning room that he had claimed as his. He yawned widely, letting his false teeth clatter together.

Feeling squeamish, Hannah took a few deep breaths and forced a smile.

'I'm on study time. I'm going to the library in a minute, I just had to get a book.'

'That's nice. Is everything okay? Only you look a bit upset. Have you been arguing with your sister again?'

'I'm fine. I'm just a bit stressed out, I've got loads of studying to do.'

'That's nice.'

Hannah was convinced that if someone said there was fire upstairs, Gerald would smile and say, 'That's nice.'

Gerald Kelly was an inoffensive man: he was small, wiry, very ordinary; he was also mild-tempered. The long relationship between him and her aunt fascinated Hannah; Gerald was as gentle and mild as Aunt Marian was nasty and spiteful, and yet he seemed to be genuinely fond of her. And he could always jolly her round when she was being bad-tempered.

The Aunt had never married and, once Gerald's ailing wife had died, had been on hand with casseroles and soups and offers to do his housework. Hannah was convinced there was nothing physical between them, that Gerald merely enjoyed being looked after and their relationship was based purely on companionship for both of them. Sometimes he stayed overnight in the winter if he hadn't remembered to turn his heating on, but Aunt Marian would bring down the spare blankets and he would sleep on the sofa. They were never openly affectionate but seemed to be such good companions she often wondered why they didn't formalise it and get married. That way there would only be one lot of bills to pay. She wondered if they were waiting until she and Julie had moved out.

'See you later.' Hannah smiled back at him, suddenly feeling kindly towards Gerald. He had after all been their saviour after a fashion in that his being around had mellowed the Aunt and protected them from the excesses of her violence.

And, of course, when he was there they were given much nicer meals and the house was heated.

'I know you're worried about leaving your sister, but don't be. I'll keep an eye on her for you, I promise. She'll be all right.'

Hannah smiled at him gratefully. 'Thanks, I know you will. I'll see you later.'

''Bye, love,' he answered as he leaned back and closed his eyes again.

8

'You're kidding me, right? This is some kind of joke . . . at least it had better be a joke even though, from where I'm standing, it's not in the least bit funny!'

Hannah lowered her eyes as Ben glared angrily at her across the dining table. She hadn't expected him to be happy at the news that her long-forgotten sister, whom he had heard about but never met, might be about to come into their lives, but she hadn't expected such an outpouring of vitriol either.

Especially as she had only told him the bare outline of her story. Ben hadn't even given her time to finish telling him everything before he erupted.

'It's not going to happen, Hannah. Not a chance. From what you've just told me, this sister and her daughter sound like bit-part players in the movie *Slappers R Us* and I will not have them coming round here with the begging bowl. Jeez, I'm amazed you can even think it.' His face reddened with fury as he banged on the table.

'That's not fair, Ben,' Hannah said calmly, careful to keep her voice even and her body language non-confrontational as she tried to carry on explaining. 'You can't just judge Julie like that without knowing the whole story. And I never said anything about her coming here. I was just explaining how I'd come across her and what a horrendous life she's had and . . . '

'That is such utter, utter bollocks!' he shouted so fiercely he made her physically jump. 'You get out of life what you put in. You had exactly the same upbringing as she did and look at you. No, Hannah. No way are we going to get involved. Don't you see enough of this sort of thing, dealing with the disgusting dregs of society all day, every day, at work? Do you want to start bringing them here as well?'

'That's not what I said or what I meant.' Hannah's voice stayed gentle and conciliatory as always despite her shock at the level of his anger. 'I just feel guilty that she has nothing and I have everything I've ever wanted. She's my sister and I let her down all those years ago. I don't see that it can hurt to go and see her . . . maybe help her a little?'

Ben shook his head fiercely. Hannah could see the veins throbbing to either side of his forehead.

'That's a ridiculous argument. If she'd wanted you to help she could have found you — you said that yourself — so obviously she didn't want to find you. Listen to me carefully, Hannah Your sister is an adult, she's not your responsibility. You're not her mother. No, trust me, you have to leave that unhappy part of your life buried in the past, where it belongs.'

When Hannah had given him the brief outline of Julie's life and explained how guilty she felt, she had expected incredulity, maybe even a touch of intolerance, but not such outright dismissive rage and it had scared her. But then, just as suddenly as he had let rip, he leaned back in his chair, breathed deeply and relaxed.

'Look, I told you when we got married that it would always be just the two of us. No family, no children, just we two. You and me, that was the deal. I was honest about it and I thought we both agreed that that was how it would be. How we both wanted it to be.' Ben managed to look hurt as he shrugged his shoulders. 'You can't move the goal posts just because you've discovered your sister is a total loser with an assortment of crazy kids. You'd never bothered to look for her before, had you? And you didn't care when you thought she was probably doing okay. Take off that stupid social worker hat of yours and think rationally.'

'Yes, but Ben, she's my sister . . . '

'There's no 'but' about it.' As he interrupted her, Ben held his hand up to her face in a stopping motion and then pointed his finger at her across the table. His hand was only inches from her face. 'What we've got, *I've* worked for, and I'm not giving even a pound of it away. Especially to a stranger who sounds like a waster and a whore.' His whole face screwed up with anger as he shouted louder, 'I mean, look at the kids. From what you've told me so far one's nothing more than a performing hooker and another's a total retard! Says it all really.' He shook his head. 'Not going to happen. I've worked hard to pay off the mortgage and get us into the comfort zone. No one is going to change that.'

He stood up and walked round the table to

stand behind Hannah. Putting his hands on her shoulders, he started to massage them a little too forcefully but she didn't say anything despite the pain shooting down her back.

'Just you and me — no one else. No long-lost relatives . . . no one. Now I'm going to get changed and then we can walk down to the pub. It's a nice evening and I could do with a pint. I'm off up North again tomorrow for a couple of days so I need a bit of R and R tonight, with no stress.'

As he left the room, Hannah stayed in her seat. Because Ben had been away working somewhere else for several days, she had given him plenty of time to relax and wind down before she had told him about Julie. Now she was cursing herself for saying anything.

The genie was out of the bottle and she wouldn't be able to put it back.

She had felt so much more confident after talking it over with Fliss. Everything had seemed a lot clearer then and, in her organised way, Hannah had decided in her mind exactly how she was going to handle it.

First, she would tell Ben because, as Fliss had said, she should be able to discuss things as important as that with her husband. Next she would contact Raymond in California who was entitled to know about his half-sister even though Hannah wasn't sure how he'd feel.

And then she would talk to Barry. Fliss had made her realise she had completely over-reacted; it wasn't her fault her sister was a client, as long as she wasn't personally involved in the case. But Fliss was right: she should declare the connection right away and admit to checking out the records.

Then, of course, she would decide the best way to go about cautiously making contact with Julie. It had all seemed so simple when chatting to Fliss. Now Hannah felt as if she was back to square one and as confused as ever.

However, disappointed as she was with Ben's reaction, Hannah still went obediently into the cloakroom, brushed her hair, refreshed her lipstick and sprayed on his favourite perfume, making sure she was ready when he came downstairs. It simply never occurred to her to go against the husband to whom she deferred on everything.

That evening she and Ben walked arm in arm to the nearby pub and, as always, sat closely side by side next to the wide fireplace that dominated the small country local. They appeared to be the perfect couple. Mostly Ben talked about his wheeling and dealing at work and Hannah listened carefully. Neither of them mentioned Julie again.

But despite Ben's public display of affection, once they were home and in bed he simply muttered a casual 'good night', switched off the lights, turned his back, and within minutes was snoring loudly, leaving Hannah to lie awake in the darkness. She and Ben rarely made love these days; it had diminished over the years until they had gradually settled into a routine of perfunctory sex two or three times a year. When it did happen it was mechanical, unadventurous and over in minutes, but she really didn't mind.

Sex had never been that important to Hannah. She saw it as just another domestic chore to be fulfilled exactly the way Ben wanted it fulfilled, so as soon they had settled into the routine of occasional sex it had actually been a relief.

* * *

'Can I speak with Raymond De Souza, please?'

'Who may I say is calling?' the smiley, female voice on the other end of the phone asked.

'Hannah Durman. I'm his sister, calling from England.'

'I'll just check if he's available. Please hold . . . '

There was a pause followed by a sudden burst of bouncy muzak.

Hannah had only met up with Raymond De Souza once and that had been several years previously; unfortunately she had built up too many expectations of the meeting and it had turned out to be a disaster. She and Ben had been holidaying in California and, at Ben's instigation, had driven to Long Beach where Ray lived with his wife Stella and their two daughters. To Hannah's horror, Ben had made no secret of the fact that he'd taken an instant dislike to them both, and the way he had rudely cut short the visit still mortified Hannah when she thought about it.

It was only after that meeting that she had realised Ben had agreed to visit in the first place because he'd anticipated Ray becoming a useful contact to have and to show off. As a salesman himself, Ben had visualised meeting up with a high-flying American counterpart and being able to indulge in some mutual back-slapping whereas, at that time, Ray De Souza was a car dealer whose business was a run-down used car-lot in an out-of-town industrial area inland from Long Beach.

He was also a mountain of a man who towered over Ben, tall and wide with a penchant for knee-length khaki shorts, loose casual shirts and brightly coloured baseball caps, a complete opposite from Ben who was always immaculately turned out.

The evening they had been invited to 'meet the friends' at Ray and Stella's, Ben had been expecting a networking opportunity with Ray and some of his business colleagues and had dressed up accordingly, insisting that Hannah did likewise. But when they got there it turned out to be a laid-back barbecue in the back yard of a very ordinary house in a very ordinary street, with Ray and Stella's friends and hordes of children eagerly scoffing mountains of barbecued steaks, huge burgers and hot-dogs dripping with onions.

Hannah had enjoyed the casual socialising but Ben had hated it and made no secret of the fact before loudly insisting on leaving after a couple of hours; he had then categorically refused to have anything to do with the De Souzas ever again.

As usual Hannah had concurred with her husband, outwardly at least. In fact, Ray often emailed her but she always deleted them just in case Ben saw them. She wasn't sure how he'd react if he knew she was still in contact with her brother.

'Yo, Hannah!' Ray's voice boomed down the line. 'Long time no hear. Gee, it's been so long I thought you'd forgotten about me! How's it going? What can I do for you on this sunny Californian day?'

Hannah smiled to herself at the greeting. She guessed the jolly-salesman pitch that he used on his customers was such second nature to Ray that he used it all the time. It was the same pitch that had successfully misled Ben!

'Hello, Ray, it's all going okay . . . or rather, it was. I'm calling because I've got some news that I thought you'd like to know. In fact, I've got good news and bad news.' She paused for a second before continuing. 'The good news is that I've found Julie . . . '

'Wow! That is some news,' he interrupted immediately. 'How come, after all this time? Is she okay? What did she say? Did she ask about me?' He fired off the questions one after the other until Hannah interrupted him.

'Hang on, Ray, here comes the bad news. I know where she is, I know all about her, but I haven't met up with her yet. Oh, Ray, she is in such an awful mess but I only found out about it by accident at work and I'm not sure if she wants anything to do with me. Or you. She is one very angry woman with just so much bad history . . . ' As she started to gabble the tale rapidly, Ray broke in calmly.

'Okay, okay, I hear you but I have someone with me right now so this really isn't a good time for a conversation like this. I've only just got into work after a few days' vacation down in Aruba. Shall we fix a convenient time for me to call you back when I'm alone? What about Ben? Does he know?'

'Yes, sort of, but he doesn't know I'm phoning you, though. It's only because I don't want to worry him, he's so busy right now . . . ' Hannah answered defensively. 'I'm around all day for you to call back, but Ray — I'd sooner you didn't tell Stella. I don't want her calling me at home and maybe getting Ben. The last time he went crazy, as you know . . . '

'Yep, I sure do know! Psycho Ben unleashed. Even on the phone way across the ocean Stella was scared . . . real scared of him.'

'It wasn't his fault, Ray. She caught him when he was working and he lost his train of thought. You know how Ben is . . . not big on family . . . and anyway I want to deal with this in my own way.'

'Good for you, Han. I'll call later when I'm alone, okay?'

After she had put the phone down, Hannah sighed. Just a couple of weeks ago her life had been uncomplicated and content. She'd had a husband who loved her even if he had problems showing it, a gorgeous home on which they had spent a lot of time and money to get it just the way they wanted, and she'd had a career that, although admittedly stressful, she enjoyed.

All had been well in her life until suddenly

thoughts of the past she'd believed safely locked away forever returned to unsettle her. Now she was feeling completely distracted. Even unhappy.

She clicked the kettle and went out into the garden to try to think it all through before she spoke with her brother again. She couldn't figure out what to do for the best. She walked down to the bottom of the carefully landscaped cottage garden and looked back at her home: the whitewashed country cottage of her fantasies, with roses round the door and wisteria up the walls, that was now a reality. She adored it.

In fact, she adored her life exactly the way it was.

Deep in thought, she physically jumped when the phone rang.

'Hannah, I couldn't wait any longer. I've locked the door and I'm all yours. Tell me about it . . . '

And so she did. Everything that she knew.

'I am so shocked, I never for one moment imagined it would be like that for the kid. What can we do?' he asked.

'I haven't got a clue, Ray, but I have a feeling we won't get a very warm welcome if we just barge on in there. As I said, Julie is angry at everything and everyone.'

'Well, we've got to do something, and do it now. Give me her number, I'll call her . . . '

'Don't push it, Ray. Let me think about it some more and I'll let you know what I'm going to do. This is all so complex, Julie's so complex, it all needs very careful handling . . . '

There was a pause before Ray answered and

then his tone was marginally cooler.

'You're confusing me now. Where do I stand in all this? Why did you call me if you want to deal with it all yourself? Do you really want me to be part of this or not?'

'Of course I do,' Hannah answered quickly, 'but it's no good crashing into her life, being all gung-ho, and then crashing out again. Are you going to jump on a plane and head over here to play at being her big brother? Be there to give her loads of fraternal advice on how to get her life back on track?'

The pause was just a couple of seconds too long. 'Sure I would, if I thought it would help.'

'No, you wouldn't, Ray. You've got a business, a wife and a family over there. Your life is where you are right now, and that's how it should be.' Hannah could feel her emotions rising to the surface again as she tried to say exactly what she was thinking. 'You were taken away from us all those years ago and had no choice but to go. I was older when I left. I had a choice. I could have stayed and watched over Julie, I could have skipped university and got a job, but I didn't. I just went, and left her to fend for herself. I was absolutely selfish then. Now I owe her.'

'Well, then, I guess we both owe her. I could have gone back to Britain anytime but I didn't.'

There were a few moments of silence when neither of them spoke. When Ray eventually did his voice too was choked.

'You keep me up to date, yeah? Maybe I can make a trip soon. I don't want us to fight, Han.'

'Me neither, Ray. I'll keep you up to speed on it all, I promise.'

Ray had only really been a part of the first years of Hannah's life, those four years she couldn't remember anything about how, no matter how hard she tried. She didn't remember her half-brother then and she certainly didn't remember what either of her parents looked like.

'His memories of those few happy years before Aunt Marian were now her memories, and she cherished every one.'

Suddenly she felt incredibly sad that Julie had none of those memories because there had never been anyone there to share them with her.

9

Julie was standing at the children's clothes stall in the local market, daydreaming while looking longingly at the tiny pair of knockoff designer jeans and the faux-fur waistcoat that she desperately wanted to buy for her daughter. She could just picture her in the outfit and was trying to work out a way of finding the money for them when Katya suddenly bounced up and down in her buggy and started shouting.

'Daddy, Daddy! Look, Daddy . . . '

At first Julie didn't register her daughter's words amid the buzz of multiple conversations going on around her, but when the words did sink in she immediately spun round to look in the direction Katya was excitedly pointing. She was just in time to catch sight of Sebastian Rumbar ducking into one of the shops that edged the market road. Quickly grabbing at the handle of the buggy, Julie pushed her way through the crowds and caught up with him as he was about to try to sneak out around the other side of the newsagent's shelving rack that ran down the centre of the shop. 'SEB! Don't pretend you didn't hear Katya calling you, the whole market heard her,' shrieked Julie as she cut him off with the pram but then stopped in her tracks as she suddenly realised there was a female beside him, her arm looped possessively, affectionately, through his.

'Hi, Julie.' Seb looked at her warily as he leaned forward and patted Katya's head.

'What are you doing here?'

'Oh, just having an enjoyable spin round the market, looking at all the things I can't afford to buy for your daughter because you haven't given me any money for her since fuck knows when,' Julie snapped back. 'You do remember you have a daughter, don't you?'

When he didn't say anything, she looked at the girl now standing slightly behind him.

'You look surprised, luv. Didn't he tell you about his daughter? This is Katya, she's three now . . . oh, and let me introduce myself. I'm Julie, the mother of the daughter.'

'Oh, yes, and I nearly forgot — I'm also his girlfriend. And you are?'

Julie held out her hand and grinned sarcastically but the girl nonchalantly crossed her arms and glanced away in apparent disinterest.

'Don't create a scene here, Julie, please, you'll upset Katya.' Smiling, Seb bent down to the buggy and leaned forward to kiss the child. 'Hello, baby, how are you? Do you want Daddy to buy you some sweeties?'

As Katya reached up her arms, Julie viciously kicked out at Seb, catching his knee and sending him sprawling backwards or to the floor. Immediately the girl held out her hands to help him up.

'I'll upset Katya?' Julie shouted. 'What do you mean, I'll upset Katya? You are just such a dick-head! Katya is already as upset as she can because you haven't been near her. You haven't even picked up the phone to talk to her, you selfish bastard.'

Julie knew she was starting to lose control; she tried hard to contain herself because of Katya but could sense that something in the dynamics between the three of them was very wrong. She felt like the odd one out and strangely intimidated by the young woman who was so obviously with Seb even though she was definitely not the type he usually hung around with. Although only in her twenties, she looked sophisticated and glamorous in an understated way with dark silky hair hanging halfway down her back and just a touch of makeup on her lips, eye-lashes and perfect cheekbones. Her jeans were well-cut and obviously designer, and the soft metallic leather handbag hanging from her shoulder definitely didn't come from the 'fake' stall further up the market.

The girl was classy and she was with Seb. Even worse, she looked as if she belonged with him. Somehow they matched.

As Julie looked the girl up and down it suddenly registered with her that Seb looked far smarter than usual in light beige casual trousers and a navy blue, short-sleeved shirt worn hanging loosely over them. His usual Nike trainers had been replaced with brown loafers that looked brand new. He also looked a lot older; more mature. It was as if he had been dressed by someone else.

Julie didn't recognise any of the clothes he was wearing; in fact, she hardly recognised him.

'Well? Nothing to say for yourself, you nasty

bastard? What about the slag here then? Does it speak or is it just a bit of thick arm candy for the day?' Julie sneered.

Motivated both by fear of the situation and the bad vibes she could feel flying towards her from both of them, Julie did the only thing she could think of and went on the attack.

Slowly the girl moved her gaze and looked directly at her, making full eye-contact for the first time.

'Oh, yes, I speak, but only if there is someone I wish to speak with.' Her English was perfect though her accent was strong. 'But you have no manners and show no respect for either your child or the father of your child so I don't wish to speak with you.' She then turned purposefully towards Seb. 'Come, Sebastian, we will be late for lunch. The table is booked for one o'clock and I know your parents will not like to be kept waiting.'

Julie looked at Seb who immediately lowered his eyes.

Everything about this confrontation was wrong.

'What parents? You told me you had no parents. Said there was no one for Katya to know. You said . . . ' Suddenly she stopped, aware that she was revealing too much.

The girl smiled. 'I think maybe Sebastian would not like his parents to meet with you. He would be too ashamed. But we will do what is necessary for Katya. She will not be deprived of her father or money for her support. Maybe she can even meet her grandparents now.'

Still Seb said nothing.

Julie tried to figure out what was going on but her brain wouldn't let her. Although Seb looked guilty, he also seemed a little amused, even flattered by the situation. The girl meanwhile looked at Julie with undisguised distaste. Julie wanted to lash out and hurt her, to wipe that smug expression off her face, but once again the presence of Katya stopped her.

'I'm talking to the organ grinder, not the monkey. Seb? I asked you about Katya. Your daughter . . . '

He smiled. 'I'll pick her up on Sunday and take her out for the day.' He looked from Julie to Katya. 'Do you want to come out with Daddy on Sunday? We could go to the seaside if it's warm . . . '

'Yeeeeessss!'

'She's not going anywhere with you . . . ' Julie interrupted.

'Well, make up your mind. You just asked what I was going to do about her. I'm still going to see her, of course I am, I was just letting the dust settle before I told you about Ciara. Now you know so . . . '

'Get this straight. You can see her but, as I just said, she's not going anywhere with you. And anyway, we have things to talk about. Alone. Without the slag there in tow!'

At that point the child suddenly shrieked loudly and burst into tears. 'I want my daddy! I want to go with Daddy!'

Julie was torn. She wanted to walk off but she knew if she did she had no way of getting in contact with him. The mobile number she had for him was already disconnected as she had discovered the previous week, and he had never had a permanent address when he wasn't with her. Or so she had thought.

As she hesitated, the girl started to walk towards the door. She grabbed Seb's hand and pushed straight past Julie, pulling him with her.

'Seb . . . ' Julie pleaded, unable to hide the panic in her voice. 'How can I contact you if something's wrong with your daughter? How can I find you?'

'I'll come round at midday on Sunday and we'll talk it all through. We'll sort it out then. I'm sorry, Julie, I was going to tell you, it's just . . . '

'Don't bring *her* with you,' Julie interrupted him. 'I'm not letting her in, this is none of her business.'

The girl turned back to her and, with a wide smile that showed perfectly straight white teeth, slowly held out her left hand, splaying her fingers as wide as she could.

'Do not call me 'her'. I am Sebastian's fiancée and I have a name. It is Ciara Rodriguez. Sebastian and I are to be married soon and he will no longer be visiting you, but I will permit one last meeting for you to make the arrangements for his child.' She switched her smile to Katya. 'Oh, yes, and Sebastian has already told me about his accidental child so it is no surprise to me that he has a daughter and that she has a mother. It is not a problem. He described you to me perfectly.'

Julie felt quite sick as she took in the glitzy

engagement ring twinkling on the girl's tanned and perfectly manicured hand, and the superior smile on her lips.

'You what? You're having me on. Seb, is this true?'

'Julie, I'm sorry, I just said. I know I should have told you . . . I was going to . . . but don't take it out on Katya. I'll come round Sunday, at lunchtime, and we'll sort it out then after you've calmed down. We have to do what's best for her . . . '

But Julie couldn't let herself respond. Even as he was speaking she turned away from them and marched off in the opposite direction, pushing the buggy aggressively along the busy pavement, completely oblivious to the angry passers-by she was barging out of the way and the hysterical child in front of her.

It took her just five minutes to make it home, half the time it usually took, but she knew that if she had slowed before she got inside her front door she would have broken down in public. And Julie Grayson never let anyone see her break down. She unbuckled Katya who was sobbing uncontrollably, lifted her out and hugged her close, all the while making soothing noises.

She had trusted Seb, let him into her daughter's life, and now he had betrayed them both; the same as everyone else had betrayed her. She decided then and there that she would never let him see Katya again. Never.

The vibes she had felt during that confrontation came back to her in a rush and Julie was suddenly very scared.

Still determined not to break down, she continued to soothe her daughter; she cuddled her, stroked her brow, and then when the sobbing didn't subside, gave Katya a double dose of the cough medicine that made her sleepy. Again.

When Katya dropped off, Julie left her on the sofa, covered with a fleece blanket, crept into the kitchen, lit a cigarette and tried to figure out what exactly had just happened. She'd always thought of herself as sharp and streetwise yet she had never seen it coming; she needed to find out how it could have happened right under her nose. Admittedly, Seb had stormed out, as he often did, but she had expected him to wander back in eventually. How could he have been having a relationship with someone else? she wondered angrily. How could he be engaged, about to be married, and never have given her so much as a hint.

Or had he?

Despite the ten-year age gap between her and Sebastian, they'd got on well together but Julie had been wary of having another man living with her and it had been her choice not to let him move in. Or so she had thought. Now she wondered if it had actually been her choice or whether he had just let her think that; maybe casual was all he had wanted, and she had played right into his hands.

A fierce crashing on the front door sent her flying down the hall to open it; she wanted Katya to stay asleep and calm for as long as possible.

'Here's young Jethro home to his mum. Julie,

I'm sorry, luv, but I'm afraid he was a bit of a handful again on the bus today. I'm going to have to record it.' The elderly care assistant who regularly travelled on the bus smiled apologetically at her. 'He hit Samantha really hard on the back of the head. I know it's not what you want to hear, especially after last time, but Samantha was screaming when we dropped her off at home.'

Blissfully unaware of their conversation, Jethro grinned happily and tried to push past his mother but she grabbed his hand just in time to stop him from darting through to the lounge and waking up Katya.

'They're going to ban him from the bus, aren't they? I just know it. I don't know what I'll do if that happens . . . my car is off the road . . . do you think they'll allocate a cab?'

'I'll put in a good word for him. I love Jethro, you know that, but I really do have to report the incident. I know he didn't mean to hurt her, he just doesn't know how strong he is and it's getting harder for me to manage him . . . '

'Tell me about it,' Julie sighed. 'I'll just have to wait and see what happens, I suppose.'

With a deep sigh, she closed the front door and led her son into the kitchen where she tried to persuade him to sit at the table.

'Please, Jeth, sit down and Mummy will get your special biscuits. Please? Special biscuits for Jethro, look.'

Julie rattled the tin but Jethro wasn't in the mood to sit still and eat biscuits. He wanted to play, he wanted to rough and tumble with Katya and torment the dog that had already run upstairs to hide under the bed. Forcefully he pulled away and made a clumsy break for the back door.

But Julie had already locked the door and put all the bolts across in advance. Despite being only twelve, Jethro Grayson was already taller and wider than his mother, and his disability meant he was completely oblivious to his own strength. He was affectionate with bear-hugs and loving with big sloppy kisses, but when he did cuddle her he didn't know when to stop and had bruised her many times. He was so big and strong it was getting to the point where Julie struggled to manage him, though she did her best.

When he couldn't get the back door open he started kicking it as hard as he could. Julie moved to stop him and tried to pull him away but he just thought it was part of the game. As he swung around he knocked her over, sending her flying across the kitchen table; because she was so light she slid straight across the shiny surface and off the other side, landing awkwardly on the tiled floor. She heard the crack of a bone as she landed but forced herself to stay conscious and calm. She tried to get up but the pain was excruciating.

'Katya . . . ' she called, praying the sedative she had given the child had worn off. 'Katya, Mummy needs you to come here.' Her voice was rising to hysteria pitch as the pain took over. 'Katya . . . ' Eventually the child wandered through, looking bewildered.

'Katya, go into the hall and get Mummy's phone out of her handbag, I need you to bring it to me. Quickly, I've hurt my leg and have to ring the doctor . . . Quickly!'

Eventually the child came back with it. 'Get up off the floor, it's dirty,' she said.

'Just give me the bloody phone!' shrieked Julie as the pain seared through her.

She dialled 999. The last thing she saw before she passed out was Katya's crumpled face beside hers as Jethro stood over them, laughing happily at this new game of pushing Mummy around the floor with his feet.

10

'I'm not staying here any longer, I'm going home.' Julie winced as she tried to sit up on the trolley but it was impossible, especially with a chunky male nurse gently pushing her back down.

'Get off me! I'm fine. I have to get home . . . my kids are there on their own.'

'Your children are okay, Mrs Grayson. Your neighbour phoned just now to see how you are. She is still with them. But you're not okay. If you get up you may do yourself even more damage.'

'But I'm fine, I'm telling you. I tripped and fell awkwardly and twisted my leg, but now I'm okay so I'm off.'

She leaned forward as if to swing her legs over the side of the trolley but once again the nurse put a gentle hand on her arm stopped her.

'Don't move . . . '

'Get your hands off me!' Julie shouted as she looked around madly for a way out.

'Please listen to me. You have to go and be X-rayed. It's likely that something is broken and if you try and walk you'll make it far worse. Please let us help you.' The nurse's voice was low and calm as he tried to reason with her.

'Oh, great. Just what I need, a fucking broken leg!'

Despite her ongoing protests, Julie finally gave in and leaned back just as the curtain was pulled aside and Autumn came in.

Julie looked at her in horror. 'What the fuck are you doing here?'

'Oh, great. Nice to see you, too, Mummy dearest.' Autumn smiled grimly.

'I said, what are you doing here?'

'The hospital rang me. They got my number from your phone. You'd tagged it 'in case of emergency'. I'm flattered!'

Julie shook her head; she was furious that Autumn was here to see her like this. 'Well, you can go again because I'm leaving now anyway. I'm fed up with lying here waiting for someone to tell me something. I can't leave Jethro and Katya, can I? You know that . . . '

'All I know right now is probably the same as you — you've maybe broken something and it could be nasty. But, hey, if you want to end up in a heap on the floor, then you try and get yourself off that trolley and out the door! I'm not helping you.'

Julie was in agony but she tried hard not to let anyone see. Every part of her hurt. She felt as if she had been badly beaten and kicked; it reminded her of when she had been in that situation before, a long time ago, but this time it was different. She couldn't have moved even if she had wanted to.

Julie found that she was in a small curtained cubicle with just the trolley and a chair; Autumn sidled past the nurse and sat down on the chair.

'I know you don't like me helping you but right at this moment you have no choice so I'm not going to play games with you. I've booked some time off work. I'll go to yours tonight and look after the kids and then we'll take it from there.'

'You can't look after the kids, you haven't got a clue! And anyway, I won't let you.'

As Autumn started to reply the curtain was pulled back again and two porters appeared. 'Mrs Grayson for X-ray?'

Suddenly Julie felt really scared as the enormity of the situation hit her. For so many years she had coped one way or another with her circumstances, with her life, but now everything was spinning out of her control. She was captive on a rickety hospital trolley, with no way of escape.

'What do they think I've done?' she asked the nurse who was still hovering nearby.

'Maybe fractured your leg or your hip, maybe nothing. We don't know for sure.'

'Only old people fracture their hips.'

'And anyone else who falls badly. But, as I said, we won't know until after the X-ray so let's get you gone and then we'll know for sure.' He paused for a second and looked at her with his head on one side. 'How did you say it happened?'

'I tripped over the table leg, fell across the top of it and landed on my side. Is that good enough for you? The floor is tiled and hard.'

He looked at her closely. 'We have to ask these things, Julie, especially as your records show you've been seriously assaulted before. We try to help . . . '

'This was nothing like that. If it was, he'd be

lying on a trolley as well, with his nuts packed in ice waiting to be re-attached. This was an accident. There were only the kids there,' she shouted, furious that the nurse thought she was lying.

'Don't get upset, Ma, now isn't the time to lose it,' Autumn interrupted, her voice gentle but firm. She looked at the nurse. 'Leave it. It was obviously an accident or, trust me, she would have said.'

Despite the fact that she still couldn't look her daughter in the eye, Julie felt grateful to have someone on her side for a change. She didn't protest when Autumn automatically followed along through to the X-ray department. Once they were outside the room and waiting, Julie reached out and grabbed on to her daughter's hand.

'Please don't let Seb use this as an excuse to take Katya away from me. Please? He's got someone else, they're getting married, and I know inside me that he's going to want to take her. Please don't let him do that. *Please?*'

Autumn smiled. 'Of course I won't. No way!'

Julie forced herself to look directly at her daughter. 'Thank you.'

'No prob, Ma.'

By the time Julie was wheeled down to the operating theatre later that night to have her badly fractured hip pinned, Autumn had already left to go back to the children and Julie was alone again with her fears and demons.

The last time she had been taken to Accident and Emergency had been when Jethro's father

had beaten her to a pulp for getting pregnant.
With Jethro.

It had been nothing short of a miracle that she hadn't lost the baby, but Julie often wondered if that beating was the cause of his disabilities. Poor Jethro, a battering from his father before he was even born. She also had to fight regularly against the thought that maybe it would have been better if he hadn't survived.

* * *

Autumn Grayson was starting to look at her mother through different eyes. It had only been a few days since the accident and already she was worn out from trying to cope with Julie's life single-handedly. She just couldn't imagine how her mother coped 24/7 with Jethro and Katya, who were both proving to be a huge challenge albeit in completely different ways. Jethro was loving and happy but absolutely unaware of his size and strength so he needed constant supervision as well as feeding and changing. Every time Autumn took Jethro into the bathroom to change him she wanted to gag; she dreaded it. Then, while this was going on, Katya constantly whined and threw huge temper tantrums just to gain her share of attention. It was a difficult line for Autumn to tread.

She understood her baby sister's demands because Autumn herself had had a chequered upbringing, but she still found Katya's neediness hard to deal with.

Her own childhood had consisted of more

time spent in foster care than with her mother, but she had been lucky, she supposed. Whenever Julie hadn't been able to cope, which was more often than not, especially once she had Jethro, Autumn had always been able to go to the same foster family who had treated her as one of their own.

Her foster parents, Alec and Jan, were much older than her mother, really more like foster grandparents. Autumn loved them and they adored her back and had constantly told her how beautiful and clever she was. She needed that reinforcement to compensate her for the lack of affection from her mother; it had helped bolster her self-confidence, and consequently Autumn had grown up feeling secure and confident of her ability to make something of herself.

In fact, she now understood her mother better than her mother understood her. When she was younger Autumn had often wondered why Julie seemed to dislike and resent her, but once she started to grow up her foster parents had helped her realise that the failing lay not with herself but with Julie. Eventually the girl had been able to accept the situation and even appreciate that her mother had led a rotten life.

Now Autumn heard the front door open and flew out into the hall just as Seb came in.

'What are you doing, letting yourself in here like that? Don't you know what a doorbell is?'

'Sorry! Julie doesn't usually mind. What are you doing here?'

'I should ask you the same question, under the circumstances . . . '

'Not that it's any of your business, but it was arranged. Your mother and I have things to talk about privately. And anyway, I want to see Katya.' He looked around expectantly. 'Where is she?'

'Julie or Katya? Who do you mean?'

'Either of them. Where are they?' He smiled his usual charming smile, but after a morning of mayhem Autumn wasn't in the mood for Seb.

'Katya's not here, she's at a friend's birthday party, and Julie is in hospital. She's had an accident. But she's fine and so are the rest of us so you don't need to bother yourself.' Autumn's tone was cool and dismissive but Seb ignored it.

'How long is Julie going to be in hospital for then?'

'Not sure . . . she's had surgery and is in traction. She said she fell but I think maybe it was something to do with Jethro. You know how rough he can be. But that's irrelevant right now. She's totally incapacitated for the moment.'

Seb looked genuinely shocked. 'Oh, wow! That seems hard on her . . . and you as well if you're having to deal with everything here. I know from experience how fucking mad that can be. What time shall I collect Katya? Tell me where she is and she can come back and stay with me. That'll just leave you with Jethro.'

'Back with you to where exactly?' Autumn asked, knowing full well what the answer would be.

'Where I'm living now. My home . . . '

'What? You and the new girlfriend, fiancée, whatever she is? Or you and your newly appeared, freshly dug up from their graves, parents? Not a chance. I'm responsible for Katya and I don't want her going off somewhere unknown,' Autumn snapped at him. 'Look, I'm sorry, Seb, but how could you do what you did to Julie? She didn't do anything to hurt you. Why couldn't you just have been honest with her?'

'She told you about me and Ciara then?'

Seb grinned sheepishly and his little-boy act suddenly infuriated Autumn.

'She told me, and I think you're a first-rate shit. It's just good manners to finish one relationship before starting another. And engaged so soon? Come on, I wasn't born yesterday, this has been going on for ages. Why didn't you tell the mother of your child, huh?'

Suddenly Seb stopped smiling.

'I've known Ciara for years, and, not that it's any of your business, Julie had a go at me just once too often. I love Katya but I'm not your mother's pet puppy, to be battered whenever she gets pissed off with her life. She is getting to be dangerous when she's on the stuff and kicks off. Well, I'd had enough of all the abuse and I met someone else. Shit happens. Now, where's my daughter?'

'Sorry, Seb, but Katya is in my care until Julie gets home. Apparently you haven't bothered with her at all recently so a bit longer won't hurt, then you can sort it out with Julie yourself. Now just go, will you?'

Autumn pointed towards the front door, hoping that Jethro wouldn't decide to leave the sand-pit in the garden and come indoors. He adored Seb and it would set him off if he couldn't go with him.

'So you think I'm going to let a stripper look after my daughter?'

Autumn laughed. 'Be very careful, Sebastian. Remember, I know where the bodies are hidden — figuratively speaking, of course. I know about you supplying my mum, keeping her as high as the Empire State Building half the time and down the other half.'

As he glared at her angrily, she laughed.

'We may not be best buddies, me and my ma, but there's not a lot I don't know about her life so if you want to push it, then do. But be afraid, Seb, be really afraid, because I am far more calculating than Julie and in the least not befuddled by any need for your noxious substances!'

'Save it, you daft bitch! I only ever got her what she asked for. She had those problems and more when I met her. I tried to help, but right now there's no one on this earth who can, you know that! My only concern is my daughter.'

Their silent eye-to-eye stand-off lasted a few seconds before, glowering furiously, Sebastian turned and walked out, muttering over his shoulder, 'This isn't the end of it, you know. I have the clout to get my daughter and I'll use it if I have to. Your mother can't look after her properly. Any court with all the info in front of them would agree with that.'

Again Autumn laughed as she slammed the door behind him though actually she felt nowhere near as confident as she pretended to be. She knew that if Seb was going to be married, and if he spilled the beans on Julie, then he stood a very good chance of getting custody of his daughter. And, secretly, she wasn't altogether convinced that it would be a bad thing.

She had no doubt at all that her mother loved Katya, but sometimes, as Autumn knew from personal experience, that wasn't enough.

For the moment she would keep Katya safe with her because she had promised her mother that she would, but Autumn wasn't convinced it was the best thing for her little sister in the long term.

11

'Barry, there's something personal I really have to do. I need a couple of hours off, can you cover? It really is important,' Hannah asked warily.

She knew the moment had come when she would have to do something about the Julie situation. Once again she had sneaked a look at Julie's records and to her horror, had seen that her sister was in hospital after an accident and likely to be there for a long time. Although she felt guilty about deceiving Ben, Hannah justified her actions to herself by arguing that she hadn't actually told him she wouldn't go, and anyway there was no way he would ever find out.

Standing up sharply, she grabbed her jacket and bag.

'Is it okay if I go? Can you manage alone for a while?'

Barry looked across his desk at her, head on one side and expression as impassive as ever.

'Probably not as I don't have eight arms and four brains, but if it's important I'll do my very best . . . '

'It is important, Barry, really it is, and I have to deal with it now while I'm in the right frame of mind. It's a now or never scenario.'

'Nothing you want to talk about?'

Hannah touched his shoulder as she walked towards the door. 'Not now. If I talk about it then I won't go, and I have to even though I don't want to. If you see what I mean! But maybe if you've got time when I get back?'

'Sure. Anything urgent that might happen while you're gone? I need to know so that I can corral someone else.'

'No more than usual, you should be okay, but if so then just ward them off and I'll sort it when I get back. I'll stay late if I have to.' She smiled. 'Thanks, Barry. I owe you one!'

'Too right you do, and you will pay me big bucks for it!' he laughed. 'I expect a chocolate cream éclair when you come back. Good luck.'

'Thanks. Talk later, yeah?'

* * *

Hannah knew the area that she now covered as a social worker like the back of her hand from when she had lived there. It had taken her a while to get used to being back and, although she was adjusting, she still felt uncomfortable here. There were just so many memories for her in these streets.

Several times over the previous few months, since she'd come here to work, she had deliberately driven past her aunt's house, her own childhood home, but had never been brave enough to stop and knock on the door. She wanted to, she wanted to accuse her vicious aunt face to face of what she now knew was the most horrendous child abuse and demand explanations for it, but she was wary of being sucked back in. Strength in the face of Aunt Marian's sheer malice had always been an impossibility for her, and the grown-up Hannah could still feel intimidated by just the thought of her.

Again she deliberately made a detour to drive past the house en route to Julie's address just a few miles away; it would help motivate her for what she was about to do. The house where she and her sister had lived together looked exactly the same as it always had although now it was noticeably tired and neglected with flaking paint on the front door and knee-high weeds in the once perfect garden. The house next-door, where Gerald Kelly had lived, looked completely different, though; it was freshly painted, with new window frames, and there were bright blue roman blinds at the windows. It looked lively and loved by comparison, and Hannah wondered again if Gerald Kelly had finally sold up and moved in with her aunt, or maybe even died. But, much as she wanted to know, she just couldn't bring herself to try to find out.

As she braked sharply to let another car pull out, Hannah shook herself back to the present and carried on her journey.

The short cul-de-sac where Julie lived was gridlocked with cars so she had to park in the next road and walk back round. Julie's house was one of a line of identical council houses built in the sixties to cope with the over-population of the area; a long line of square joined-up boxes built on land that had previously been a grassy open space where children had played.

The people who lived in the older, pre-war houses opposite had resented the newcomers from the start and there was still a famous division between the two sides of the road: the owners or private tenants on one side and the council tenants on the other. Historically and irrationally, each side hated the other despite the fact that it was a relatively trouble-free road where children still played in the small playground that had been built to compensate the residents, and most of the neighbours knew each other, by name.

Hannah walked along counting down the numbers until she reached the one she wanted. Without hesitating she turned into the already-open gate, walked up to the door and knocked firmly.

When there was no answer she knocked again and waited, but still there was no reply. She turned away, not sure if she was disappointed or relieved that no one was home. The file had told her that Julie's eldest daughter, the child Julie had given birth to when she was really only a child herself, was looking after her half-brother and -sister. Hannah wondered about the loyalty, and also the capabilities, of a daughter who had clearly been neglected herself and had consequently spent most of her own childhood in care.

As she reached the gate she came face to face with a young woman pushing a buggy who was about to turn up the path. They stopped, face to face, and instantly Hannah knew who this was. It was almost as if she recognised her although they had never met. Hannah could see herself at twenty in this girl and was shocked; she had expected to see a young Julie, not a replica of herself.

'Can I help you?' the girl asked politely.

'I hope so. Are you Autumn Grayson?'

'Yes, I am,' she replied confidently. 'Who wants to know?'

Hannah smiled. 'It's a bit complicated. Can we talk inside rather than out here?'

'Not if you don't tell me who you are and why you're here, no. It's not my home to invite strangers into . . . '

'I'm not a stranger. Well, not really. Look, I don't want to shock you but I'm your mother's sister. I'm Hannah. I don't know if you've heard about me? You're my niece.'

'And how do I know that what you're saying is true?' Autumn asked suspiciously.

Hannah dipped into her bag and pulled out a photograph, the last one of the two girls together, taken by her friend's mother the day Hannah left for university. After a close look at the photo and then the woman in front of her, Autumn nodded her head slightly and walked up to the front door, pushing the buggy ahead of her.

'You'd better come in then. I was worried you might be here because of this one.' She looked down to the sleeping child. 'Her father reckons he wants custody. I've been expecting the social workers to turn up and want to take her away, especially as Ma is incapacitated,' she said over her shoulder as she put the key in the lock.

'Actually I am a social worker,' Hannah admitted with a grin, 'but, believe me, that's a complete coincidence. Though it is how I found out about Julie . . . I saw her in the office a few weeks ago, but she didn't see me. I recognised her straight away even though it's been so long.'

Autumn led her through into the kitchen and pulled out a chair. 'I guess you know all about my brother Jethro then? He's the biggest headache for Ma. I adore him, we all do, but he's too much for her. Unfortunately, no one will consider the alternative of something like boarding school.'

'I know a little about him,' Hannah said. 'I know he has a learning disability . . . '

Autumn laughed. 'Ooohh, I just love that expression! It conjures up an image of him maybe being a bit behind with his reading or having a little problem with his maths.' She shook her head. 'But I don't want to go into all that now, I just wanted to explain why the house looks so empty and rundown. It's not that my mother doesn't care, it's not neglected, it's just Jethro. He wrecks everything.'

'Hey, you're talking to someone who understands. Really I do.'

'It's so hard. I don't know how she copes, I'm knackered already. Tea or coffee?'

'Either. Whatever you're having.'

Hannah watched as the young woman moved around the kitchen and wondered again how she could be Julie's daughter. They were chalk and cheese. Julie was tiny, angry and hyperactive; Autumn was tall, graceful and calm, with an assurance way beyond her years. Hannah suddenly wished she had had that much self-confidence at this girl's age. At any age, in fact.

As if aware that she was being scrutinised, Autumn suddenly turned round and looked at Hannah.

'Why have you never been in touch? I mean, I knew my mother had a sister but she's never talked about you. I know nothing about any of her family or her childhood other than that it was so crap she never wanted to talk about it. And she didn't. Ever. To her it was all in the past. Gone.'

Hannah could feel hot, unwelcome tears starting to prickle behind her eyes.

'She's right, it was crap, and to my shame I walked away from it and left her behind. Then she ran away and disappeared, and that was that. We went off in opposite directions and never came back to each other. I do regret it . . . I regret it so very, very much.'

'So why now? I know she's in hospital but we've had far worse than that over the years . . . '

Hannah smiled sadly. She knew she couldn't excuse herself but she wanted to try to explain. 'I didn't know about any of that, I had no idea. Before I saw her in the office, I hadn't got a clue where she was or what she was doing. Shall I start at the beginning?'

'That'd be the best way, I reckon.' Autumn's smile was wide and without any trace of malice. ' 'Cos, as I said, I know zilch. My mother doesn't actually like me very much so I never really bothered to ask anything because I knew she wouldn't tell me anyway!' She laughed at

Hannah's shocked expression. 'It's okay. I understand her and I'm used to it. Go on. Tell me all about it.'

Hannah gave her niece a brief outline of her and Julie's early lives and the fact that they had an American half-brother before explaining what she herself had gone on to do.

'I never knew,' Autumn said sadly. 'She never said a word . . . '

'But that's enough from me for the moment,' Hannah interrupted, desperately not wanting to upset the girl any more than she already was. 'Tell me about yourself . . . what do you do?'

'My job? I'm a lap dancer at a club in Soho. An upmarket gentlmen's club they call it, but that's really just a way of justifying the exorbitant charges.'

Hannah wondered if this statement was a challenge. 'How interesting. Do you enjoy it?' she asked with a show of interest rather than any other reaction.

'I do actually. And I enjoy the salary that comes with it. I try to help Ma out but she sees everything I do as a criticism of her, which of course it isn't.' Autumn paused and looked thoughtful. 'Although, thinking about it, she's right in a way. I try not to judge but I don't understand her lifestyle and habits . . . then, if I had to put up with all of this every day, *I'd* probably need a bit of help to get me through!'

'I guess you mean the drugs. How's she doing in hospital? I mean, it must be an involuntary detox for her . . . ' Hannah stopped mid-sentence, suddenly aware she may have overstepped the mark. 'I'm sorry, it's nothing to do with me, I know . . . '

'That's okay. But, no offence, if you knew all this about her, then why haven't you offered to help before now?'

'I told you, I've only known for a short while, just a few weeks, and anyway it's difficult for me. You see, my husband can be somewhat anti-family and he doesn't want me to get involved . . . '

Hannah stopped short when she realised that Autumn was looking at her almost with amusement. For a split second, Hannah was the child, her niece the observant adult.

'That came out all wrong, I didn't mean it like that,' she back-tracked nervously. 'It's just that neither of us has any family so it's always just been the two of us. He just doesn't want to . . . '

'It's okay,' Autumn interrupted her with a knowing smile. 'I understand. Really I do. Your husband doesn't want you to get involved with any long-lost, scummy East End relatives.'

'That's not true! It's not like that at all . . . Ben is a good man and his main concern is me. He just doesn't want me to get too involved and then be hurt if it all goes wrong.'

'Do you have any children?' Autumn asked.

'No. Ben and I decided a long time ago not to have any. We're happy as we are, just the two of us, and anyway I had to have a hysterectomy a few months ago so it's not even an option any more.'

At that moment Katya started squirming in her buggy. 'Mummy . . . where's Mummy?' She looked at Autumn, her face screwed up, obviously ready to cry at any moment.

As she looked at the child Hannah's heart flipped and she felt an unexpected rush of emotion as she realised that, despite all Julie's failings in life, she was at least fortunate enough to have three children.

Autumn unclipped the harness and the child jumped out but suddenly stopped dead and looked at Hannah.

'Who's that?' she asked.

'That's Aunty Hannah, Munchkin. Do you want a drink or something? Some lunch?'

'No. I want my mummy!'

The stamping foot and the sulky pout reminded Hannah so much of Julie when she was a child that it physically hurt.

'Hello, Katya.' She smiled down at the little girl who was refusing to make eye contact with anyone.

'Go away, you . . . ' Katya toddled over to Autumn and buried her face in her legs.

'Mummy'll be home soon, when she's better.' Autumn leaned into the bag behind the buggy. 'Look what I got you while you were asleep.' She held up a small doll and Katya smiled as she reached out for it.

It was a baby doll dressed in a pink all-in-one suit and with a dummy in its mouth, just an ordinary little plastic baby doll, but Hannah couldn't see that. She saw a ragdoll, a big floppy ragdoll that Julie had carried everywhere. She also saw Aunt Marian with her dressmaking scissors and a wide grin, snipping away slowly as

Julie screamed in grief and pain.

'What's wrong, Hannah? Are you all right?'

Hannah suddenly realised she had tears streaming down her cheeks. She jumped up and ran over to the kitchen sink where she flicked cold water over her face.

'I'm sorry. I shouldn't be here, this is too much . . . '

'Hey! It's okay. Really, it's okay. Whatever happened, I'm so glad you found us, we're family . . . '

Hannah froze momentarily as she felt Autumn's arms wrap gently around her at the same time as a tiny pair of hands hooked themselves around her leg.

That was the moment Hannah dissolved completely.

12

Every part of Julie Grayson's body hurt; she was strapped up, hooked up, in traction, and only able to move the top half of her body. The strong painkillers helped but they were nowhere near as good as the morphine she had been given immediately after the operation.

'Nurse,' she shouted as loud as she could. 'NURSE! I keep buzzing for someone . . . can't any of you hear this fucking buzzer?'

Julie was in a side ward with four beds that was right next to the nurses' station. The other three women in the room with her always managed to look engrossed in something when she started shouting.

Usually the nurses responded to her quickly because otherwise she disturbed the whole ward, but this particular day they didn't. She could see them rushing back and forth but, although her common sense told her there was a crisis of some sort, she didn't care. She hurt all over and she wanted it to stop.

'NURSE!' she shrieked again before collapsing back on to her pillows. The pain from shouting was almost as bad as the pain throbbing in her head, and she cursed her stupid accident.

Julie knew that it wasn't Jethro's fault because he had had no idea of what he was doing, but it didn't stop her from resenting him for putting her here. Her frustration at the situation was compounded by Jacob, Jethro's social worker, who had been in to see her and confirmed eagerly that Autumn was doing a great job with the children. He had thought it was what Julie would want to hear but it had only made her more furious. Once again the ever-perfect Autumn had proved herself to be better than her own mother, and Julie envisaged Katya being taken away from her and handed over to Seb and his slut as a result.

Without her usual intake of drugs she was becoming increasingly paranoid; she had only ever viewed her drug use as the result of her situation, so convinced that she needed something to get her through every day that she couldn't imagine her life any other way. She was sure she was in control of her habit and had gone into orbit when the counsellor who came to see her in hospital had gently suggested that her habit could actually be making her life worse rather than better.

Julie looked up at the ceiling. If she could just have something now then she could relax instead of feeling as if she was wired into the mains. She wondered if she dared ring a friend and ask them to bring something in. It had been too long with not even a fix of nicotine or a swig of vodka to help her along.

She needed some help.

'Yes, Julie? What is it now?' The nurse who'd appeared from around the corner marched up to the bed, making no attempt to hide her own irritation. 'You have to consider the other patients, you know. It's not just you in here, I've got a whole ward full out there.'

'No, I don't have to consider anyone else! I only have to consider *me* and *my* pain. I'm in agony here and you're doing fuck all about it . . . '

The nurse looked down at her watch.

'I'll be bringing you your meds at eleven. In another half an hour. I'm sorry, Julie, but I can't give it you any earlier . . . you know that, we have this conversation several times a day. We're doing our best for you.' She straightened the sheet on the bed automatically as she spoke.

'Get off me!' Julie snarled as she flicked the woman's hand away. 'Do you enjoy seeing me like this? Get your kicks from watching me beg for pain-relief, do you? You power-crazy, dried up old bitch!'

'There's no need for that,' sighed the nurse. 'Now I've got a seriously ill patient who needs my care so I'm going. I'll bring your meds at eleven, like I said.'

As the nurse moved away, Julie shouted angrily after her, 'Bitch!'

She hated that woman, and at the moment she also hated Autumn for being perfect, and Jethro for putting her in hospital and emphasising her inadequacies. But most of all she hated Seb for proving that her judgement was still crap. Only the thought of her gorgeous Katya made Julie's life worthwhile at that moment.

Closing her eyes, she forced herself to concentrate on something else as she tried to distract herself from the pain wracking her bones. It was that pain that reminded her of Vera.

On the day she walked purposefully away from the only home she had ever known Julie felt no regrets, but nonetheless she was apprehensive and aware that the future for her looked precarious and lonely. As she marched down the road with just a rucksack and enough cash stolen from Gerald's wallet to last her a few weeks, she deliberately didn't look back but promised herself that one day she would return to that house and make her aunt pay for what she had done; one day she would get her revenge. But in the short term she knew she had to try and forget about what was now the past and focus on finding herself a job and somewhere to stay.

Focus on starting a new life.

She headed straight up to the West End of London and Piccadilly Circus where she had heard that most runaways gravitated to, and where she hoped she might pick up some tips on what to do next.

Julie was still only fifteen, and although she had tried hard not to think about it she was also several months pregnant. Because she'd told no one it had never been confirmed but she was streetwise enough to recognise all the signs; when she did think about it she just viewed it as an irritant that she could deal with when the time came. It certainly didn't bother her unduly. She knew there were people everywhere who wanted babies and intended to hand hers over for adoption the moment it appeared. It had even crossed her mind that she might be able to sell it. She certainly didn't harbour any sentimental feelings towards the thing growing inside her.

When Julie arrived at Piccadilly Circus her first feelings were of excitement and freedom. She had finally escaped from the Aunt's house for ever and she was determined that they would never find her; she would make sure that neither the Aunt nor Hannah the Great Betrayer would ever track her down and take her back. But as the day wore on she realised that she didn't have any idea what she was going to do for her first night of freedom, let alone the rest of her life. With only a thin blanket she had snatched off her bed at the last minute and a small waterproof tarpaulin screwed up in her bag. Julie's romantic idea of sleeping on the street was becoming less attractive by the minute.

Standing against the wall between two shops, with her arms crossed defensively and her shoulders hunched, she was just starting to feel very nervous when an eccentric-looking, middle-aged woman approached her. She was tall and stick-thin with long salt-and-pepper grey hair loosely woven into a plait that hung over one shoulder. Her clothes were ill matched and layered for warmth, she wore worn-out corduroy trousers tucked inside green wellington boots.

'Hello, my dear. I hope you don't mind my speaking to you but I've been watching you for a while and you look a bit lost. I wondered if I could help you? It can be really quite frightening here when you're alone, especially at night . . . '

Julie looked at the smiling woman suspiciously. 'I'm fine, I can look after myself, and anyway, what's it to you?'

'Nothing really.' The woman smiled sadly. 'I just like to keep an eye out here sometimes. My own daughter was here once, maybe not in the same circumstances as you but she was here . . . '

'And?' Julie's response was nervously sarcastic.

'And nothing, except that I like to help if I can. It's absolutely none of my business what you do, but if you want somewhere safe to stay for a few nights, there's a hostel for young girls not far from here, run by a private charity. They won't ask any questions and it's safe there. Just while you find your way.' She gave Julie a piece of paper. 'I can see you have only just arrived in London. Please be careful, my dear. God bless.'

With that the woman walked off into the crowd, but a few minutes later Julie spotted her talking to another young girl who was standing on her own a short distance away. She watched and waited and then, after the woman moved on again, went over.

'Was that old bat harassing you as well?'

The girl looked at her curiously.

'No, not really harassing. Just another do-gooder who means well, I guess. There are loads of them hanging around here, nearly as many as there are nasties but sometimes it's hard to tell the difference. Word is she's one of the good ones, though; a bit loopy but okay. She gave me an address for somewhere to stay for a couple of nights.'

'Me too. Are you going?'

'I'm not sure, are you?'

'Dunno. Fancy a Coke somewhere? I feel a bit strange, I only got here today.' Julie laughed but it sounded hollow and nervous. Dusk had turned to darkness, and despite the bright lights and crowds of people, the area suddenly seemed spooky and she was starting to feel afraid and alone.

'Yeah, I guessed that. Look, there's a McDonald's over there. We could share a hot drink if you like. I'm Mandy, by the way.'

'I'm Julie.'

Both girls simultaneously hoisted their weighty backpacks on to their shoulders and crossed over to the well-lit familiarity of the fast-food restaurant. As they walked along together, Julie looked at Mandy surreptitiously. She guessed the girl was a little older than her, maybe around eighteen, and she looked as if she had been around longer. Her hair was already forming into dark blonde dreadlocks and she looked generally grubby, but her teeth were white, her skin clear and her accent decidedly upper-class. It was as clear-cut and perfect as the accent of the woman who had approached them.

'Where have you been staying?' Julie asked.

'Here and there. And on the streets. The doorways aren't good, though, even as a last resort. There's always someone wanting to nick whatever you've got, and if you haven't got anything they beat the crap out of you in frustration. Hence I think we should look at this place.' Mandy still managed to laugh as she described what had obviously happened to her. 'Might be somewhere safe for a few nights until there's a decent squat up for grabs . . . '

After getting to know each other superficially over a shared cup of tea, the girls made their way to the address on the card, which turned out to be exactly the opposite of what they had envisaged.

After chatting about it on the way, they had been expecting a run-down hostel in a backstreet so both hesitated as they looked in awe at the white canopied entrance to what seemed to be a large private house near Earls Court. Two ornate concrete pillars flanked the wide steps that led up to double front doors.

After a few moments' silent hesitation, Mandy pulled Julie up the steps behind her and rang the bell; as they waited the girls edged closer to each other warily.

The door was opened by the woman who had spoken to them earlier.

'Hello, girls. Come on in. I've only just got back — I'm pleased you decided to come here. I was so worried about you both, out there alone.'

'Why us? Why did you only ask us?' Mandy asked almost aggressively as they edged inside the vast entrance hall.

The woman smiled. 'Because you both look too young to be out on the streets and, much as we'd like to, we can't help everyone out there.'

The girls instinctively sidled in together and Julie smiled as Mandy muttered out of the corner of her mouth, 'If they're religious nuts here then I'm off.'

Julie could see that the woman had obviously heard but she didn't comment.

'Now if you decide to stay you'll both have to share a room with two other girls, there are bunk beds in all the rooms. Shall I show you? Oh, and I'm Vera Smythe. Do you want to tell me your names? We don't want all your personal details but we do need to know just enough to keep a record of who's staying here. Fire regulations and all that. It's all absolutely confidential, I promise you.'

Julie and Mandy introduced themselves but still stood close to each other, unsure of exactly what was going on.

'Now, would you like to have a quick look round before you make your mind up? We've had two girls move on today hence my offer to you two . . . '

'The only rigid rules we have here are no boys, no alcohol, and no drugs on the premises,' Vera told them as she led them slowly up the ornate staircase. 'Oh, and we lock the doors at night. Not to keep you all in but to keep the others out. This is a safe house and we like to keep it that way.' She laughed; it was a deep throaty sound that instantly told of too many cigarettes.

At each turn in the stairs she stopped to cough and catch her breath and the girls waited politely behind her.

'The dreaded weed . . . it gets me just about here, hence the stool halfway up.' She smiled as she hugged her chest tight and tried to catch her breath.

The house was enormous and four floors high.

The decor inside and out was a little rundown and neglected but it felt homely nonetheless and was clean and warm.

'What do you reckon?' Julie whispered to Mandy who was obviously the more streetwise.

'I reckon it beats the back doors of John Lewis into a cocked hat! Some luck or what?'

They discovered that six rooms were used as bedrooms and each accommodated four girls; the rooms were always full but girls could only stay here for four weeks although sometimes, if there was a vacancy, Vera would let them return. But during that time, Vera and her friend Barbara, who lived together in the basement flat, helped them try to find alternative safe accommodation.

Despite the boarding-school atmosphere in this house of girls, Julie loved it there and was dreading moving on. When Barbara stopped her on the stairs one morning, Julie started to panic.

'Ah, Julie, dear, I was just looking for you. I'd like to have a word with you . . . would you mind coming down to the flat? It's more private there.'

Apprehensively, she followed Barbara out through the front doors and then down the steps to the basement flat that doubled as an office for the two women. It was fiercely untidy and cluttered with papers and files in piles on the enormous desk and all over the floor.

'Come on in.' Barbara smiled and held the door back for Julie to enter. As she set foot in the room she was jumped by a large hairy blue Persian cat who stood up on his back legs and put his front paws on her knees, pushing aside an equally large tabby moggy. Both cats were mewing and purring excitedly.

'Excuse the babies.' Barbara smiled. 'They do so love visitors! Now have a seat, dear.'

Julie sat down nervously on the edge of a large battered armchair, a cat perched on each arm, and hunched her shoulders defensively.

Barbara sat down opposite and smiled at her.

'Don't look so nervous!' she said comfortingly. 'I don't bite, as you know, and if you don't want to talk about this you don't have to, but Vera and I couldn't help but notice that you appear to be more than a little bit pregnant and we are worried about you.'

Julie froze. That was the last thing she had expected to hear.

'What makes you say that?' She asked, trying to appear nonchalant.

'I'm a middle-aged woman of the world, dear, I notice these things, but if you really don't want to talk about it then that's fine. We do try not to interfere, but at the same time we like to help. We just wondered what your plans are . . . '

'I'm going to have it adopted as soon as it's born. I don't want it!'

'And what about the father? Does he know?' Barbara's tone was neutral as she asked the question.

'No. I was raped.'

'Okay. Well, we can talk about that another time, if you want to, but in the meantime you need to see a doctor and there's no way Vera and I can let you go off and fend for yourself in *that condition so we've made an executive decision. If you want to, you can stay here for the time being, until you have the baby.'*

'Julie felt her eyes filling up. She had been dreading leaving the hostel that was laughingly nicknamed 'Vera's Gaff'.

'We'll do everything we can and will expect you to help us out in return — maybe do a bit of office work for us. You're a bright girl, and Vera and I both hate admin. Look at all the paperwork on that desk! We've been ignoring it for months because Vera isn't at all well so I'm sure you'd be a great help . . . What do you think?'

'Julie . . . are you okay, Julie?' The concerned voice broke into her thoughts and she opened her eyes to see the nurse looking down at her.

'You were miles away them. I've brought your meds. And you've got a visitor.'

Julie turned her head and saw Seb sitting beside the bed, smiling.

'What the fuck are you doing here?'

'I'm here to talk to you about Katya and where she's going to live. My lawyer is in the waiting room.'

'Don't give me that crap! You can't afford a fucking lawyer . . . '

'No, but my parents can!'

'Fuck off.'

'Not a chance!' he laughed.

13

Julie tried hard to fix her mind on exactly what Seb was saying but it was difficult. Her head felt as if it was full of cotton wool and her muscles felt as weak as if she was a hundred years old. The strong medication the nurse had watched her swallow had quickly started to take effect and she could feel herself drifting away gently but fought against it. She knew she had to try and stay alert and focused on what Seb was saying.

'Come on, Jules, be logical about this. You have to admit that it's got to be the best solution for everyone, especially Katya. I mean, you can't look after her properly at the best of times, and now, with you like this . . . Look at you. You're going to be out of action for months.'

She stared at him. Even with her blurred vision she registered that he was once again smartly dressed and well groomed, completely unlike the Seb she had known for so many years. He looked like a stranger.

'What is it with this Ciara bitch then? How did all this shit happen without me noticing?'

Seb looked at her quizzically and snorted. 'Do you really want to know? Normally you have no interest in anything other than yourself. In fact, that's *why* you didn't realise. You notice nothing apart from that.'

Julie looked at him hard and shook her head.

'Just tell me. I have a right to know, I thought we were together.'

Seb smiled but Julie could see it was more in amusement than nostalgia.

'No, you thought we were together whenever it suited you! Anyway, I've known Ciara for ever, she's a distant cousin by marriage. My parents always wanted me to marry her but I wasn't interested. I didn't want the traditional marriage thing. But then the last time you kicked off it just happened to coincide with her coming to stay in London. She visited my parents, so did I, and that was it really. We fell in love. She's a nice, gentle person.'

'Fell in love, my arse! I'm guessing she's got money somewhere, somehow. You told me you had no family and no money yet she's flashing a great big fuck-off engagement ring. You said often enough you loved me . . . '

'I was addicted to you, Julie, I had to have you, you were my heroin, but I'm over that now. I can see you for what you are.'

'You bastard . . . '

Seb ignored her interruption and carried on as if she hadn't spoken.

'I knew my parents wouldn't approve of you. I mean, look at the state of you. And you're such a scummy gobshite, especially when you're pissed or drugged up . . . '

'Fuck off!'

'See what I mean? Anyway, I never told them about you or Katya, but now my parents know about her they want to meet their granddaughter, and Ciara loves children. She doesn't work so she can give Katya plenty of time . . . something you can never find for your kids.'

'You bastard,' She repeated, slurring her words angrily, 'I bloody well never stop working. Anyway she's my daughter and you're not taking her from me and giving her to the next girlfriend in line like a pet puppy. I won't let you. I'll go to court if I have to . . . ' Julie's voice started to crack. 'You're not doing this . . . I'll sue the arse off you.'

'What for? Wanting to take care of my daughter while her mother is in hospital?' Seb laughed. 'Anyway, you're being dramatic now. I'm not kidnapping her, I don't want to whisk her away and hide her from you for ever, she can go back and forth between us. Ciara and I have a nice flat, and we can take Katya on holiday and for days out. Other parents do that when they split up and it works.'

'I'm not other parents. Katya is my daughter, *mine*, and you and the slag are not having her!'

'No, she's *our* daughter,' Seb snarled. 'I always did the best I could for you both but still you treated me like shit on your shoe. The same way you treat everyone. And then you blame it all on your upbringing? Yeah, right! I've discovered you're really not a nice person, Julie, and I don't want my daughter growing up like you.'

'Well, that's tough . . . '

'For you, yes, it is tough. I'm going to collect Katya from Autumn and take her with me. End of. Unless you want me to bring my lawyer in here and serve papers on you as an unfit mother? Everything is drawn up, ready and waiting. Not to mention that she's currently in the care of your other daughter who is nothing more than a prostitute.'

'Fuck you *and* your lawyer . . . '

Seb laughed sarcastically. 'Oh, no, Julie, that's your party piece — fucking around with everyone. Well, no more with me you don't, and certainly not with Katya.'

As if in a trance she watched silently as he quickly stood up and rushed angrily away from her.

Julie felt her eyelids closing slowly. She was exhausted and overwhelmed but she didn't think for a moment that Seb really meant his threat. It was just another row. He didn't really want Katya, he was having his strings pulled by his new girlfriend. He wouldn't do that to Julie, and even if he tried she wouldn't let him.

Katya was the light of her life, the daughter she adored and who she was going to have all to herself.

Unlike her first daughter.

'I can't do this.' Julie screamed as Barbara held her hand tightly and tried to soothe her. 'It's horrible. I don't want it . . . I just don't want it! Cut it out and get rid of it.'

'You can do it, my darling, you can do it.' Vera had tried to calm her. 'Just breathe deeply and hang on . . . it'll be worth it in the end, you'll see. It's always worth it, whatever happens afterwards.'

'But I don't want it . . . ' Julie wailed. 'I'm not keeping it, I hate it.'

She had expected an uncomfortable time during labour — many of the girls who'd passed through the hostel had gleefully told her all about the pain and suffering that was heading her way — but she had never thought the experience could possibly be so long, so painful and so traumatic. Vera and Barbara had counselled and supported her through the pregnancy but nothing they had said or done had prepared the naive young girl for the reality of a labour and birth that had been made so much worse by her small frame and immaturity.

As a result, Julie had cussed and kicked and created noisy chaos throughout the whole labour, reaching a crescendo during the actual birth after which she had collapsed exhausted.

'I don't want to see it!' she cried, over and over, adamant that she was giving the baby away as soon as possible. But after she had calmed down, more out of weariness than compliance, she had taken her child when the nurse handed her a wrapped bundle. Julie didn't want to look at the baby, she really didn't, but curiosity had got the better of her. And then she had looked down into the deep blue eyes of a little baby girl with a warm pink face and rosebud lips that, just a few minutes after birth, appeared to be smiling.

How she had been conceived was suddenly irrelevant. Julie realised that the tiny little being in her arms was the only thing she had ever had that was truly hers alone. She decided, then that she would keep her baby, come what may.

'I'm going to call her Autumn,' Julie told Vera and Barbara, 'and I'm going to love her and give her everything I can. No one is going to treat her the way I was treated. No one.'

A few days later, Julie and Autumn went back to the hostel to live in the spare room in the basement flat.

No one really knew the precise relationship between Barbara and Vera though there were many insinuations about them being lesbians. Julie didn't know and didn't care. The two women took care of her and loved Autumn as if she were their own.

Julie discovered that the reason the hostel had been started was because Vera's own only daughter had been a runaway who had been found dead in an alley at just seventeen years old. The needle was still in her arm.

After that Vera had turned her family house in Earls Court into a hostel and that had been the start of it.

The end of it had come when Autumn was just four months old. The origin of the fire was never really confirmed but it gutted the house and both Vera and Barbara died inside of smoke inhalation as they tried to get everyone out.

Julie, who had quickly escaped from the basement, could only stand on the pavement on the opposite side of the road with Autumn in her arms and watch.

Julie came to with a start as the pain that gnawed away at her body intensified once again. It took a few moments for her brain to clear and for her to recall Seb's visit and the accompanying conversation: he was going to take Katya!

'Nurse,' she shouted. 'Nurse, please, I need the phone. I need it now, it's urgent . . . '

When no one came immediately, Julie could feel her panic rising. Her head had cleared and she realised now that Seb had meant exactly what he had said. He was going to take Katya away from her.

After what seemed like an age a head appeared around the corner of the ward. 'Yes, Julie, what is it now?'

'I need a phone. I have to ring my daughter, Autumn. My baby's father is going to take her away . . . '

'I'll ask one of the Care Assistants to get it for you. Have you got any change?'

'Yes, in my purse. I've got some coins for the phone in there, in the drawer.'

The nurse moved round to the cabinet where Julie had her personal items stored and opened the drawer.

'Julie, what on earth is this?'

'What's what?' she asked.

'This.' The nurse held up a transparent package containing what looked like a small amount of talcum powder and waved it in front of Julie's face. 'Is this what I think it is? What on earth are you doing with this on the premises? Have you no idea how dangerous this is when you're on such strong medication anyway?'

Julie could feel the panic rising in her throat. She knew instantly what was going on. Seb had planted a packet of cocaine in the drawer just to strengthen his case for custody of Katya.

'That's nothing to do with me — I swear I didn't know it was there! I didn't have a clue. Seb was just here, he must have put it there . . . '

'Well, Julie, I believe he put it there but I don't believe you didn't know. I'm going to have to report this. We can't have drug dealing and using on the ward, for heaven's sake.' The nurse shook her head in disbelief.

Julie laughed. 'Give me a break! Would I be in this state if I was using? Come on. And anyway, who are you going to report me to? You can't exactly chuck me out, can you? And the police won't give a toss about that amount . . . '

In a flash, Julie was fiercely angry again. Sebastian Rombar was not going to get away with this.

'I'm sorry, I need the phone . . . can't you see what's going on here? That bastard has set me up. He planted that here so he could justify taking Katya away. Please get me the phone so that I can warn Autumn. She's looking after her . . . *please!* I have to warn her.'

She could see that the nurse was still unsure what was going on but nonetheless she called out across the ward, 'Can I have the phone over here now, please? As quickly as possible.'

Julie twitched nervously until someone appeared with a payphone on wheels and plugged it in. She dialled Autumn's mobile number. 'Seb was here, he says he's going to take Katya, he's planted stuff in my locker . . . '

14

It was mid-afternoon when Hannah, flushed and dishevelled, ran back into the office. 'I am so sorry, Barry . . . I just got side-tracked. I'll come in tomorrow instead of working from home, I'll make the time up, and you can stay home and catch up on paperwork.'

'No need to apologise, it's no big deal.' Barry smiled. 'Just for a change nothing out of the ordinary happened . . . well, nothing I couldn't deal with. And I really, really don't want you to come in tomorrow! No offence but we've got those reports to get done and you're so much better than me at that sort of thing. My computer skills are zilch, as you know. You stay home and do them in peace, I'll man the front line. It suits me.'

'Okay,' Hannah agreed wearily. 'But I still owe you one.'

'Well, in that case, I'll finish writing up these notes and then I'd like to make an early getaway if poss. I promised to pick number three daughter up from gym club if I could get away in time.'

Barry looked back down at the papers on his desk and carried on writing as Hannah dithered over what to say next.

On the spur of the moment, she took the bull by the horns.

'Barry, have you ever come across a woman

called Julie Grayson when you've been on duty? She's the mother of Jethro Grayson, a young lad with severe learning disabilities. He goes to Farrowfield School, he's twelve . . . '

Barry looked up and chewed his lip thoughtfully. 'Not that I know of, but that means nothing really. We see so many different people, my mind goes blank sometimes when I see my own mother.'

'She's really loud and aggressive. They live at . . . ' Hannah paused ' . . . hang on a sec.' She went round to Barry's desk and typed the details on his keyboard then pointed at the computer screen. 'Here . . . this family here.'

'Still no, I'm afraid.' He shook his head. 'Give me another clue.'

'Small and blonde, three kids altogether, well known in reception for causing a rumpus when she wants something?' Julie looked at his face expectantly then shrugged. 'Oh, well. Anyway, I've discovered that this Julie Grayson is my sister. I haven't seen her since she ran away from home at fifteen just after I went off to uni and then . . . boom. I saw her in reception causing mayhem.'

'Oh, wow, Hannah! That is so weird. How did you feel when you saw her? And what did she say when you told her?'

Hannah pulled a face. 'I didn't talk to her. I hid behind a filing cabinet and watched secretly from a distance. How bad is that?'

'Do I want to know why you didn't just call her over and say hello?' Barry looked bemused.

'Because . . . because . . . oh, I don't know

why. Lots of reasons. She was so awful, she was embarrassing, and then I was going on holiday and when I eventually discussed it with Ben he said I shouldn't have anything to do with her. He's right, it was all such a long time ago . . . anyway, now you've probably guessed why I'm telling you. I've been checking her confidential files. That is such a big disciplinary thing, isn't it?'

Hannah walked back round to her own desk that stood at right angles to Barry's, and slumped down in her chair. She knew she was about to cry and bit her lip to stop herself as she watched for Barry's reaction.

'What is going on here, Han? A bit of self-flagellation? There's guilt over your sister, guilt over Ben, guilt over checking out a file, guilt over being late back, guilt over eating a biscuit . . . Where has all this guilt sprung from all of a sudden?'

'But it's against all the rules. *I'd* certainly pull someone up for spying on a family member, it's an abuse of trust and position. You know the rules. It's a disciplinary.'

'Yes and no. That's something we've all done at one time or another — it depends why exactly we do it. You didn't have any ulterior motive other than to check this woman was really your sister, did you?'

'But . . . ' Hannah tried to protest as Barry carried on speaking.

'No buts. Declare on record that she is your sister to avoid any future conflict of interest and that is good enough for me. But there's something else you're not saying here, Hannah. What's the real bottom line with all this? You've found your long-lost sister. It should be, 'Whoopee!' '

Hannah paused and nervously fiddled with the ends of her hair, a throwback to childhood when she would lie in bed and chew it until the ends were ragged and she felt sick.

'Well, it is, sort of. That's where I went today — to see her children because I knew from the notes that Julie herself is in hospital. She's had an accident and her eldest is looking after the other two.'

'That's a start then, isn't it? Meeting her children?'

'Absolutely, and I'm so glad I went. Now I want to go and see Julie in hospital, but she's really angry about everything in her life and I just know she'll guess I've been digging and then she'll make a complaint about me. Julie always was very volatile and it seems she hasn't changed over the years . . . ' Hannah knew she was gabbling but somehow she couldn't stop herself.

'And? You can live with that, I'm sure. Blimey, all of us get a couple of complaints a year against us, it comes with the territory.'

'And Ben has told me not to get involved with Julie and her family. He went a bit crazy about it actually.'

'Oh, I see where you're coming from now.'

'What do you mean by that?' Hannah glared at her colleague defensively. 'I mean, when I really think about it, I can see his point. They do seem to be the family from hell.'

'Maybe,' Barry said gently, 'but you're part of that family, aren't you? If you want to go and see your sister then that is what you should do. Ben should support that.' He paused. 'And, of course, I'm sure he will in time.'

As Hannah shrugged she saw her colleague glance down surreptitiously at his watch.

'Oh, my God, you wanted to leave early! Go. You go now. I'll put the files away and lock the cabinets.'

Barry grimaced. 'Thanks. We can talk whenever you like, but think about this. She's your sister, she's family, and she's in need right now. I'm sure Ben will be okay if you give him time to get used to the idea of some new family members.'

'GO!' Hannah ordered, then grinned as Barry backed out of the room bowing and making forelock-tugging gestures at her.

As he pulled the door closed behind him, Hannah's mobile started to ring. She pulled it out of her bag and flipped it open. Ben.

'Hi there, darling,' she said softly, 'I was just going to ring you. How goes it? When will you be home?'

'That's why I'm calling you — to let you know there's no need to rush home and put my dinner in the oven. I've got to go further afield than I'd expected. It's a pain but the boss has only just phoned and told me so I'll be another couple of days. Hopefully, I'll get back on Friday night if I can race the traffic. As soon as I finish here I've got to head up to Newcastle of all places. Bloody miles away. Wales, Newcastle . . . I don't know . . . '

‘Oh, Ben, you’re going to work yourself into the ground at this rate. Still, I guess work has to come first.’ Hannah forced herself to keep the disappointment out of her voice She had been hoping to have some time with Ben, maybe talk him round about Julie.

‘Too right it does. This is one big deal for the company and I’ve been chosen to close it ASAP. It’ll be a good bonus. Anyway, behave yourself now!’

‘Of course. You too. Love you . . . ’

But as she spoke the words the phone was disconnected and a little warning light of jealousy starting blinking behind her eyes.

Despite wanting to trust her husband one hundred per cent, Hannah’s insecurities always bubbled up when ever he was away overnight. When Ben had changed his job and they had first moved to Essex, he had only ever worked inside the M25 and had been home every night. But then he had been promoted and sent further afield. Now that he was a national manager it was even further and sometimes he was away the whole week, only making it home at weekends.

Hannah tried to clear her mind of her nagging doubt. She couldn’t imagine what she would do if Ben ever left her. He had been her whole life since she was eighteen years old. Just him and her. The thought of ever being on her own was just too horrific.

Hannah’s fantasy vision of her new life at university hadn’t been matched by the reality. She had found the noisy, busy atmosphere unexpectedly difficult. Always a loner at school, she wasn't used to making friends and the crowds of boys and girls from all walks of life completely overwhelmed her. She took to hiding herself away to study on her own.

Her favourite place at the beginning of the first term had been the library where she could sit with her head down and ignore everyone, but then she had discovered the campus bookshop and its young assistant manager.

Ben Durman was always friendly to the nervous, mousey young student who took refuge amid his bookcases. Within a very short space of time, Hannah had developed a serious crush on the confident young man who plied her with coffee and biscuits, and talked to her about worldly things she had previously known nothing about. She loved the time she spent in the back of the shop with him, and she loved the way he talked to her as if she was an adult. Right up until the day she had left, Aunt Marian had always treated her as a stupid child, not worth bothering with.

But underneath the worldly-wise exterior that Ben presented to an adoring Hannah was someone with a huge chip on his shoulder about being a working man earning a living, while all the students he served seemed to him to lead a hedonistic life of Riley. They all tolerated him because he worked in the bookshop, but he had no real friends. He was often to be found in the student bar or at parties, pontificating about how much of a shock they were in for when they went out into the real world and had to work for a *living. Secure in his arrogance, Ben was blissfully unaware that they laughed at him behind his back.*

Hannah rarely went to the bar and never went to student parties but, flattered by his personal invitation, let herself be persuaded by Ben to go to a Christmas party before they all went their separate ways for the holidays. The night turned into a disaster very quickly when Hannah, after downing a couple of glasses of innocent-looking punch to calm her nerves, felt desperately ill. The other students raised their eyebrows at her naivety and pointed her towards the toilet, but Ben rose to the occasion, took charge and led her back to her room.

He got her a bucket, tended her, tucked her in her bed and then slept the night on the floor beside her. Hannah had woken the next day with her first ever hangover; she had never felt so ill or so embarrassed. All she wanted to do was curl up and die. However she was also deeply, deeply in love and within a few weeks had moved into Ben's tiny flat. They had been together ever since. Just the two of them. Hannah couldn't imagine a life without Ben simply because he was her whole life.

Hannah's mind wasn't on work, though she did her best to keep focused until the end of the working day by clearing up lots of loose ends in the office that needed little concentration and allowed for less accuracy.

Her thoughts flitted back and forth between Ben and Julie. She was upset that her husband had phoned at the last minute to say he wasn't coming home, but at the same time also wondered if she might just be able to take advantage of his absence and go to see Autumn and Katya. The girls had made such an impression on her that Hannah just wanted to see them again. Regardless of what Ben had said.

As she tried to figure out what to do for the best her mobile jumped into life in her jacket pocket.

'Hello, is that Hannah? It's Autumn here . . . Julie's daughter? Seb has been round and taken Katya and I don't know what to do! He turned up here with someone official-looking and that was it. You're the only person I know who might be able to help. Ma is going to kill me when she finds out!'

15

By the time Hannah had fought her way through the East London rush-hour traffic, Autumn was already in tears, having just suffered the full force of her mother's vitriolic anger down the phone-line from the hospital.

Because she had first fallen asleep and then had to fight to convince the nurse that she really did need the phone, by the time Julie had got through to Autumn it was too late. Seb had already been and gone, taking his daughter with him. He had turned up on the doorstep with two hefty-looking young men in tow and simply barged through the front door as soon as Autumn opened it, snatched Katya and walked straight out. The whole episode had only taken a couple of minutes and, because Autumn had been so shocked, few words of any relevance had been spoken.

Katya had naturally been delighted to see her father so had gone with him quite happily. Autumn had been left to deal with a distraught Jethro who was equally delighted to see Seb but who had gone into meltdown as soon as he realised he had been left behind.

'Thanks for coming.' Autumn was fighting back tears as she let Hannah in. 'I didn't know who else to call. Ma knows he's taken her, she's absolutely steaming. She said that Seb went to visit her in hospital to tell her he was taking

Katya and also planted some Charlie in her locker for good measure. Bastard! It's a shame she didn't let me know in time, I could have taken Katya and hidden her somewhere. Anywhere.'

Hannah gently guided Autumn back into the house and then followed her into the kitchen.

'Okay. Now we need to try and figure this out calmly.' She put her briefcase down and pulled out a chair. 'Tell me exactly what he said when he was here. Did he say anything to identify the men with him? Have you seen them before?'

Before Autumn could answer there was an almighty crash upstairs.

'I have to go and see what Jethro's up to first, won't be a sec . . . ' Autumn took the stairs two at a time.

'Bugger! He's pulled the shower off the wall,' she shouted down. 'Can you give me a hand? There's water pumping down the wall and spurting everywhere.'

Hannah rushed up and was confronted on the landing by Jethro, fully clothed and soaking wet from top to toe.

'Hello, Jethro.' She spoke softly. 'I'm Aunty Hannah . . . '

The young man laughed and reached forward to hug her. Hannah automatically went into social-worker mode and turned sideways so that, as he wrapped his arms around her, she still had room to manoeuvre within the hug and could escape his iron grip when she was ready.

'Jeth, let go.' Autumn looked at Hannah and sighed, then she pulled a scrunchy out of her pocket and tugged her damp hair back into a pony-tail. 'He's broken the shower completely, just ripped the fittings away. That's all we need, no shower!'

'Never mind.' Hannah spoke more confidently than she felt. 'We can easily get it replaced. Let's get him dry first, he's soaked through.'

Reaching out, she took Jethro by the hand. 'Come on, me laddo, you need some dry clothes. Show me where your bedroom is.'

As Autumn sorted through his clothes, Hannah looked around the boy's bedroom. Apart from a huge cardboard box of toys in the corner, there was only his bed and a large old-fashioned tallboy with cupboards at the top and drawers underneath. His bed was equally large and dated. There was a metal grid at the window, and the built-in airing cupboard in the corner had a padlock on the doors. Autumn noticed Hannah taking it all in.

'I know it looks crappy in here but Ma gets him the old furniture because it's so much sturdier than the modern chipboard stuff. He can demolish that in a few days . . . can't you, Jeth, hmmm? Come on now, be good. You have to be good when we have visitors, don't you? This is Aunty Hannah come to see you, so best behaviour . . . '

Without saying anything, Hannah helped the young woman strip Jethro down, dry him off and re-dress him in fresh clothes. All the while, Autumn murmured reassuringly and kept gently stroking his head to keep him calm.

Once he was changed they took him

downstairs to the lounge and Autumn clicked the TV on.

'I'm just going to put a DVD on for him. He loves cartoons so he'll sit still for the duration. Sometimes he'll lie on the sofa with his cuddle-blanket and watch for a couple of hours. We can talk once he's settled. I'm sorry about all this.'

'Don't be sorry, I'm impressed by how brilliant you are with him. I really don't know how you do it.'

Hannah felt distinctly shell-shocked after seeing Jethro in action. Reading about it was rather different from being confronted by it.

'And, of course, I also don't know how your mother copes.' Hannah sighed as Autumn came back into the kitchen. 'This is a horrendous situation.'

'It's only in the last year or so that it's been as bad as this. Hormones, I guess. Jeth used to be very placid and easy-going, but he's nearly a teenager now so there's all the puberty business starting.'

Autumn held her hands out in front of her despairingly.

'And I really don't know how much longer I can stay here, I have to get back to work. At a push I could have taken Katya to stay with me and got a baby-sitter, my partner wouldn't have minded for a short while, but I just couldn't manage Jethro, that's for sure.'

'We'll figure something out for him,' Hannah tried to reassure Autumn who looked so young and tired. 'Maybe we can find somewhere for him to go in the short-term . . . I'll have a think . . . but first, tell me about when Katya's father turned up. Tell me everything you can remember, exactly what he said. Everything.'

Autumn looked a little fazed when Hannah got her notebook and pen out of her bag but Hannah just smiled. 'It's okay, I know from experience how easy it is to forget things unless you write them down immediately. I just want to help, remember that. I want to do everything I can . . . '

Autumn smiled and related as carefully as she could the way it had happened, but it didn't take long to tell. It had happened so quickly.

'And I know that Ma is telling the truth about Seb planting drugs in her locker. There's the fact that he turned up here at more or less the same time, and if it was her own stash no one would have stumbled on it by accident. Trust me, she's far too experienced at hiding her stuff to let a nurse come across it!'

Autumn's laugh was humourless and Hannah could feel the young woman's frustration. Again she marvelled at the way Julie had produced such a down-to-earth and loving daughter. She wanted to hug her and love her but knew it was too soon for anything like that.

'Looking at you, I reckon I have more of your genes than Ma's,' Autumn suddenly blurted out. 'We look alike, we think alike . . . or at least we seem to so far. Nature vs nurture, eh? Who knows the answer?'

'Do you know anything about your father,

Autumn?' Hannah asked. 'Have you ever met him?'

The girl pulled a face and shook her head. 'I know nothing about him at all. Whenever I asked, Ma just said he was a passing fling when she was at school and that was it. She said she couldn't even remember his name and without that I have nothing to go on.'

'Have you ever wanted to try and find out about him? What about your birth certificate?'

'The old favourite, 'Father Unknown'. Lovely! I've thought about pursuing it at times, but then I think, what would be the point? I am who I am, nothing will change that. And, of course, it would really send Ma into orbit if I asked about him again.'

Both of them laughed together then, each understanding the other's powerlessness when faced with Julie's volatility.

'Have you got any family photos? I mean, I obviously had grandparents . . . your parents. I'd love to know what they looked like. I'd like some sense of self, I suppose.'

'No, I haven't, sadly. Our aunt took everything and that was it.'

Hannah had a sudden flashback to their time with the Aunt and remembered that incident with Julie and Josh, when she'd nearly caught them in bed together. For a moment she wondered whether to say anything but common-sense told her it wasn't her place to interfere, and certainly not at that moment. This was strictly between mother and daughter.

'Autumn, I'm sorry but I'm going to have to

go now. I know it sounds petty in comparison but I have two cats shut indoors, Ben is working away, and the neighbour I could normally call on is away for a couple of days.'

'No problem,' the girl interjected quickly. 'I understand. I love cats but I don't have one because they are such a tie, and anyway I don't have a garden.'

'I'm a bit of a sad old woman, I suppose. Mine act like babies and I treat them as such! But, in the meantime, do you want me to try and find somewhere temporary for Jethro? Maybe emergency foster care? I can talk to his social worker tomorrow. I should also go and see Julie about Katya. We can't just intervene without her permission, Seb is the father and has rights before us . . . '

'No, don't go and see Ma yet.' Autumn looked as if she was about to panic. 'I know her skewed thinking. She'll decide it was all your fault . . . that you're in this with Seb. I just know she will, you being a social worker.'

Hannah allowed herself a laugh. 'Oh, well, no change there then. Okay, I'll wait until you think the time is right.'

'But I agree about Jethro,' Autumn continued. 'I can't stay here much longer. I want to help Ma but I have to get back to work. Aside from my responsibilities to the club, it's a case of no work, no money in my profession. But don't do anything without telling me first. We're in dangerous waters here. Ma is quite capable of going for both of us.'

Hannah hugged the girl. 'I'll call you

tomorrow after I've put some feelers out. Good luck!'

'Thanks.' Autumn looked at her and smiled. 'I hope we can sort this family thing out. Even though we've only just met, I already feel I know you so well. I want to meet Ray, too, and of course I'd love you and Ma to reconcile . . . '

'We will sort it out, Autumn. We have to, all of us, but it's going to take a lot of work and some clever manoeuvring.'

Once she was in her car, Hannah leaned her head back in her seat and took a few deep breaths before driving off.

Suddenly her life was as complex as it could possibly be. She knew Ben would be furious if he found out she had got involved, but suddenly that didn't seem quite as important as it would have done a few short weeks ago. She had always agreed with him about not needing family, the same way she had always agreed with him about everything, but now she wasn't so sure she could do what he wanted.

The door had been opened to family, her family, and she didn't think she could ever slam it shut again.

16

Autumn Grayson saw her brother Jethro off on the school bus, tidied up the house as best she could, walked and fed Bitzer the dog, and then, with a deep sigh of relief, called a cab to take her back to her apartment in the West End.

More than anything she wanted a luxurious, peaceful soak in the bath and a cup of real strong coffee from the espresso machine. She had long ago moved away from the life that her mother led and it was always a culture shock to her when she re-experienced the manic chaos that was the norm there. Autumn had always tried to be supportive of her mother, and wanted to help her as best she could; what she didn't want was to have to keep going back there and be reminded of the various times in her life that held uneasy memories for her.

Her childhood hadn't been all bad, especially the times with her foster parents whom she still visited. She had matured very young and moved on from it all, both physically and mentally. It bothered her that Julie had never tried to do that. Not properly. Instead she just accepted it as her way of life.

Autumn felt really guilty about Seb taking Katya because she knew it would devastate her mother, but deep down she still thought it might be the best thing for the child; maybe Seb would treat her as a living breathing person rather than a doll to be dressed up and shown off. Her own escape had turned out to be the best thing for her.

Julie Grayson just wasn't cut out to be a mother.

Autumn realised she was back to her own life as the cab turned the corner and pulled up outside the building where she lived. The elderly caretaker, ensconced in the corner sorting out the mail, smiled as she went in through the main security doors of the apartment building and headed towards the lifts. 'Good morning, miss.'

'Morning, Frank, how's it going?' she called back as she walked past his ancient desk in the corner of the lobby. But she didn't wait for an answer, just waved to him as the lift doors opened and then slid inside quickly, pressing the button for the fourth floor. Usually she ran up the stairs but after no sleep the night before she was too tired to contemplate even one flight, let alone four.

'Leon?' she shouted as she opened the front door. 'Are you here?'

She hadn't really expected him to be but nonetheless Autumn felt a wave of relief sweep over her when there was no response. She didn't want to have any conversation at that moment, and she certainly didn't feel like having sex. She wanted peace and quiet and some time to herself.

She loved Leon and enjoyed his company, but it was an affectionate love based on companionship and convenience rather than real passion. Autumn Grayson didn't believe in heady passion, although she was excellent at faking it, and had no intention of allowing it into her well-ordered life; she had seen how life-consuming passion could be and much preferred to remain in control.

Because of that, Leon Browning, her boyfriend of two years, suited her perfectly. He was a millionaire entrepreneur and businessman and Autumn had met him when she first started at the Soho club, two days after her eighteenth birthday. Although it was strictly against the rules to date customers, an exception was made for Autumn because Leon was one of the owners of the club and therefore above the rules. He had interviewed her and the attraction between them had been instant. Autumn had been drawn to his darkly handsome looks that owed much to a distant Irish heritage while Leon had been drawn to the leggy young dancer with a confidence and serenity far beyond her years.

The fact that he was thirty-five years older than her with a wife and two young children settled in an elegant county house in Surrey, and an ex-wife and two adult daughters, both older than Autumn, in a townhouse in the centre of Edinburgh, seemed irrelevant. Autumn knew that if she wasn't his mistress then someone else would be. That was the nature of Leon. His first wife hadn't been keen on this arrangement and that was why they divorced, but his second wife accepted it as a small price to pay for the luxurious lifestyle she enjoyed.

There was nothing that Autumn didn't know about Leon and actually it suited her that he had a wife in the background; she was perfectly happy in her role as his mistress and made no demands on him for anything else. She had no interest in marriage and children, didn't want a legal commitment, all she craved was emotional security and financial independence. Leon gave her the luxury of both.

The small but desirable apartment, tucked away in a side street on the borders of Soho, belonged soley to her although Leon had helped considerably with the purchase, and the generous allowance he gave her towards the bills and expenses allowed her to save and invest a huge chunk of her own earnings.

He also treated her well, respected her. Autumn was determined she would never end up in the same situation as her mother, being used and abused by all the men in her life.

As always when she came home after a visit to her mother's house, she looked around her own home, checking every room and making sure everything was as it should be. Only then could she relax.

After a deep bubble bath and a short nap in her own bed, she dressed, pulled her hair back into a pony-tail, applied a touch of lip-gloss and a huge pair of sun-glasses, and strolled the short distance to the club where she worked most evenings of the week.

During the day the glamorous venue where the rich and famous liked to party looked completely different. The lights were all on high and the girls were practising their routines dressed in an assortment of dancewear and with hardly any make-up on. Despite being the same people, they bore little resemblance to the minimally dressed, heavily made-up girls who took to the stage nightly dressed as exotic birds in just a few strategically placed but easily removed feathers and wearing elaborate head-dresses. Each girl wore a different colour or shade of outfit: Autumn's signature costume was bright emerald green, as was the G-string she stripped down to.

'Autumn, my gorgeous! Where have you been? Your fans have been distraught. They're all missing you tons and harassing me for information . . . '

She laughed. 'Yeah, right. Like they really give a toss who it is in front of them. It's the tits and arses they recognise, not the person.'

'Such a cynical old head on such young shoulders! I mean it. Every night someone asks about you . . . the guys from the Japanese bank, the hunk with a habit from *EastEnders*, even your regular loner with the comb-over. They all wanted to know where you were.'

'Ah-ha. The wonderful big tippers from the bank . . . I suppose I could say I've missed them as well, after a fashion,' though maybe not the others!'

She smiled widely and patted her back pocket.

Simon laughed and carried on stocking the mirrored bar that stretched the length of the room. Night after night the young man camped it up and strutted around behind the bar as part of his work persona, when in reality he was a gentle family man with a wife and four children back home at the maisonette they all shared in South London, from where Simon commuted back and forth on his mountain bike. It was a life that was Autumn's worst nightmare but he was happy and she admired him for it.

'Leon's not here by any chance, is he?' she asked.

'No, I haven't seen him for yonks actually, but I'm guessing he'll be here any minute. It's auditions today, isn't it? Very important auditions, I understand, friends of friends . . . all secret squirrel and pre-chosen! Nudge nudge, wink wink. No Job Centre applicants here, my dear. No, no, no. Nowt so common.'

Autumn laughed.

'Yes, it is audition day, and, yes, there does have to be a weeding out as you well know, but I'm not going to be here. I won't be back at work until next week. I'm just passing through to touch base really, let everyone know I'm still alive and kicking. I don't want you all forgetting about me.'

'As if we could ever forget about you, Autumn, as if!'

She didn't explain her absence and Simon didn't ask.

The Birds of Paradise Club, popularly called Birds, was a spacious upmarket place in Soho that was discreetly divided into several sections. It was an inconspicuous property from the outside, just one of many similar buildings in the area. There was the entrance and a small bar at street level, then downstairs was a nightclub that stayed busy into the early hours with top DJs at the decks. The clientele was mostly well off and moderately famous and the carefully trained doormen were very selective about who was allowed over the threshold courtesy of their superficial membership policy.

There was rarely any trouble in Birds and certainly never any of the notorious paparazzi photographers although they did congregate outside in the early hours, hoping to catch *the* shot that would make them a fortune.

Through to the rear and up a level, away from the night-club but within sight of it, was the semi-private dancing area where there was something going on all night. The overpriced drinks were served by gorgeous young men and women, all trained to flirt and charm but equally adept at avoiding the groping hands that reached out despite the many signs displayed throughout the club that stated emphatically 'No Touching. No Contact'.

In this area the erotic dancers, wearing only removable feathers, alternated between performing in wire cages suspended from the ceiling and dancing around the shiny stainless steel poles that rose up from raised platforms to the mirrored ceiling.

Autumn was a natural dancer and very ambitious. In just over two years she had progressed from part-time in the cages on stage to full-time in the elite area where dancers performed privately for guests in intimate booths. That was where she was most happy because that was where the big money was.

As Autumn walked the length of the building

to the offices at the back she was greeted affectionately by everyone. Birds was her security blanket and she felt at home there. This was her family.

Suddenly her mobile trilled in her bag.

'Autumn? It's Hannah. I've spoken with Jacob and he can place Jethro in a small residential home in Hampshire for a few weeks until Julie is up and running again. It's a really nice place, I'm sure he'll love it there. What do you think?'

'Oh, God. I don't know what to say . . . Can I have a think and call you back?'

'Sorry, love, it's now or never. These places are like gold-dust and there are others in need. We're jumping the queue as it is.'

Autumn felt panic starting to rise. She wanted to say yes, for everyone's sake, but knew her mother would be furious. It could even be the final nail in the coffin of their relationship. She didn't know what to do.

'Autumn? Can you hear me? What shall I say? I have to get back to Jacob right away.'

She took a deep breath. 'Okay, go for it. I'll deal with the backlash when I have to. How will he get there?'

'I'll have to call you back on that — you may have to take him. If so, I'll try and get time off to go with you. They may also have to talk to Julie as his mother . . . '

'But I'm his temporary guardian. Ma will never agree.'

'I'll see what I can do. We may even have to go and see her together.'

'Oh, bugger. That'll go down like a cup of cold sick!'

As she clicked the phone off, Autumn slumped down on to one of the velvet banquettes in the VIP area and put her head in her hands. She had let Seb take Katya and now Jethro was going away, albeit only for a while. She had promised her mother she would take care of them but she hadn't been able to. It had all been too much for her. Nevertheless, she knew only too well that Julie would never forgive her. She would assume that her despised daughter had done it on purpose. Once again Autumn had failed.

'Sweetheart, what's up?'

Autumn looked up to see Leon standing in front of her, hands in his pockets and a frown on his forehead.

Quickly she stood up and beamed a wide smile. 'Just the family stuff I'm dealing with but it's nearly under control.' Reaching out, she snaked her arms around the back of his neck and kissed him sensuously on the mouth. It was affectionate yet sexy at the same time. 'I've missed you. How was the meeting yesterday? I had hoped maybe you'd be waiting for me when I got back home this morning . . . '

He pulled her tight against him. 'Plans are going good but the nitty-gritty is so boring. The money men always seem to live up to the reputation they've earned — they really are investment wankers at heart.' He laughed and looked at her. 'I missed you this morning as well. I wanted to be with you too . . . '

They each loosened their hold on each other

at the same time. Autumn knew what Leon was thinking so she grabbed his hand and pulled him through the fire doors on to the landing at the rear and down the stone steps to the dancers' dressing room in the basement. Forcefully she backed him against the bare brick wall and undid his zip. He was already rock hard in anticipation, and when she kneeled down and took his prick in her mouth he put his hands behind her head and wrapped his fingers tightly in her hair. He pushed hard against the back of her throat and immediately started to moan.

It was all over in seconds.

'Leon!' a voice shouted from the top of the stairs. 'Leon, are you there? Come on, man . . . '

'What's up, Simon?' he called as he quickly zipped himself up and tried to make his voice sound normal.

'The girls are arriving for interview and there's no one here to interview them. Mr O'Brien has called, he's not coming so you're it.'

'Give them a coffee and let them wait. If they want the job, they'll wait all day if necessary. Happily!'

Autumn and Leon giggled quietly like two naughty children caught out behind the bike sheds.

'Shhh!' He put his forefinger to his lips. 'We'll embarrass Simon! I'd better go. We need a couple of them to start tonight so time is of the essence. Will I see you at home later?'

Autumn pulled a face. 'I've got to go back to my mother's. There's no one else to deal with it all. I know it's inconvenient but we'll soon be back to normal, I promise. Katya is with her father now and Jethro is going to a residential unit.'

Leon kissed her on the cheek almost chastely. 'You're a good girl, Autumn, I admire the way you deal with your responsibilities without making a big fuss about it.' Then he shouted up the stairs: 'On my way, Simon. I've just been in the dressing rooms checking out some outfits . . . '

They went up the stairs together.

'I'll call you later. Love you,' Autumn told him.

'You too.'

To avoid any embarrassment with Simon at the top of the stairs, Autumn left through the club's back exit. It opened on to a filthy rubbish-strewn alley where Leon's car and chauffeur were waiting. As she sank back into the leather seats, Autumn smiled to herself.

She loved her life.

17

Long Beach, California

After the shocking conversation with his half-sister had ended, Raymond De Souza pushed his vast leather chair back, put his size-12 crocodile-skin-clad feet up on the paper-strewn desk in the huge trailer he used as his office, and steepled his fingers together in thought.

Ray liked having a trailer as an office, and even though his business had taken off in the past few years still had a trailer at each of his three car dealerships. When his wife had cautiously suggested he upgrade to expensive purpose-built premises, saying he needed to promote a different image, he wouldn't even consider it; insisted it helped him remember not to take anything he had for granted. After watching his father's various business ventures rise and fall dramatically over the years, Ray wanted to stay alert. He had worked hard to get where he was now and wasn't going to let it slip through his fingers through over-confidence.

To Ray, the trailer was a constant reminder of where he had come from, and the struggle to escape that place. He was never going back.

The rhythmic hum of the air-conditioner started to irritate him so he went outside for some fresh air despite its being hot and humid with more than a touch of hazy smog in the atmosphere. His memories of Julie and Hannah, his mother and the step-father he had loved as much as his own father, were surprisingly sharp. He still mourned what had ultimately turned out to be the loss of every one of them. It was almost as if his whole family had been wiped out in the accident rather than just the two adults. During her call, Hannah had not only told him all she knew about Julie and how things were for her at that moment in time, she had also told him about their shared past. For the first time ever he had learned about their abysmal life with their Aunt Marian in the London House of Horrors.

Ray's instinctive reaction had been to rush off and book himself a flight to London, to see what he could do, but then commonsense had kicked in and he'd realised that it would be acting on a whim rather than for a purpose. Also, he wasn't a free agent — he had a business to take care of, a family to consider. He would have to tell them all about the return of Julie, his baby sister, now a thirty-six-year-old mother of three with more problems in her life than even he could imagine.

But even though she was his baby sister, they were also total strangers to each other. It had been excruciatingly hard for Ray at fifteen to lose his mother and step-father. He'd never ceased to be grateful that his birth father had come up trumps and whisked him off to the States. Although he had never been excluded or treated differently by his mother and step-father in England, he had always *felt* excluded purely by virtue of the family dynamics. When the girls were toddlers, he had already been suffering the pangs of an insecure adolescence. Then, after the accident, he had been taken off to another country and another family where once again he had felt like the intruder in an established family unit. Hence, without knowing the true circumstances, he had always resented the fact that the two girls, full sisters, had stayed together in England.

But as a tall, good-looking adolescent, naturally sporty and with a British accent, Ray had soon found himself in high demand with the American girls. Before too long he had all but forgotten about Hannah and Julie, thousands of miles away. He had always assumed that they too were happy and cared for, despite the lack of communication. Now he knew that it had been completely the opposite for them.

He opened the trailer door and shouted to a figure in the distance, 'Jim? I'm taking the rest of the day off. You're the boss now so get your ass in here. And I want you to phone round all the others and keep them in line too.'

'Hey . . . are you feeling okay, Ray? Are you sick? You never up and take a day off.' His right-hand man and best friend for more than twenty years started to walk over in Ray's direction.

'I'm fine but something urgent has come up. Anyway, there's a first time for everything, Jimbo. You can get me on the cell if it's real urgent. If it's not life or death, then you can deal. No giving any vehicles away, though, I know you and your kind heart!'

Ray knew his friend was curious but he wanted to talk to his wife Stella about it all first. Throughout their marriage he had never kept any secrets from her, either business or personal, and had no intention of starting now, regardless of what Hannah wanted. As far as Ray was concerned, if she didn't want her husband to know what was going on then that was her problem. He wasn't going to pander indirectly to a man he disliked intensely. The man who had been so rude to both his wife and himself in front of all their friends and neighbours.

He could in no way comprehend why any woman would allow her husband to treat her as badly as Ben did Hannah.

Ray had always tried hard to be the best husband and father he could. He had met Stella when they were both at college and they had been together ever since. Now the kids were off-hand and semi-independent, they had time for themselves and, better still, more money. Business was good, the kids were doing well, and Ray was happy with his life. They had even discussed semi-retirement and moving from the large family house on a gated development in Long Beach to a beach-front condo.

On the drive from the car-lot to home, Ray tried to figure out what to do about the situation in England. He wanted to be involved and he wanted to help. Like Hannah, he felt guilty, but for different reasons. He felt bad for not making any effort over the years to check on his baby sisters; he knew he should have done, but life and the Atlantic Ocean had got in the way. Now, he thought, maybe he could make up for that neglect.

As always he smiled as he reached his home and turned his car on to the wide driveway. The tall, grey-and-white pseudo-New England mansion was a visible mark of his achievement and he never failed to enjoy looking at it as he pulled into the drive. He had paid for this house and everything in it with good old-fashioned hard work and was proud of himself for never having compromised the integrity that underlay all his business dealings.

'Stella?' he called as he let himself in through the front door. 'Where are you, honey? Big surprise coming up! I want to talk to you about a trip to London . . . '

As he headed towards the kitchen he glanced sideways into the family den. It took him a moment to absorb the scene in front of him; to realise that Stella was frantically throwing on her clothes and that a man Ray didn't recognise was trying to get out of the full-length windows.

Instantly his instincts kicked in. He threw himself across the room and wrapped his arms around the man's neck, pulling him backwards. Only then did Ray realise the man was wearing just his boxer shorts and holding his shoes and clothes.

'Stella? What's going on here?'

He looked at his cowering wife as he continued to hold on to the near-naked figure only half-heartedly trying to escape from the grip of this man who was twice his size.

'I can explain,' Stella muttered as she pulled

her tee shirt over her head.

'Who *is* this?' Ray looked from his wife to the man and then back again as he tried to make sense of the scene being played out in front of him.

'Let him go and I'll explain. Let him go, Ray, you're hurting him!' Stella was shouting hysterically, her voice full of fear.

'No, I'm not hurting him, not yet, but I will hurt him real soon if you don't explain what you were doing with him in my den with no clothes on. And it won't only be his neck, I'll break every bone in his slime-ball body . . . '

'Please, Ray, let him go.' She stepped towards him, her tee shirt and slacks back in place.

'Tell me who he is, Stella. Tell me exactly what's going on here.'

'I can't.'

The man yelped as Ray tightened his stranglehold.

'Okay.' Stella held up her hands in defeat. 'He's one of the golf pros at the club. He was giving me private lessons, this isn't what it seems . . . '

'Name?'

'I can't . . . '

'You can.' Ray tightened his arm just a little.

The man yelped again. Then: 'Denny! My name's Denny,' he croaked, speaking for the first time.

Ray loosened his grip and let him step away.

'Lessons in what, Stella? What exactly was he giving you lessons in?' Ray laughed but without a trace of humour.

'I'm sorry. I'm really sorry . . . '

As big fat tears started to roll down Stella's face along with her mascara, Ray shook his head.

'Get out of my house right now, mister golf pro, and stay the hell away from my wife.' The young man started to pull his trousers on as he backed towards the windows. 'Just get out of here. You can go get dressed on the road. Maybe a truck will come along and flatten you. Save me the trouble.'

As Denny ran for it, Stella looked in his direction. Ray saw the expression on her face and suddenly the full realisation of what was going on hit him. Stella was in love with the rat.

'Go with him, Stella, if that's what you want.'

Ray spoke calmly to her over his shoulder before walking through to the kitchen where he'd been heading originally; he wished he had never come home early, wished he had never glanced into the den, and he really wished he had never learned what he knew now because his whole life had been turned upside down by it.

On auto-pilot he poured himself a cup of coffee and went outside to the pool. The water shimmered in the bright sunlight, enhancing the gold mosaic classic Cadillac that Ray had insisted on having inlaid on the bottom. It had cost a fortune but it was another symbol of his success and he loved it. When the wave machine was turned on the car looked just as if it was moving, driving through the water . . .

'Ray?' Stella whispered behind him. 'I'm so sorry.'

'Sorry you did it or sorry you got caught? How

long has this been going on?'

'Not long. It just happened.'

'These things don't just happen. Attraction happens. You look at someone and there's an attraction, but if you're married you don't do anything about it. You can't help being attracted but you can help following it through.' He paused for a second as the enormity of what was going on hit him. 'You followed it through, didn't you? In our family home, you made the choice to have sex with another man.'

He looked at Stella, his wife, and for a moment saw a stranger; there was something different about her expression, something he didn't recognise, something he didn't like.

He could feel a huge, over-powering rage building up inside him and for a moment was frightened that he would not be able to contain it. Ray had never laid a finger on his wife in anger; in fact, he had never laid a finger on anyone. His usual modus operandi in the face of trouble was to walk away. He pulled his phone out of his pocket and scrolled to a number.

'Jimbo? It's me. Can I come stay with you for a few days? I'll explain later.'

Without another word he went up to the master bedroom, pulled a suitcase out of the closet and quickly filled it with clothes, shoes and toiletries.

When he got back downstairs, Stella was standing silently by the front door. She looked sad but made no attempt to stop him leaving.

'I'll be in touch,' he said without looking at her. 'Or my lawyer will.'

18

'For fuck's sake, leave me alone. I'll do this my way.' Julie bit her lip and gripped the frame tightly with her sweating hands as she tried her best not to cry with the frustration of it all. 'Just get away from me. I want to walk and get out of this shithole so I don't need you talking to me like I'm a five-year-old who doesn't know jack shit . . . '

'Language, my dear.'

'Arraggghhh!' Julie banged the frame on the floor. 'If you call me 'my dear' once more, I'll wrap this thing right around your neck. I'm not your dear . . . '

She was progressing quite well but the pain was still overwhelming. It wasn't just the physical pain in her pinned hip, it was also the lingering pangs of withdrawal from everything except the strongest painkillers the Registrar could prescribe. At that moment she would have given anything for a hit of something to help her along. For the first time in many years she was having to cope each day without anything enhancing to lean on. No alcohol, no illegal substances, no cigarettes even except on her brief trips out of the ward. And it was hard.

Since the incident with the cocaine in her bedside cabinet, the drugs counsellor Sabine had visited her every day. Thanks to her gentle and persuasive manner, Julie had calmed down considerably. Now she was out of traction and in a wheelchair, Sabine would wheel her outside to have a cigarette, which helped. They talked and for the first time Julie felt that someone was on her side; that another person truly understood how she had got caught up in all this. For the first time in her life, Julie had someone she could confide in.

But at this particular moment in the hospital's rehab unit she didn't want to be doing any of it; she hated the exercises and she hated the physiotherapists who were doing their best to help her exercise. However, she knew she had to co-operate and get herself mobile if she was ever going to get back home and fight for Katya.

The physio-in-charge was a no-nonsense woman who was obviously good at her job but her people skills were non-existent. She sent Julie, who called her the Dragon Lady, into a frenzy every time she appeared. However, the male physio who assisted her, and sometimes filled in for her, had the knack of making Julie laugh. Just one raised eyebrow, a slight twitch of his lips and a witty one-liner, could immediately warm the atmosphere and calm her down.

While she was busy banging her walking frame and raging at the Dragon Lady, Neil started quietly humming 'The Hokey-Cokey'. It was so very silly, Julie couldn't help but smile through her anger.

In a different environment she wouldn't have given Neil a second glance. He was tall, way over six foot, and stick-thin, with lanky brown hair and a strange goatee beard that missed being trendy because it was straggly and sparse. But in the confined hospital environment where everything was alien to her, she found herself drawn to him. Even to the extent of looking forward to her sessions with him.

As he hummed, Julie started to move her foot.

'Now that's more like it, my little pearly queen. 'Left leg in, left leg out, in out, in out, shake it all about . . . ' '

Julie laughed out loud and moved quicker.

There was definitely something about him that attracted her, though she could never have explained what.

At the end of the session, Julie asked him to wheel her outside for a cigarette.

'Ms Grayson, that is so out of order.' He sucked in his breath dramatically. 'Are you suggesting I encourage you to partake of the evil weed?'

'Give me a break, man. I'm clean for the first time in fucking years, there's not a grain of anything illegal in my bloodstream and not a drop of alcohol either . . . you can't expect me to ditch the ciggies as well, can you? Come on. I've been so good here today.'

The Dragon Lady looked from one to the other of them and glared darkly. 'I'll pretend I didn't hear this conversation. Honestly! Sneaky cigarettes behind the bike sheds at your age. Neil . . . back at two on the dot.'

As he wheeled her out through the doors at the side of the hospital and into the open air, Julie breathed in deeply. 'This is so much better than the delicate aroma of disinfectant and piss.

And I can smell someone else having a quick fag, too. God, even a bit of passive smoking feels like heaven to me right now.' She made a show of scenting the air as he wheeled her along.

Around the corner adjacent to the car-park was a small smoking area. As soon as the wheelchair crossed the painted line, Julie was already lighting up the cigarette she had clutched in her hand.

'Ah, this is wonderful. Fancy a puff, Neil?'

'Not in uniform. I daren't.'

'Well, take it off then. You've got a tee shirt on underneath. I won't tell.'

He pushed her over to beside the bench and, after slipping off his white tunic, sat down beside her and surreptitiously shared her cigarette.

'It's like being at school this, trying not to get caught having a drag. Sad! Anyway, how's the fight to get your daughter back coming along? Any progress?'

'No. There's not a lot of point in me doing anything while I'm in here and can't look after her anyway. If that bitch-from-hell eldest of mine had done her job properly, I wouldn't be in this mess.'

'You can't blame her, Julie,' Neil commented lightly. 'She would have had no legal clout against the child's father, would she? If he wanted to take his kid then she really couldn't stop him.'

'She could have tried harder . . . ' Julie paused when she saw Neil's expression. 'Okay, okay. I know you think I'm being unfair on her.'

'I do, but it's none of my business really.

Maybe you could try looking at it from Autumn's point of view. Maybe she just didn't know what to do. She's not much more than a kid herself, is she?'

Julie thought about it. 'I suppose you're right. It's just that she's such an arrogant superior rich bitch sometimes that I forget she's only twenty. She talks to me like she's my mother, not my daughter.'

Neil didn't answer, just passed the cigarette over to her and leaned back, savouring the warm rays of the sun on his face. Julie knew he was deliberately avoiding saying anything too confrontational.

'And another thing! She let Jethro be put into care rather than look after him herself. What a fucking cop-out that was. Even took him down there with the social worker. Selfish bitch. Just so she could get to work on time.'

Still he didn't respond.

'You think I'm a cow, don't you?'

'Of course not.' He looked at her and smiled. 'No comment, Madam Moooooooo. You have to figure that one out for yourself.'

Julie reached out and batted him on the shoulder. 'Pig!'

Neil laughed and stood up. 'I'm going to leave this farmyard and get a cup of mud from the machine then I have to return you to your cell. Stay here, young lady, or you'll be in real trouble.'

Julie studied him as he walked away. She knew he was separated with two young children, and that he lived back with his parents. He was also the same age as her to within a few days. But that was all she knew other than that he was good company and could make her laugh and walk, despite the pain.

As she quickly lit another cigarette, determined to make the most of her freedom, she noticed a shadow fall over her.

'That was quick,' she said. 'No queue?'

As she looked up, expecting to see Neil, she saw Autumn.

'What the fuck are you doing here? Don't I get any privacy? I close my eyes, I open them, and there you are.'

'I was on my way in when I saw you from across the road. How are you?'

The question was polite and formal but Julie didn't answer, just took a deep drag of her cigarette and then blew the smoke in Autumn's direction.

'I need to talk to you about something, Ma . . . it's important.'

'Nothing to talk about. And don't call me Ma. You no longer exist to me. You gave my kids away.'

At that moment, Neil came back with a polystyrene cup of coffee in each hand.

'I see you've got company, shall I leave you to it?'

'Don't bother, she's just going.' Julie took another drag of her cigarette and looked off into the distance.

'No, I'm not going. I've just got here and I have to talk to you . . . '

'Fuck off, Autumn. I just told you, there's

nothing to talk about. You've betrayed me once too often.'

'I've *never* betrayed you. Not once. Never,' Autumn stated firmly but with a slight tremor in her voice.

Neil handed Julie a cup and then held his hand out. 'Ah, so you're Autumn. I'm Neil, your mother's physiotherapist. Well, one of them.'

Autumn smiled and took his hand. 'Nice to meet you, even if it's going to be short and sweet. I've been dismissed.'

Julie felt a strange pang of jealousy as she noticed Neil, and several other passing males, looking appreciatively at her daughter who as always looked casually gorgeous in jeans, strappy sandals and a tight pink top. Meanwhile, she herself was wearing a scraggy grey tracksuit that hung off her and had her hair tugged up in an unflatteringly tight pony-tail.

Neil held out his cup of coffee to Autumn. 'Here, you have this, I'll get another later.' He sat down on the bench and patted the seat between him and Julie's wheelchair. 'Are you parked in the car-park?'

Autumn smiled and sat down. 'No, I don't have a car. In fact, I don't even drive. Living in London, there's no need. A mini-cab dropped me off.'

'More money than sense,' Julie muttered. 'Fucking minicabs. Rich bitch!'

She looked at Neil expecting him to smile, but he didn't and she saw something different in his eyes. Disapproval? Disappointment? She wasn't sure but it certainly made her feel unusually awkward.

'Do you want me to leave you two alone?' he asked. 'Maybe Autumn could take you back to the ward, Julie. I've only got another ten minutes on the stop-watch then it's back to work for me. Things to do, patients to see.'

Julie's automatic aggressive retort stuck in her throat. She suddenly realised she didn't want Neil to think badly of her. It was a very strange feeling.

'No, it's okay, we'll talk here for a few minutes then you can take me back.' She shifted her gaze from Neil to Autumn and tried her best to sound civil. 'So, what's so urgent? I thought we'd said everything. You dumped my kids. Your own brother and sister. End of.'

'I didn't dump them, as you very well know. I had no choice but to let Seb take Katya, and Jethro is only in respite until you're well. The dog's gone next-door. I managed for as long as I could, I'm just not as capable as you. I'm not used to it.' Autumn was close to tears.

'Too right you're not used to it! But that's no excuse for what you did. Anyway, what is it that's so important now? I want to get back to the ward. Don't want to miss my afternoon nap, do I?' Julie's tone was cold and dismissive.

Autumn hesitated then stood up. 'It doesn't matter. I'd better go now. I'll see you soon.'

With a half-hearted backward wave she was gone.

'Typical Autumn. Things don't go her way so she throws a tantrum.' Julie shrugged. Neil clicked the brakes on the wheelchair and started pushing.

'Sounds familiar!' he commented quietly. 'Anyway, I thought she was very polite. A credit to you, in fact, if I may say so. Now I have to get back to work so I'm going to deposit you on the ward and leave you to it. I'll see you in Physio tomorrow. My, you have such a busy life!'

'You do think I'm being unfair, don't you?' Julie tried to look over her shoulder at him but couldn't see his expression.

'That's for you to decide. I'm not a shrink. I fix bodies not heads!'

'I wonder what she wanted?'

'Why not ring and ask?'

'I wouldn't give her the satisfaction.'

'In that case you'll never know, will you?'

He helped her from the wheelchair into the bedside chair and then left her wondering whether she could swallow her pride and ring Autumn to ask what it was she had come for.

19

Without a word, Ben leaned forward, picked up the remote control from the table and changed the channel on the TV.

'I was watching that, Ben,' Hannah commented gently. 'It's very nearly finished, can't I just watch it to the end? You were asleep . . . '

'Yes, well, I'm awake now and I'm not watching that crap.' He frowned angrily. 'It's puerile television for the mentally subnormal — the sort of people you work with. When I've been out working hard all week, the last thing I want to do is sit in my own house watching something I don't want to watch.'

Without looking at her reaction he scrolled through the channels. 'There must be something half-decent on here somewhere. Maybe the Discovery Channel has got something on scuba. Not that you're interested in that any more.'

Although she didn't know why exactly, Hannah was sure Ben was trying to start an argument, so she didn't respond. He just carried on talking at her while channel surfing. She thought about all the programmes she hated that she watched without saying a word. Ben was definitely Mr Remote Control and she never disputed his choices. She never disputed his choices in anything.

'I think I'll give that Declan bloke a bell and see if he fancies a week away somewhere. You couldn't be arsed to join in last time so no point in taking you again. I might as well go with someone who'll enjoy it. Your half of the cost was a complete waste of money when we went to Egypt, wasn't it, hmm?'

Still Hannah didn't respond but this time, instead of her usual submissive acceptance of 'Ben being Ben', she started to feel angry at his unjustified goading. It was a slow-burning anger and it was completely out of character but it was there under the surface nonetheless.

'Yes. That's what I'll do,' he continued. 'I'll give Declan a bell. He was good company on the dive boat. Better than you, that's for sure. He's got a sense of adventure *and* a sense of humour,' Ben said nastily as he clicked the TV off and stood up. He automatically straightened his shirt and designer jeans, flicked his fingers through his hair and snatched up his mobile phone and keys from the long low glass table.

'Right. Shift yourself. There's bugger all on the telly, we might as well go to the pub. There's a live band tonight.' He looked down at the shirt he was wearing, held his arms up and sniffed his armpits before shaking his head. 'I need to change this shirt. Have you washed and ironed the new black one yet? The one I put out last weekend?'

Since the changes in her life, Hannah was finding her time spent with Ben increasingly difficult. All she wanted was to be able to tell him about Julie and her life, to rave about Autumn and little Katya and Jethro; she wanted him to share in her excitement at discovering her family; the family that, however dysfunctional, she now knew she wanted in her life.

She wanted to share it all with him and have his support, but she knew now that would never happen. So, rather than risk slipping up and saying the wrong thing, she had been keeping quiet about everything except the most mundane, domestic issues.

The last time she had broached the subject, to try to explain about Julie, her life and her children, he had flown into a rage and forbidden any further discussion of it. Ben had no sympathy for anyone he perceived as weak or immoral, and he had decided that Julie and Autumn were both. He just did not want to know anything about them. It had been a strain keeping her feelings about this locked up and Hannah was starting to feel it.

But in his usual self-obsessed way her husband hadn't even noticed her unhappiness or discomfort, and that also bothered Hannah. It made her realise that he didn't actually listen to or take notice of her at all; that she really had very little say in their life or their marriage.

Ben alone organised their weekends, their hobbies, their holidays, and everything to do with the house, from choosing the curtains and deciding where the furniture stood in the rooms to picking out which CDs and DVDs to buy. He made all the decisions, and spoke to her as if she was incapable of anything but the most basic domestic tasks. Most hurtful of all was the way he derided her career, something she had worked hard for, first to qualify and then to win several promotions. In his derogatory eyes, though, she may as well be stacking shelves in a supermarket.

Hannah had thought she understood him, that it was his own insecurities that made him the way he was, but now he was making decisions about her family that she felt only she was entitled to make. Hannah was starting to feel bullied and, probably because of everything else that was bothering her, she felt unusually irritated by her husband's attitude. It was as if she had had a light-bulb moment. For the first time she could see herself and her life in full-colour clarity. She could finally see that she wasn't a normal wife, an equal partner, a lover or even a friend; she was more like an obedient doormat.

'I don't want to go to the pub tonight.' The words came out of their own volition. Hannah quickly smiled to take the edge off them. 'But you go. Your shirt's hanging up in the wardrobe. I've had a hard week at work as well, you know, and now I just want to relax in front of the TV. I'm really tired.'

Ben laughed. 'Don't be silly! Come on now, chop-chop. A bit of lippy and a clean blouse and you'll soon be raring to go.' He started dancing around in front of her, wiggling his hips and waving his arms around. 'Saturday night is party night . . . '

'No, Ben. I've decided. I'm not going. Not tonight. I really don't want to, I'm too tired.' Hannah breathed deeply. She had never stood up to him before about anything and really wasn't sure how he'd react. Scared, she looked up at him but she didn't see Ben — all she could see in front of her was Aunt Marian, holding the bamboo cane and swishing it against her other hand, grinning spitefully in anticipation of the beating she was going to inflict.

'Come on, Hannah. We're both going. Now go and get yourself ready.'

Ben laughed as he stood in front of her. He reached out and took her arm, trying to pull her up from the armchair. Angrily she snatched her arm away.

'I said, I don't want to go, Ben, and I'm not going. Please don't pull me around.'

Still laughing he reached down, grabbed her arm again and pulled harder, really tugging at her forearm.

'Stop it! You're hurting me . . . '

'Well, get your lazy fat arse up off that chair then. I said we're going to the pub and we are. Get up.' His tone changed in an instant from humorous disbelief to undisguised anger.

Again that unwanted memory of the bamboo cane flashed up, along with a sickening wave of guilt for letting both Julie and herself down, time and time again, because she was always too scared to stand up to their bullying aunt.

Suddenly it was important to Hannah that she made a stand.

'Ben, I'm not going but it's really not that big a deal. So let go of me. *Now.*' Her tone was quietly determined but her heart was thumping so hard and fast she was sure he could hear it. But still he tried to force her up out of the chair and this time she felt her shoulder pulling painfully in its socket.

'I said, let go, Ben. You're really hurting me . . . ' She struggled to escape but he just gripped tighter and pulled harder. 'Bloody well let go of me now!' she shouted, far louder than she'd intended to as she tugged her arm back again.

And he did. He let go and stepped back, a look of shock on his face. 'You cheeky bitch, how dare you talk to me like that? What's come over you?'

Hannah then stood up of her own accord and looked at him quizzically as she rubbed her shoulder and then her forearm where the marks of his fingers were already starting to glow red. The pain gave her a strength she hadn't known she possessed.

'I don't want to row with you, Ben, but I'm not your obedient servant or one of your minions at work — I'm your wife. I'm a grown-up, and I can make my own decisions. Now, as I've said, I'm not going to the pub but you are more than welcome to go on your own.'

For several seconds there was an angry stand-off with Hannah forcing herself to keep her ground and Ben feeling slightly wrong-footed because her outburst had been so unexpected. Hannah was inwardly terrified, though.

'I can't believe you just said that,' he said finally, the words laced with anger.

'Oh, come on, Ben, be reasonable.' She shook her head in disbelief. 'I said I didn't want to go to the village pub, I wasn't saying I wanted to have sex with the whole of the West Ham football team! Now you go and have a drink with your friends and I'll stay here and relax. I'll see you when you get back.'

'Last chance, Hannah, I mean it.' Ben looked her in the eye and glared at her meaningfully, as if she was a defiant child.

'No, Ben, this is silly. I don't want to go and I'm not going. You can't force me . . . '

Barely were the words out when his hand shot up and cracked her so hard on the side of the head it made her ear buzz. The blow was so forceful and unexpected that her head bounced from side to side and Hannah stumbled away from him, her ear ringing.

'Ben! What on earth do you think you're doing? You hit me . . . I can't believe you hit me like that, you bloody well *hit* me . . . '

For a few moments he stood in front of her and tried to stare her out but then, when she didn't look away, he turned on his heel and walked out, slamming the front door behind him so fiercely that the glass in it rattled alarmingly.

He didn't look round, but if he had he would have seen his wife sit back down on her chair, brow furrowed in shock, unable to comprehend what had just happened between them.

She had always known that Ben had an underlying streak of nastiness and a short fuse when crossed but, although he had intimidated her psychologically before, he had never physically harmed her.

Hannah's first instinct was to run after him. If he hadn't struck her then she would have. But even with her blind spot when it came to Ben, she could see that something had changed irrevocably. Ben had just crossed the line, and she knew that if she went after him now she would be tacitly implying that he had done nothing wrong.

After a couple of hours spent sitting in the darkened and silent room, waiting for Ben to come back and apologise, Hannah eventually went to bed but she couldn't sleep. She watched the bright green numbers on the digital bedside clock click over until she heard him come in noisily at just after three; she guessed from his stumbling footsteps on the stairs that he'd been drinking all this time, probably in the pub and then on somewhere else, but at least he was home.

Again she waited, still hoping for an apology, but within a few minutes of his clambering clumsily into bed beside her she heard snoring. She lay there for the rest of the night, wide awake but scared to move for fear of waking him.

The next morning, Hannah heard him get up early but instead of elbowing her in the ribs and shouting 'Rise and shine, time to cook my Sunday full English', as he usually did at weekends, he went straight downstairs. She threw her clothes on and followed him but he ignored her completely; he didn't look at her, speak to her or even respond to her tentative attempts at conversation. It was as if she wasn't there.

Whistling as he banged around in the kitchen, he made some toast and coffee for himself and ate it with the newspaper held in front of his face before going outside, leaving Hannah to clear up the debris.

Next thing, she heard his car start up with the engine revving louder than usual before the inevitable wheel spin on the gravel.

She knew his silence had been meant as a punishment and that he expected her to grovel and apologise to him but she forced herself to stand firm. If she wanted things to change, she knew she couldn't back down now.

But giving in to Ben was a hard habit to break.

20

After he had left, Hannah angrily tackled the housework as a distraction and cleaned the cottage manically from top to bottom as if her life depended on it. By late-afternoon, when he still hadn't come back, she started to worry and went round to see Fliss, the only person she could easily confide in.

'Well, good for you, my dear.' Her friend smiled approvingly when Hannah told her she'd stood up to her husband. 'It's high time you did that. Standing your ground is no bad thing when you know you're right.'

'I don't think I agree, not now,' Hannah sighed. 'It's caused such an atmosphere. He didn't say a word to me this morning, blanked me totally.'

'Well, when he does speak to you, I hope the first word he says to you is sorry. It was unforgivable of him to hit you. Absolutely unforgivable.'

Fliss was so indignant she stamped her foot hard on the quarry-tiled floor, causing a gentle echo around the stripped brick walls of the kitchen.

'Well, he didn't exactly hit me . . . not really hit me,' Hannah started to backtrack. 'It was more of a slap. I don't think he meant to hurt me, just to stop me from arguing. He usually hates rows of any kind. I had the feeling he was trying to start one, though, that he wanted an excuse to storm out. He's unhappy about something but I don't know what . . . '

'Don't even think about downplaying it my dear,' Fliss interrupted sharply. 'I can see the bruises on your cheek from here. The marks of his hand are imprinted on your face and your arm. If you were my daughter, I'd . . . I'd . . . well, I'd make sure he never did it again. Never, never, never, should a man touch a woman. It's the sign of a bully and a coward.'

As always, Hannah's first instinct was to stick up for Ben. She had been doing it for so long that it was second nature to her.

'I think he's stressed. He's working such long hours at the moment, driving all over the country . . . ' she began tentatively.

'No excuse.' Fliss tutted. 'We're all stressed, especially you, what with your sister and all! Ben needs to grow up and stop being so self-centred. He should be supporting you right now, not making you feel guilty.'

Her remedy for everything was camomile tea. She handed Hannah a mug with the teabag still gently infusing. Hannah took it gratefully and, as she turned, caught sight of herself in the pine-framed mirror on the dresser. She looked awful. Apart from the inflamed cheek, she was noticeably paler than usual with grey-blue circles under her eyes and inflamed nose-to-mouth lines that made her look even worse than she felt. Where she had tugged her hair back and pinned it up at the back she looked older than her years and definitely older than Ben. She had taken to wearing long flowing skirts and tops to try to cover up her shape, and as she looked at her friend's reflection beside hers she realised with a start that she and Fliss could probably pass for sisters. Even more disheartened, she looked away quickly.

'But Ben just doesn't see it like that. He's always been a very macho, in-charge type of husband, and I accepted that. It's me that's trying to change the status quo but now I'm scared. He cuts out anyone who upsets him, has had nothing to do with any of his family since he fell out with them as a teenager, and doesn't have any real friends, just casual acquaintances. What would I do if he cut me out the same way? I'd have no one.' Her voice trembled at the thought.

'And neither would he,' Fliss interposed quickly, 'so I doubt for a second that he's that daft or vindictive. He has far too much to lose. He wouldn't throw everything away on a whim, I'm sure.'

Hannah's answering smile was watery. 'I think you're wrong, Fliss, I think his pride would make him do it. Ben never backs down. Ever.'

'Look, I know he's not perfect, far from it, but I can't imagine not having him in my life. It's just the two of us, it always has been from the word go. I've never been close to anyone else apart from Julie all those years ago.'

'Then I'm sure you'll sort it out between you. Once he's had a bit of a breather, he'll realise exactly what he stands to lose if he ever lays a finger on you again.'

Fliss smiled and touched Hannah's face gently where the outline of Ben's hand still shone red.

'Now, in the meantime, tell me all about your sister and her family. Disregarding Ben and his silliness, this must be so exciting for you . . . I'm so looking forward to meeting them all! With my children and their offspring living further afield now it'd be nice to have some youngsters around again.'

Following her chat with Fliss, Hannah felt more positive; she was determined to make Ben understand her point of view and set off for home full of enthusiasm. But when she got back, he wasn't there.

And he didn't come home that night either.

When she repeatedly called his mobile and he didn't answer or respond to her messages, she guessed that he must have gone somewhere for the night and then headed straight off to Wales for work. Before their argument, he had told her that he would be away from Monday to Wednesday that week but she couldn't believe that he would just go off without telling her and deliberately let her worry about him.

By Friday, five days later, when it was nearly the weekend again, Hannah was up the wall with worry that there was still no sign of Ben. And as he still wasn't answering his phone, she called his office.

She had never been allowed to have anything to do with his work place or colleagues, so knew he'd be furious with her, but she was worried sick by and now had to speak to him.

'Ben Durman?' the male voice on the other

end of the phone queried after she'd told her tale of a non-working mobile and a family crisis to three different people. 'I think there's some mistake. You've rung the wrong company, Mrs Durman. Ben hasn't worked here for nearly a year.'

After an initial hesitation, Hannah's response was good. 'Oh, whoops, sorry!' she laughed. 'I must have got the numbers for Ben's work muddled up in my phone and clicked the wrong one. I'll delete yours immediately.'

She desperately wanted to ask more. 'And your name is?' she asked. 'Just so I can tell Ben when I explain what an idiot I've just made of myself at his old company.'

'Andy Greenward, but he won't know me. I'm actually his replacement — I was drafted in from another branch after he . . . ' the man paused just long enough to make his point ' . . . after he had to leave the company. He left rather suddenly so I doubt anyone here has heard from him since. I'm sorry, I never met him and he never met me.'

'Oh, well, nothing to be sorry about,' Hannah said hurriedly. 'I just can't believe I screwed up like this. I'm blushing as we speak.'

She slowly put the phone down and tried to think. None of it made sense. Why hadn't he told her he'd changed his job? He'd changed it before, that was part and parcel of life in the sales industry, a couple of years and then move on. But Andy Greenward had said 'Ben had to leave'.

Hannah didn't understand and couldn't figure it out.

She wandered through the cottage again as she had done constantly over the previous few days. It suddenly felt strange, almost as if it was somewhere new, somewhere different. She found herself looking at and gently touching things, as if it was her first time here.

The pristine magnolia walls everywhere, the highly polished stripped floors throughout the open-plan downstairs, the pale lemon carpet upstairs, which was so thick you could see the footprints in it. There were a few carefully selected ornaments dotted around on radiator covers and shiny glass shelves, but there was nothing personal apart from one framed wedding photograph on the mantel-piece in the sitting room and a photographer's photo of the two of them taken in Mexico on a boat, holding their scuba gear.

It was all so perfect. Maybe it was *too* perfect, she thought as she analysed it with fresh eyes. She thought about the fact that they had no real friends, only casual acquaintances, and hardly anyone ever set foot inside this immaculate cottage other than Fliss, the weekly cleaner from an agency, and the occasional tradesman — and even they had to leave their shoes in the porch.

She thought back again to when they were first married. Ben had said from the very start that they needed only each other and, desperate to be with him, Hannah had agreed willingly. Only now, twenty years later, did she start to wonder if she'd made the wrong decision. She desperately wanted to help Julie and be part of her life and knew that she couldn't let Ben stand in her way this time.

It was something she had to do.

Her mobile rang and she snatched at it as if her life depended on answering it.

'Hello?'

'Hi, Sis. It's Ray. How do you feel about me taking a trip over to see you? I'm taking some time off and really want to meet up with you and Julie. Just me. No wife, no kids . . . I've decided it's time for a family catch up. Life's too short to keep putting everything off.'

'Oh, Ray, that'll be great. But just you? Why no Stella?' Hannah replied with an enthusiasm she didn't feel.

'I'll explain all when I get there. Let's just say I've had a wake-up call and discovered that maybe life's too short to work twenty-four/seven. I'll email you all the details when I've confirmed my travel plans.'

After the call ended, she phoned Autumn.

'Guess what? You know you said you wanted to meet your Uncle Ray? Well, he's just called and he's coming over from America soon to visit . . . '

'Oh, bugger, bugger, bugger! That's bad timing. Ma wants to discharge herself. She's steaming mad, and needless to say it's all my fault. Again. I don't know what to do. I was hoping you could help before Julie really goes into meltdown. She's heard from Seb and . . . '

'Bad timing indeed.' Hannah laughed for the first time in days as she interrupted Autumn. 'In fact, it couldn't be any worse!'

And then she laughed, louder and harder, until she started to cry.

'Hannah? Hannah? What's going on? What's wrong?' Autumn asked quickly.

'I'm being over-emotional. I guess it was the thought of Ray coming over on top of everything else . . . you know, Julie, you, the children.' Hannah sniffed, trying hard to get control of her emotions. 'But I'm okay really. I just have a lot of stuff to sort out.'

'Where are you? Are you at work?'

'No, I'm at home, I've taken a couple of days off.'

'Have you got time for a coffee? I can get a lift now and be there in no time. We could be each other's sounding boards.'

'I'd love to, Autumn, but I'm worried Ben might come home . . . you know, I told you he doesn't want me to get involved with Julie again.'

It was her niece's turn to laugh.

'Well, if he does turn up, you can just tell him I'm the new Avon Lady! I won't mind.'

21

It was the middle of the night but Julie was wide awake and feeling increasingly wired. Despite the medication, her brain was in over-drive so when it got to three a.m. and it was obvious that sleep wasn't going to be an option, she just accepted the fact and lay staring hypnotically at the anaemic hospital ceiling, trying to analyse her current feelings about everything from being incapacitated in hospital to secretly fancying her physio, a man who was the complete opposite of every other she had ever had in her life.

As the days passed she spent more time thinking than she ever had before and could feel herself slowly becoming institutionalised; despite the pain of both the injury and the withdrawal, there was a sense of security and lack of responsibility in hospital that she was actually enjoying after all the years spent coping with everything on her own. It was a respite from her normal life but, much as she liked the feeling, Julie was sharp enough to know that it was a false sense of security that was enveloping her. No matter how cocooned she felt now, she was all too aware that the same old problems were still out there, waiting for her, and possibly getting worse.

After working hard with Neil, she could manage to get around the ward on crutches and was determined to discharge herself soon so she could at least get Katya back with her. After Seb had taken her from Autumn, he had sent a couple of reassuring text messages, promising to bring the child to visit, but he had never appeared and then his phone had been set permanently to voicemail. Julie had left regular messages and texts but he never responded to them and she now had no idea where her daughter was. Julie knew her beloved daughter would be safe with her father but that wasn't the point. She wanted her child with her. After the traumas of being a teenage mum, with her daughter Autumn in and out of care, and then the huge problem of coping with her brain-damaged son, Julie had seen Katya as her redemption. Her chance to prove she could be a normal mother. She adored her youngest daughter and the thought of never living with her again was just too much to bear.

As she lay, still and silent, in the dark, depressing hour before dawn, she considered again Neil's advice about Autumn. It was difficult for her openly to acknowledge that she was being unfair to her eldest daughter but she had given thought to his suggestions and views and decided that maybe she would call Autumn and ask her to visit again. She knew the girl would come if she was asked to; she always did. Julie knew deep down that she was lucky Autumn didn't hate her, and would have loved to be friends with her, but the chasm between their lives was now too wide. It was hard for Julie to accept that while Autumn was, and always had been, a good daughter, she herself had definitely not been a good mother in return. Hence the seething resentment she had always felt towards her and indeed to the foster parents who had become the substitute mainstay of Autumn's life. This had become so deeply ingrained in Julie that it was easier now to blame them for all the ills in her life than it was to look closely at herself.

Everything was clearer to her now she was drug-free and not quite so irrationally angry all the time, and as a result she wanted to try to get some sort of rapport going with her eldest daughter. She intended to try but wasn't sure if she would be able to follow it through.

'You'll have to come with us now, dear, there's nowhere else for you to go and you've got a baby to consider.' The social worker hesitated as he saw the look of terror on Julie's face. 'We just want what's best for you both. If you don't want to come, then at least let me take the baby somewhere safe, just for the moment. You wouldn't want her to live on the streets. You know that's not a good environment.'

The man's voice was kindly and his stance relaxed but, because of the horrific tales she had heard during her time with Vera and Barbara, Julie was convinced that they would immediately snatch her baby away from her, put her in foster care and then have her adopted. As she stared at him mutely, Julie was convinced she would never see her baby again if she agreed to go with this man.

As soon as word had got round that the hostel

was ablaze, two social workers had almost immediately turned up to try to sort out what to do with the group of vulnerable young girls who were now all homeless. They had quickly noticed Julie clutching Autumn and she instantly became their prime concern.

'Okay.' Julie smiled tearfully back at the man. 'I'll come with you. I'm just going to say goodbye to my friends.' She indicated the group still standing there in shock, looking at the doused fire. They had all watched in horror as the bodies of Vera and Barbara had been carried out and placed on stretchers, their faces covered, and now the girls were starting to get hysterical.

Julie went over to them and huddled close. 'I need to get away from here . . . they want to take Autumn and put her in care. Please help me! I can't let them take her. She's all I've got.'

'You can come with me,' one of the girls, Sasha, whispered to her, 'I know somewhere we can go. I was going there when Vera found me. Just do as I say . . . '

It only took a few seconds for the streetwise girls to crowd around Julie and shelter her from the watchful eyes of the social worker. Loudly they all said their goodbyes, with much kissing and hugging, moving around like a pool of human quicksilver until they were nearer to the street corner.

The noise level rose for an instant, there was one final flurry as the group parted, and then Julie, holding Autumn, and Sasha made their escape down a side-street. They ran, criss-crossing through back streets and narrow passageways, until they thought they were safe.

'I'm going to a squat I know about.' Sasha was breathing so heavily it was a struggle for her to get the words out. 'I haven't been there before but I've got a friend there. She says it's really shitty and you have to earn your keep but it's better than the street, especially with a kid. You up for it?'

Julie's lungs were screaming for air and Autumn was screaming in hunger and fear after being bounced relentlessly up and down in her mother's arms as she ran.

'Thanks for helping me get away, I don't know how I'm going to cope without Vera and Barbara. It's awful . . . Vera wouldn't have stood a chance in a fire with her bad chest. It must have been agony . . . '

'You've got to close that door and move on, girl. That's life on the streets. Always moving on, never getting too attached. They were okay, I suppose, but they were just a couple of fucking do-gooders with too much time and money to spare. There are plenty more like them out there. Don't know why the daft old bats do it . . . '

'Vera's daughter died on the streets. She was a runaway who died a horrible death on the streets. Vera was just trying to stop it happening to other girls.' It upset Julie that Sasha, anyone, could dismiss the two women so easily.

Sasha shook her head. 'It's tough, I know, but shit happens. Come on, let's go.'

Julie bit her tongue; the other girl's unsympathetic stance made her want to cry but she was too scared to argue with her in case she went off on her own. Instead she quickly changed the subject.

'I have to get some food and stuff for Autumn. What shall I do? I've got a couple of pounds in my pocket but that won't last long. She's got no food, no nappies, I couldn't get anything out of the house . . . '

'Let's just get to the fucking squat,' Sasha snapped impatiently. 'My mate's got a kid there, maybe she'll help you out overnight. If not you'll have to nick it all from somewhere. Now come on, I'm not hanging round while you go all sentimental.'

Sasha was only fifteen but looked a lot older, having already spent a couple of years on the streets. She wasn't a lot taller than Julie but she was twice as wide and her head was shaved down to her skull.

Julie was scared of her but she also thought it was safer to be with her than to be against her. Or, even worse, be out there on her own with a baby.

The squat was a large boarded-up house in Hammersmith with no electricity or gas. It reeked of human waste, body odour, candle wax and stale tobacco laced with marijuana. There was an assortment of filthy mattresses and bedding and two old paraffin heaters that filled the place with acrid black fumes. A fire burned in an open grate piled high with unrecognisable debris.

Julie hated it, there from the moment they were allowed in through the door but she knew she had no choice. She couldn't turn and run.

A few days later, when Autumn was screaming with hunger, she was left with no option other than to succumb to the whims and fancies of Garth, the man in charge of the squat. Sex for money was the deal, and Julie took it, in order to feed her baby. Garth was older, wiser and very manipulative of the young women in the squat whom he controlled by whatever means he could. He supplied them with drugs to keep them amenable, sent them out to beg, pimped them when he needed money to pay for the drugs, then battered them and used them himself whenever he felt like it.

Julie had naively followed Sasha through the door of a free-for-all house that was nothing short of a brothel, taking her baby daughter with her and instantly placing her in danger.

Her immediate relief at getting away from the social workers had clouded her judgement and she had quickly been sucked in. She soon discovered that she was especially welcome because Garth loved having babies in the squat; it meant he had total control over their mothers. A raised hand, a verbal hint or even a dubious glance towards Autumn or Francine and the women did exactly what he wanted.

However, despite the deprivations of this environment and the horrendous things she had to do there. Julie soon acclimatised herself to it; she felt accepted and almost secure living with the other girls who helped to protect Autumn and the other child, Francine, who was three years older than Autumn. She had grown used to living with girls at Vera and Barbara's hostel, and in a strange way felt the same way in the squat. They all looked out for each other and the two children. Julie had been there for several weeks when, after a late night spent working and using, she slept through until lunchtime the next day. When she finally came round the house was empty and Autumn was screaming, her face red and tear-stained. She'd been wearing the same nappy for twenty-four hours.

Julie snatched her up and headed out to steal some formula milk and nappies but as she stood outside the doors to the large High Street chemist's she noticed the way passers-by were looking at her, with a mixture of distaste, disapproval and sympathy. She glanced down at herself and saw that not only were her jeans and sweater filthy, they were also caked in something unsavoury, maybe vomit, and her baby was wrapped in a coarse and stained piece of old blanket that smelled nearly as bad as the dirty nappy.

At that moment something clicked in her brain. She thought of Vera and Barbara and could only imagine how upset they would be to see her and Autumn like this. Instead of stealing she turned away and headed for the local police station.

'I can't look after my baby properly, can you help me? I haven't got anywhere to live,' she told the surprised officer on duty.

A sympathetic policewoman rushed out to the nearest shop for some nappies and essentials, gave Julie her first square meal for weeks, and *took care of them both until a social worker arrived. She had already set things in motion and straight away drove them both to the South London home of foster carers Alec and Jan O'Leary, who had agreed to take on both mother and daughter temporarily.*

The experienced foster carers loved Autumn and did their best to cosset Julie and help her, but it wasn't enough. She had tasted another life, one where she could earn money and get high, so after just a few weeks back in the real world she walked out, leaving Autumn behind.

Julie went back to Garth and the squat of her own accord.

Julie snapped herself back. It had been a long time since she had thought about that time in her life and she didn't like revisiting it. Despite being just a child herself then she had had to make huge decisions and had always self-destructively made the wrong ones.

As soon as it started to get light she got out of bed and reached for her crutches. A night of hard thinking had left her feeling more positive.

'Where are you off to, Julie?' a nurse asked her as she hobbled past.

'I've got a phone call to make and I need a ciggie.'

'You should really have someone with you when you go outside, just in case you fall, and you haven't had your medication yet . . . '

'Well, that's just tough, because I'm going and I'm going on my own. This isn't Holloway, you know, I'm not under a bloody restraining order.

I'll be in the smoking zone if Brad Pitt calls for me.'

But she'd barely made it down the corridor to the main doors when her phone beeped with a text message.

Ciara and I are getting married next week. Katya is to be a bridesmaid and will stay with my parents while we're on honeymoon. She is happy living with us and wants to stay here so that is what's going to happen.

Julie's newfound self-control disappeared in an instant as she completely flipped; after screaming at the top of her voice, she tried to put her crutches through the safety-wired glass at the top of the doors. When that didn't work she just battered the doors and walls randomly.

'Fucking bastards!' she screamed, over and over, as she lashed out. 'They can't do this to me. They can't . . . I've got to get out of here now! I'm going to kill him. I'll kill him and her before I let them do this to me. He can't take my daughter, he can't . . . '

Mad-eyed, she peered around as the nurses thundered down the corridor towards her. It was as if she was suddenly unsure where she was.

'I've got to go *now*. I'm going home. I've got to find my baby. I'm fucking out of here *now*.'

It took three nurses to calm her down sufficiently to find out what was going on, then one of them went back to the desk and phoned Autumn.

22

When she heard the crunch of tyres Hannah instantly jumped up and looked out of the window just in time to see Autumn climbing out of the back of a sleek black Mercedes with gleaming wheels and darkened windows. As she closed the car door it quickly drove off and was away down the lane before Hannah even got to open the front door.

As the young woman walked quickly across the drive, Hannah couldn't help looking her niece up and down and wondering again how Julie could have produced such an elegant and self-assured daughter.

She also couldn't help feeling extraordinarily envious.

'Ding-dong. Avon calling!' Autumn smiled cautiously as she stepped inside the porch and kissed her aunt affectionately on both cheeks, making her blush with pleasurable embarrassment; Hannah just wasn't used to anyone being tactile with her. 'You sounded so weird on the phone, I was worried. Hope it's nothing I've done . . . '

'Of course not. And I'm fine, really I am.' Hannah smiled as cheerily as she could. 'I guess it just suddenly got too much for me. What with finding you all, and then Ray wanting to come over from the States before I've even had a chance to meet Julie again . . . '

'I know what you mean. I feel overwhelmed by it all, too, but I'm hoping it'll all come good eventually.'

'I'm sure it will.' Hannah forced a smile and reminded herself that Autumn was still virtually a stranger to her; turning, she led the way through the wide open-plan lounge and into the kitchen and dining area at the rear of the property.

'Come through . . . everyone always seems to end up in the kitchen here,' Hannah said as she signalled to one of the chrome and acrylic chairs that were pushed neatly under the shiny black table. Everything in the retro 1960s kitchen and dining area was either chrome, black or white, and every surface glistened with sparkling cleanliness.

'This is such a beautiful house — I love it! The mix of old and new is so clever. When I'm too old to be a dancer any more then I'd love take up interior design. I was good at art at school. I was going to go on to college but . . . ' Autumn stopped and looked around her with interest. 'Eventually I'd like to divide my time between my little apartment in London and a country cottage with a huge garden . . . and a donkey and a goat, of course!'

'And your boyfriend?' Hannah looked at her curiously. 'Is he countrified as well or is he a born and bred city boy?'

'Oh, it's not a relationship like that,' Autumn replied quickly, 'we just have an arrangement. I'm not into the whole marriage and baby thing, and I know I never will be. I've seen what it does to people. Anyway, Leon has other commitments. It's a part-time relationship which works for both of us even if it is different from the norm.'

'Is that why you didn't want to bring him in and introduce him then?'

'Oh, heaven forbid, no!' Autumn laughed. 'That wasn't Leon, that's his driver. Leon is working at the club all day so the car and driver were free for me to use. Better than a mini-cab.'

She stopped short there and Hannah could see she didn't want to give too much away; she guessed immediately that Leon was married but didn't make any comment. 'But that's enough about me,' her niece continued quickly. 'I came to have a coffee and a natter. I could tell you were really pissed off about something.'

Hannah paused, unsure how much to say but in need of a sympathetic ear just the same. 'Well, yes, I am actually. It's Ben.' She shrugged as if it wasn't all that important. 'I don't actually know where he is and I've discovered he's not been entirely truthful with me. Several things don't stack up yet I'm sure there must be a logical explanation . . . '

'Okay. So when did you last see him?' Autumn asked.

'Sunday morning. He went out quite early, he wasn't talking to me, and he hasn't been back since unless he came and went while I was in with Fliss. We'd had a big row on Saturday night. We've never rowed like that, ever; it was a humdinger . . . '

'Go on, tell me it was all about Ma and me,

ike we're the Addams Family?'

Hannah very nearly lied, she wanted to, but then thought better of it. 'Yes, indirectly, it was, unfortunately. But then, that's Ben. That's just how he is.'

'I must admit I guessed something had happened as soon as I saw the mark on your face. Ma used to have marks like that sometimes after being battered.'

'Oh, it's nothing like that! Oh, heavens, no,' Hannah said, casually tugging her hair forward over her cheek to cover the mark. 'I know it sounds bad but I was horrible to him and he just flipped momentarily. Anyway, now I can't get hold of him.' She paused for a second. 'And there's worse . . . '

All her good intentions of putting up a brave front disappeared then as the tears welled up again and she blinked rapidly to hold them back.

Autumn looked at her sympathetically. 'I tell you what, how about I put the kettle on and then you can tell me everything that's happened? I'm sure there's a simple explanation. There usually is, for most things.'

As Hannah went through to the cloakroom to wipe her eyes, Autumn quickly familiarised herself with the coffee-making paraphernalia. Everything in the kitchen was kept neat and tidy, almost obsessively so; the worktops and surfaces were almost bare and the contents of the cupboards regimentally stacked and canisters labelled. Even the fridge was sparkling and orderly, down to the last yoghurt pot facing the right way.

'I don't know why I'm telling you all this, I bet you're fed up already . . . you've only just met me and my credentials aren't that good so far, are they? Two nieces and a nephew I didn't even know existed, and a sister who hates me.' Hannah managed a watery smile. It felt very strange to be talking intimately with her niece but somehow she already felt comfortable with her.

Autumn pulled a face. 'Hey! We'll all sort it out, I'm sure. Leon's favourite expression is, 'Life's a bitch and then you get over it.' Though, of course, he doesn't have to go to the hospital and face the wrath of Ma once again like I do. Unless she discharges herself in the meantime.'

'You don't think she will, do you?'

Autumn shook her head. 'I hope not! But who can tell with Ma? She is desperate to get Katya back from Seb so anything is possible, and now he's announced by text that he's getting married and Katya is to be bridesmaid! I mean, the tactless bastard. I know Ma was pretty vile to him but she *is* Katya's mother and loves and misses her desperately. But anyway, we can talk about that next. Tell me about Ben first.'

Hannah took a deep breath and told her all she knew about Ben's disappearing act and his not being at work for a year.

'So where do you think he is when he's not working?' Autumn asked. 'He must be going somewhere for the several days and nights a week he's away. He must be sleeping somewhere and earning something . . . I hate to ask this, but have you checked your bank accounts?'

'I can't. They're all in Ben's name.' Hannah felt embarrassed as she said it; suddenly it sounded ridiculous. 'I always use my credit card – well, it's Ben's credit card, he pays it. All the bills are paid by direct debit and he gives me a cash allowance.' She could feel the tears starting again as she spoke faster and faster to justify the situation. 'Oh, God, it sounds so stupid when I say it out loud considering that I work, but it's just how it's always been and there was never any need to change it. I can buy what I need, I've never gone without . . . I don't *need* to know the details. Ben is the one with the accounting brain.'

'Maybe it was okay once but you need to change it now. Just in case. At least you'll be in charge of your own money, your own salary. Financial independence is so important for a woman.'

Hannah managed a wry smile. 'How come you're so sensible and worldly-wise? Both me and Julie, the should-be grown-ups, seem stupid and childlike in comparison!'

Autumn shrugged. 'I had to grow up very young and it probably did me good. And I also had . . . still have . . . wonderful foster parents. But don't tell Ma I said that, she hates them. Of course!'

'We had a rubbish upbringing but we both reacted to it differently. I really want to get to know Julie again and if Ray is coming over maybe that will smooth the way a little. He wasn't part of our upbringing by Aunt Marian so she can't resent him as much as she does me.'

'It's your call, when you're ready. She'll definitely go ape-shit but that's her style as you know!' Autumn stood up. 'If in doubt, shout, is Ma's reaction to everything. Shall I pour the coffee?'

As she walked across the kitchen to get the cafetière she glanced back into the lounge appreciatively.

'Is that a photo of you and Ben over there? Can I have a look?'

'Sure, that's our old wedding one. God, we were only kids back then, I was probably younger than you are now, and that's a more up-to-date one of us when we were on holiday in Mexico last year, looking a bit touristy with all our scuba gear at our feet. It was a hotel photographer. He charged a fortune but it's a great photo!'

Autumn walked through and picked up the frame.

'This is Ben?' She frowned incredulously as she peered at the photo more closely then turned it around towards the light to get a different angle and a better look.

'Yes, of course it is. You sound shocked. What's wrong? I thought it was a good photo,' Hannah said surprised by the question.

'Nothing's wrong,' Autumn muttered distractedly, 'no, nothing. It's a lovely photo, you both look so happy. Ben just isn't how I imagined him, that's all.'

'How did you imagine him then? Tall, dark and handsome?' Hannah smiled.

'Taller . . . older maybe . . . I don't know. I just

had a totally different mental picture of him. You know how it is when you've never met someone, you have to make your own mental image.'

Still Autumn didn't turn back round; she replaced the frame then took her phone out her pocket and clicked through the menu. 'I could have sworn I heard my phone beep with a message just then . . . ' She fiddled about with her phone for several more seconds before clicking it shut.

'Do you know anyone he could be staying with?' She continued. 'He just has to be somewhere when he's not here.'

'I haven't got a clue,' Hannah confessed as they walked back to the kitchen. 'I've racked my brains and can't even imagine where he could be. We don't have friends and family as such. There's no one.'

'Has he got an address book?'

'I'm not sure if he's got a written one. He uses his BlackBerry all the time, it's attached to him . . . '

Autumn looked worried. 'Please cover yourself, Hannah, just in case. You know, my foster mother always used to say 'knowledge is power', and I think that applies to you here. You have to find out where you stand. Have you checked through the mail?'

'No. I never open anything unless it's for me personally, and anyway . . . '

'Well, maybe you should. You're his wife and he's been lying to you. Surely you're entitled to do some digging and find out what's going on?' Autumn interrupted her sharply. For the first time Hannah sensed irritation in the younger woman and, although she felt embarrassed, she could also see that Autumn was right. She had been naive to the point of stupidity.

Hannah thought for a moment and then, without saying anything, went through to the conservatory and picked up the pile of mail that lay on Ben's desk. Every day she had been automatically placing post on this pile without really looking at it, but suddenly she realised that there did seem to be a lot of mail for just a few days. A lot more than usual. Again she felt stupid for not having noticed something so obvious.

She turned it over in her hands. 'I don't know if I can do this. It's a breach of faith . . . surely we should trust each other? Without that . . . '

'It's a breach of faith for your husband to piss off and not tell you where he is! It's a breach of faith for him not to tell you about losing his job. You are entitled to know what's going on. You're a married couple. Equals. Though I know it's none of my business,' Autumn said as Hannah went back into the kitchen with it all.

Hannah started tearing envelopes open and putting the pieces of paper into separate piles.

The pile of unpaid bills mounted as did the pile of final demands and threatening letters. Feeling sick and faint, she then went through to Ben's desk again and used a knife to break into it before pulling out everything from the drawers.

The eventual outcome of a long and nerve-wracking session of sorting, sifting, checking bank and credit-card statements and adding up, was the devastating realisation that Ben was up to his neck in debt. He owed thousands on credit cards alone, was overdrawn at the bank and, even worse, so far behind on mortgage payments that their house, which had apparently been secretly remortgaged, was now under threat of repossession.

Hannah couldn't take it all in.

She could see that they actually had very little and owed a lot. She didn't understand what was going on.

23

'I'm really sorry, Hannah,' Autumn said once it had got to mid-afternoon, 'but I have to go. I have to see Ma and try and do something about Katya, but I don't want to leave you on your own. I mean, supposing Ben comes back?'

'I'll be fine, really I will. I know I have to approach things systematically and there's no way I can sort this lot out in a day.' Hannah smiled sadly. 'Guess I know where I stand with Ben now, eh? Filed carelessly under 'not important'. If he comes back then I'm ready to deal with it. Fliss is coming over in a while anyway, I've given her an outline.'

'Okay. I'll call you later and let you know how Ma is and where it's at with Katya and Jethro.'

'Good luck! I'll be back at work next week, needs must and all that, so I'll have a chat with my colleague about Katya then. See what we can do about finding her.'

'Okay . . . and good luck to you, too. Don't take any bullshit from Ben if he comes back.'

Autumn kissed her aunt and let herself out. As she walked towards the waiting car that had just pulled up she saw someone clambering through a gap in the hedge; she guessed it was Fliss so walked over and held out her hand.

'Hi there, I'm guessing you're Hannah's friend Fliss? I'm Autumn, her niece.'

Fliss laughed. 'There'd be no denying that, my

dear. You are so much like her, you could be mother and daughter.'

'Thanks. I don't know what Hannah's going to do about all this,' she whispered to Fliss as they walked slowly from the hedge to the back door. 'The whole thing stinks of something really, really dodgy. I'm worried what might happen if her husband does come back over the weekend.'

'Do you think we should call the police? I mean, if he thought he was about to be found out with all these goings-ons, he might even do something to himself. Hannah would be devastated and would, of course, blame herself. The little shit can do no wrong in her eyes.'

'Oh, he doesn't appear to be the suicidal type to me . . . far too arrogant. No, there's more to this than meets the eye, I just know it. I think he's playing away. In fact, I'm sure of it . . . '

Fliss frowned. 'Hmmm. I suppose anything's possible. Anyway, I'll go and see what Hannah wants doing. I always knew Ben was a bad 'un, from the first time I met him. I never trust bullies and he is one of the worst I've met. A psychological bully and a complete control freak, but she can't see it.'

'What do you know about him?' Autumn asked lightly. 'I mean, as a person. His hobbies, social life, friends . . . '

'I know he's fond of scuba-diving, but apart from that I always thought he was a workaholic who loved his job and was good at it. They have no friends to speak of. They are very isolated socially. Why do you ask? Do you know something?'

'I'm just trying to get a mental picture of the man as a person . . . '

'All I can say is that as a person he stinks! He's just plain nasty. I'm very easy-going but I dislike him intensely and there are not many people I'd say that about.' Fliss stopped her vilification of Ben and turned to Autumn. 'But changing the subject . . . Hannah told me all about you and it's so nice to meet you even if the circumstances are less than ideal. Hannah has no one except Ben, which isn't healthy. I hope you and your family are going to stay in her life?'

'Oh, I certainly will. I feel attached to her already and I think we'll all get on just fine once the ice is really broken, though I must admit my mother is going to be a very hard nut for Hannah to crack.'

* * *

Once back at her apartment Autumn went straight through to the carefully designed tiny study tucked away inside what was once a large storage cupboard; she fired up her PC and then pulled out her mobile phone and clicked through the menu. Peering at the small screen, she studied the photos she had surreptitiously taken in Hannah's house. They were photos of the scuba-diving picture of Hannah and Ben but the images weren't quite clear enough on her phone for her to really focus on so she downloaded them to her computer.

As the photo sprang to life on her screen she stared at it in fascination.

'I knew it . . . the bastard!' she said out loud as she turned on the overhead spotlight and studied the image of Ben Durman.

Quickly she made some notes of dates and times before she forgot them then picked up the phone and called the day manager at Birds.

'I need to see some CCTV footage from the past week. Is it possible for me to scan through? I'll clear it with Leon but other than that it's confidential so please keep this between us for the moment.'

Again she studied the photos, one after the other; there was no doubt in her mind that the man standing alongside Hannah in the photograph was also a regular at Birds. The man who regularly requested Autumn to dance for him privately, and always tipped over the odds.

Autumn had always been able to switch off while in the company of the men she danced for. It was just a job to her, and the men merely customers paying for a service; she saw it as no different from serving in a burger bar or selling handbags — except that it was considered more glamorous and the pay was a lot better. She didn't find it erotic or sexually exciting but skilfully acted her part every night: writhing, pouting and tempting everyone equally, even the women who were often included in the parties of drunken City businessmen who regularly turned up late on Friday nights after winding down in the local pubs and bars.

Up until this point it had all meant nothing to her, but suddenly the thought of her aunt's husband getting his kicks from watching her gyrating in front of him made her feel quite nauseous.

Autumn shook her head to get rid of the unwanted image and then called a cab to take her to the hospital to see her mother.

* * *

Early the next morning, Leon turned up to find Autumn already up and dressed and again studying the photo that was now filling the screen of her laptop.

He moved her hair aside, gently kissed her neck and then looked over her shoulder. She could smell his familiar, very expensive after-shave; he only ever used Dior and just a whiff of it made her feel secure and comfortable. She loved him even if she wasn't in love with him. Autumn Grayson had never been in love with anyone. 'Who's that?' he asked.

'Well, it's my new-found aunt and her husband. I went to see her yesterday and it seems that perfect hubby has disappeared, leaving her with a stack of debts she knew nothing about. She thought he was working away from Monday to Friday, but he certainly isn't working where he said he was — if he's working anywhere, of course. All very spooky . . . '

'And you're worried because . . . ? I mean, you hardly know this aunt yet.' His tone wasn't exactly dismissive but it was curious.

'Well, I'm worried because I saw this photo on her mantel-piece and nearly passed out. I'm sure this is the bloke who regularly comes into the club on his own and always wants either me or Holly to dance for him. The geeky one who tips really well but only drinks non-alcoholic beer.' She spun round on her chair and looked up at him. 'Leon, what should I do?'

'Difficult call that, but I'd suggest doing absolutely nothing so far as your aunt is concerned. Confidentiality is our unique selling point and going to a gentlemen's club isn't against the law, is it? Most of our members are married. Once our confidentiality goes so does the reputation of the club.'

'I do know that, Leon,' she snapped a little more fiercely than she had intended. 'That's why I'm telling you and no one else. You know I'd never do anything to harm you or the club, but I am worried about the implications if it is him. Implications for the club and, of course, for my aunt. I mean, how could I possibly dance for him any more? It's just too tasteless!'

'Well, if he's as skint as you say he is, he won't be coming to the club anyway so problem solved. He doesn't have a tab, does he?'

'God, no. He's small fry!'

Autumn shut her laptop down and snapped it closed. 'You're right. This is none of my business! I've missed you lately, you're working too hard. You know what they say about all work and no play . . . '

Leon quickly pulled her up from the chair. 'Well, my beautiful bird of paradise, I'm here now so we may as well make good use of the rest of the morning for which I am totally yours.'

Autumn smiled as she fell into his arms and

sighed seductively. 'What are we waiting for then?'

She was a brilliant actress with a high IQ and understood absolutely that Leon loved every moment of having a gorgeous young woman adore him and do whatever he wanted.

After a long slow morning spent making love they went for a meal at his favourite restaurant, just a few doors away from the club. It was small, discreet and tucked away in an exclusive mews courtyard. Both staff and regular diners treated them as a couple there. It was 'their' restaurant where, by agreement, neither of them ever went with anyone else, however innocently.

'Well, it's back to the grindstone in a minute, I'm afraid.' Leon smiled as they sipped their brandy. 'I'm going to be there tonight as well. There's a meeting and this is the only time we're all free at short notice.'

'What about? Or shouldn't I ask?' Autumn smiled.

'Mostly about upgrading security. There seem to be more nutters about than ever before and they all want to get in here and have a grope! However, it's also time to have a think about maybe adding a new feature to the floor. Clubs like Birds can start to feel tired and then the punters move on to the next new place. We need to keep up with the trends, keep an eye on the competition. So we're going to have a brainstorming session. Any ideas?'

'Well, since you ask, I'd suggest new costumes. They are getting a bit tatty now as well as outdated. Familiarity breeds contempt and all that. Maybe the punters need to be seduced by the ambience all over again . . . '

'But we don't want to change the name of the club so you'll all have to stay as gorgeous multi-coloured birds.' Leon laughed and touched Autumn's hand as it lay on the table.

'I know that, but we could maybe upgrade them . . . be a bit more luxurious? Bigger and better feathers maybe with a touch of velvet? And some new cages? A different shape and style perhaps . . . why not Mediterranean? You know, like the cages they have hanging on balconies in Italy and Spain? Get rid of the modernist steel and go a bit retro.'

'Sounds feasible. I'll put it to them. And there's one more thing . . . ' Leon paused and smiled.

'And that is?'

'How would you like a promotion? I've been giving it some thought and I reckon you should now be in charge of all the girls, we could use a Senior Bird, and I want you to be part of the unofficial board. That way you can be in on the meetings and have a say and a proper salary. A minor say, of course, and no voting rights unfortunately, but it would be good to have a voice from the floor.' Leon looked at her expectantly, waiting for a reaction.

Autumn stayed as calm as she had always trained herself to be when faced with good news or bad; it wasn't her style to jump up and down and scream even though she wanted to. Being as ambitious as she was, the new role Leon had suggested was exactly what she wanted even if it was unexpected. 'Would I still dance? That's where the big money is for me. The tips.'

Leon shook his head. 'I don't think that would be a good idea if you're going to have control of the other girls, but the salary I have in mind would more than compensate for the missing tips.'

'I thought you didn't mind me dancing?'

'Up to a point I don't mind, of course. It would be hypocritical of me, after all. But I don't think that, professionally, you can do both. The other girls would resent it. It's up to you, but I know it would be a good career move for you.'

He looked away and signalled for the bill. 'Anyway, I'll mention it at the meeting and then if the others agree, as I'm sure they will, we can talk again. I can't stay in town tonight but I'll drop you home after closing.'

He signed the slip and they stood up together. 'Work, my darling. Let's go.'

Autumn didn't want Leon to know how excited she was about the possibility of such a huge leap forward so she changed the subject to something more neutral. He took her hand but as they strolled along the busy pavement to the club, she could tell that Leon's mind was no longer on her, it was already on thoughts of the business. She didn't care because her own mind worked in exactly the same way.

As they turned into the doorway, the bouncers almost stood to attention and then stepped back deferentially and unhooked the red restraining rope to let them through.

Walking into the club on Leon's arm, Autumn

shivered with happy anticipation of her potential promotion and the possibility of having a more important role to play in the club.

It was only once she was in her dressing room getting ready that she remembered her mobile phone had been switched off since the early-morning when Leon had arrived at the apartment. She clicked it on and found several missed calls and dozens of text messages from her mother, screaming about being discharged and needing her door keys.

Autumn sent a short text.

Working at the mo. Will be at hospital at 11 a.m. xx

She then quickly switched it off again before her mother could reply. She wanted to think about Leon's proposition in depth and in peace. She knew the others would agree and that it would happen; no one ever said no to Leon.

That night, as she danced her way around the private booths, she scanned the customers as best she could but there was no sign of the regular she was looking for, the man she now knew was Ben Durman.

24

'She's not answering her phone and she's got my bloody house keys! Have you told her to lie doggo so I can't go home tomorrow?'

Julie was crashing around her bedside cabinet, gathering her belongings and stacking them at the end of the bed. The doctors had finally agreed she could go home, on condition she had some help and providing Jethro didn't return for a few weeks. Her son's social worker had made arrangements for him to stay in residential care for the time being and Julie had promised faithfully to keep all her pre-arranged after-care appointments. Soon she would be out and able to get her daughter back from Seb.

There were drugs clinic appointments, physiotherapy appointments and outpatients appointments, systematically planned out for the next three months. But all Julie could really focus on was seeing Katya again.

Everything was in place for her to go home but she couldn't get hold of Autumn to let her know, which was a bit of a problem as she had told the nursing staff that her daughter had agreed to help her at home.

Neil laughed. 'Well, hardly. Why would I want you to stay here and cause any more mayhem? And anyway, how would I know how to contact your daughter?'

'Duh!' Julie pushed him on the arm playfully.

'From my notes, of course, the ones you write in every day of the week nearly . . . my loser-of-the-century life history. The crap stuff that you all spout about me and my psychopathic family!'

'Oh, yes, I could have done that, couldn't I?' Eyes wide, Neil looked upwards and placed his index finger on his chin. 'But, as you well know, I didn't. She's probably busy and has switched her phone off. Just leave her another message. You're not going home until tomorrow so there's plenty of time. Shall I take you for one last whizz to the ciggie corner? For old times' sake?'

Julie smiled. Neil had the ability to calm her down and make her laugh.

'Good idea. And a wheelie would be nice. Those crutches have just about done my arms in, though I guess they'll come in handy for beating the crap out of Sebastian Rombar when I see him . . . the lying, cheating, child-stealing bastard!'

'You've caused enough problems already with those crutches. They are called mobility aids, they're not meant to be weapons of mass destruction, you know.'

Laughing, Neil grabbed a wheelchair from the corridor and Julie carefully lowered herself into it. She had learned a lot about inner resilience over the years but these few weeks in hospital had pushed her to the very limit of it; however, she had made it through and was pleased with herself for that.

The surgeon had told her she would continue to need physiotherapy for several months, and maybe even need more surgery, but she wasn't as worried about that; hers had been a freak accident, with the break made worse because she had been so thin and weak. Now, for the first time since she was a teenager, she was completely drug-free and sober; she had put on some weight that had fortunately gone on in the right places, and even let the volunteer hairdresser at the hospital cut her hair short and spiky before adding both high and low lights.

She looked different and she felt different; she just wasn't completely convinced she could carry on being different once she was away from the security blanket of the hospital and back in the real world, with temptation just a phone call away. Julie desperately wanted to leave this place but at the same time was scared of how she might react once she was back in her old surroundings with all the accompanying problems.

'I don't know what I'm going to wear once I'm away from here. The only clothes I've got that fit are trackies and even they're getting tight now. Obesity here I come! My arse is spreading by the second. If I move one cheek, I'll black out the South East of England!'

'Hardly! I think you look really great.' Neil smiled at her and followed up with: 'Will we keep in touch once you've gone back home, do you think? I mean, apart from physio?'

'Dunno.' Embarrassed, Julie concentrated hard on her cigarette. 'What do you think?'

'Well, I'd like to. Maybe we could go for a drink once you've settled back at home. It's going to feel strange for a while. For both of us.

I'm really going to miss you.' He sounded nervous and Julie was fascinated to see a deep red blush start at his neck and spread all the way up to his hairline.

'Actually, I'm a bit scared of going back to my old life. You know . . . I've got to keep away from so many things, so many people who were my friends but who use. I don't want to start doing drugs again but I'm scared that I won't be strong enough to resist. I may even have to try and move, maybe get an exchange somewhere.'

Neil gently stroked the back of her hand with one finger and Julie felt as if she'd suffered an electric shock.

'It'll be hard but I'm sure you can do it. Both for yourself and your kids. Everything is in place to keep you clean and well, if you keep all the appointments at the drugs clinic. And, of course, your appointments with me.' Neil paused and stared at her. 'You know, right now I really want to kiss you . . . but I also don't want the sack! And I don't want you to think I'm taking advantage of you.'

'What, you mean because I'm in a wheelchair and can't leg it?' Julie giggled nervously under his intense scrutiny. She actually felt quite girly.

'I think I have to do a home visit tomorrow evening, just to check you're settling in okay on your first night home. Would that be all right with you, Ms Grayson?'

Before Julie could answer her phone beeped.

'It's Autumn,' she said, staring at the screen, 'she's going to pick me up tomorrow morning.

Hope she brings the goddamned keys with her . . . '

Neil was still staring at her quizzically.

'Oh, okay, home visit tomorrow then, Mr Physio. Bring a bottle of Diet Coke and a packet of fags!'

Neil smiled. 'So this is your last night in a hospital bed, surrounded by all the crashing and banging and interminable noise. Bet you're going to miss it?'

'You're forgetting where I live,' Julie laughed. 'This has been peaceful by comparison. No screeching of tyres as the idiots race down the road and do handbrake turns. No gangs of hoodie kids outside on the wall, lobbing beer cans into the garden. And, best of all, no loud music rattling the walls.'

'Hmm. Do I need to bring a bodyguard with me tomorrow then?'

They both laughed and Julie wondered again at her overwhelming attraction to this man she would previously just have laughed at if he had suggested they get to know each other.

All her life she had managed to get involved with losers and controllers and now she found herself fancying someone who was ordinary and normal with a career and a personality. But she was also intuitive enough to wonder how she would view him once she was out of the confines of the hospital and he was out of uniform.

'Okay, Grayson. Back to your bed right now. You've got an exciting day ahead of you tomorrow.'

* * *

Aware that her mother would be like a cat on hot bricks, Autumn turned up at the hospital bang on time.

'Where have you been?' Julie asked when she appeared at her bedside.

'Nice to see you, too, Ma.' Autumn smiled, determined not to take the bait. Her new position with Birds had been confirmed: she was going to be the Senior Bird and would also be part and parcel of the everyday running of the club; her future was secure. No more dancing round lecherous drunks, no more smiling and pretending to fancy them as they tucked twenty-pound notes into the elastic of her G-string. Now she was going to get paid even more *and* she got to keep her clothes on and have authority in the club in her own right.

No way was her mother going to spoil her mood today.

'Have you got everything packed? I brought an extra holdall along just in case. You must have a lot of stuff here now after so long.'

'Neil's already lent me a perfectly good case . . . ' Julie started to snap, then to Autumn's amazement stopped for a moment before continuing in a much softer tone ' . . . but I could use another one. Thanks.'

'Okay, well, if you want to chuck it all in we can get going. I've got a cab waiting.'

During the short drive from the hospital to her house, Julie didn't stop talking but Autumn knew it was because she was nervous about going home.

'The house was such a tip when I left it . . . have you done anything to it? Did you clear up? Maybe that's why Seb took Katya, because you did bugger all when you were there. And the bills . . . I bet there's no gas or electricity . . . '

On and on she went but Autumn didn't respond. As the cab pulled up outside her house, Julie started on her again.

'You don't have to come in. I'm perfectly capable, you know. I've managed all these years . . . '

'Ma,' Autumn said as she helped her mother up the path to the front door, leaving the cab driver to follow with the bags, 'just for once, will you shut up and listen to me? I'm coming in with you, whether you like it or not, and then we can sort everything out. Just stop going on and on at me about everything.'

'Oi! You shouldn't be talking to your mother like that, you should show her some respect,' the middle-aged cabbie piped up from behind them.

Autumn spun round on him. 'Do you want a tip or not? If not then feel free to carry on interfering.'

For the first time that she could remember in ages, Julie laughed. Really laughed.

'Fucking hell, Autumn, for a split second there you sounded just like your mother's daughter!'

Autumn joined in the laughter for a few moments then stopped. 'Before we get inside I want you to know that I haven't been interfering, but when I was staying here Jethro got really frustrated and caused a lot of damage so there's some new things . . . but if you don't like it then you can always change it.'

'New? Such as?'

Autumn pulled a face. 'Such as nearly everything! He really went into Incredible Hulk mode!'

She paid the grumpy cab driver and put the key in the lock, helped her mother inside and waited for the eruption.

But it never came. As Autumn put the kettle on, Julie slowly manoeuvred herself around the house on her crutches and looked at the new furniture, television and DVD player, and carpets. In the kitchen there were new appliances and crockery: upstairs new beds and wardrobes in all three rooms.

'This must have cost you thousands,' Julie said calmly as her daughter appeared in the kitchen doorway. 'What exactly did Jethro do?'

'He went from room to room smashing everything. I think it was because you weren't here. He didn't understand . . . that's when I knew I couldn't cope. But he's so happy in Hampshire now. He's got lots of space and is with other children with similar disabilities. I'll take you down there to see him whenever you like.'

Julie was struggling to sit down at the new pine kitchen table so Autumn took hold of her arm and helped her lower herself. She felt her mother start to pull away and then relax.

'He can be a bit of a bugger can Jethro, I do

know that!' Julie smiled. 'Now, shouldn't you be at work?'

'Not until this evening. I'll make a cuppa . . . oh, and I brought you these.' Autumn pulled several packets of cigarettes out of her bag. 'I know you won't be able to get out for a while . . . '

'Thanks.'

There was an almost companionable silence as Autumn made a pot of tea and put the new mugs on the table. The eruption she had expected over all the replacements didn't come; in fact, her mother was unusually quiet.

'Are you okay, Ma? Are you cross about the furniture? I could have left it and given you the money, but then you'd have come back to chaos. I didn't know what to do for the best.'

'No, Autumn, I'm not okay. In case you haven't noticed, I'm back here but without my kids. Okay, so Jethro is happy where he is, but I want Katya here with me and I don't know where the fuck she is! I don't even know where that bastard Seb lives. Now I'm home, I've got to find her. Any suggestions?'

Autumn sighed. 'Not really, but I'll do what I can. Tell me everything you know about Seb and I'll make some enquiries.'

She wrote it all down but there was precious little real information.

'Are you still in a good mood with me, Ma? I mean, can I tell you something without you going into orbit?'

Julie looked at her suspiciously. 'I don't know, depends what you're going to say. Is something wrong with one of the kids? Are you pregnant?'

'Nope. Nothing like that. Now I want you to chill . . . really chill.' Autumn paused and then carried on, 'I've met Hannah, your sister, and your half-brother Ray is coming over from America shortly. They both want to meet up with you. Hannah especially.'

With her head down, Autumn gabbled the words very quickly before looking up to see her mother staring at her, mouth open and momentarily speechless.

25

'I don't want to know! I don't want to know so shut up going on about it. I'm not interested in any of them.' Julie put her hands over her ears. 'This is all too much. Are you deliberately trying to upset me?'

As Autumn had anticipated, her mother had erupted, but it hadn't been as bad as she had expected. At least Julie hadn't thrown her out of the house and cursed her at full volume down the street as she had done in the past. As soon as the impact of Autumn's words hit her, she had ranted and raved, predictably enough, but eventually had calmed down enough for Autumn to be able to tell her the facts about meeting up with Hannah.

'So the Queen of Brown-nosing is a bloody social worker, eh? Now why doesn't that surprise me? That is just so Hannah — all sweet and sugary on the surface and a traitor underneath. I bet she loves snatching babies and locking up kids.' Julie gesticulated wildly as she ranted on and on. 'Has she got a huge arse and floppy tits? Nah, doubt it if she's got no kids. Not that I care. She could drop dead tomorrow and I wouldn't give a monkey's bollock. I hated her then and I hate her now . . . and *you're* just like her!'

Autumn tried to ignore the insults; she knew it was just her mother's defence mechanism when she felt backed into a corner, but still it hurt.

It always hurt.

'Hannah's all right actually. You'd probably get on with her if you gave it a chance. And she *is* your sister.' Autumn tried to make eye contact but Julie wouldn't look at her. 'At least think about it. She regrets such a lot about that time with your aunt, she told me all about it. But it was a long time ago, and we all do things we regret . . . '

'Is that the royal 'we'?' Julie laughed sarcastically. 'I mean, what have *you* ever done wrong? What could *you* possibly regret?' Momentarily forgetting her hip, Julie got up abruptly from her chair and nearly fell over as her own weakness surprised her. She pointed her finger in Autumn's face. 'Now you listen to me. I never want that aunt of mine mentioned. Never. I hope she's dead and buried and covered in maggots — the filthy, dirty, conniving bitch! And as for Hannah . . . she doesn't know what really went on then because she just stuck her nose in a book and ignored most of it. She didn't give a toss about me just so long as *she* was okay.'

Julie started scratching nervously at her head, a subconscious throwback to when their aunt would tell them that nits ate their way into children's brains at night after burrowing in through their ears.

'Ma, I can understand how you feel about your aunt, but Hannah is different surely? She was just a kid as well.' Autumn tried to keep her voice quiet and reasonable. 'I mean, she's your sister and Ray is your brother. Both of them are your blood relatives, and both of them really want to see you. Not that I've met Ray yet, of course.'

'Half-brother,' Julie snarled. 'He's only a half-brother, and he never bothered to keep in touch. Pissed off to America and forgot about us. No, I'm not having anything to do with either of them. Don't forget the Aunt was a blood relative as well!' Julie sank back down on to her chair, the crutches crashing to the floor at her feet. 'Anyway, end of conversation. That part of my life is over, all of it. Over and done for ever. I don't have the energy for it.'

'Okay, it's your decision.' Autumn sighed, aware that now wasn't a good time to pressure her further but happy nonetheless that she had sown the seeds. 'I don't know what you intend to do about food but there are some microwave meals in the freezer to start you off, save you having to cook right away.'

'Much use they'll be as I haven't got a fucking microwave!'

'Yes, you have. Over there. I thought it might help, save you bending down to the oven, though I guess you could always ring pizza delivery,' Autumn said carefully, all the while watching her mother's face, studying the expressions she knew so well.

'Oh, my great and wonderful daughter, you are just so perfect, aren't you? Little Miss fucking Perfect!'

Autumn smiled widely, put her hands on her hips and tilted her head winsomely to one side. 'Yes, I know, Ma. Sometimes it's just such a challenge being as perfect and gorgeous as I clearly am, but I do the best I can to cope with it.'

To her surprise she noticed that Julie nearly smiled and wondered if maybe the best way to respond to her mother in future was to fight fire with fire. Maybe she had always been too submissive, too scared of the rejection that was always eventually meted out. Maybe it had taken the accident to make things change. She hoped so.

'I've sorted out your bills as much as I can without interfering. Everything is over there on the worktop and it's all pretty much up-to-date. I'm going to have to go to work now but if you need anything ring me on my mobile.'

'Well, of course I'll ring the mobile. Like I've got any other number for you anyway. Or address. But who gives a toss about that? All I want is Katya back with me. She belongs here, not with that scumbag who calls himself a father. Can you do that, eh? You're so bloody capable, can you do the one thing I really want you to and get my daughter back for me?'

'I can't promise but I'll see what I can do, though now you're out of hospital and able to care for Katya again, you ought to go to a solicitor to sort out your legal position. I don't know the procedure but I bet Hannah could help you . . . if you'd let her.'

Julie stared defiantly at Autumn.

'Give it a rest. If you want to play Happy Families then go ahead, I can't stop you, but I like being on my own. Same as I've always been.

I don't need any of you, least of all my ex-sister.'

'That's your choice, of course. I'm off then.'

'Don't forget about Katya.'

'As if I would. And I haven't forgotten about Jethro either. I care about both of them,' Autumn snapped defiantly.

'You've told me he's fine but I don't know what's happening to Katya. She's my baby girl and she should be here with her mother, not living with fucking strangers'.

Unsure as always whether these poison darts were deliberately or accidentally inflicted, Autumn didn't reply although she wanted to scream, What about me? I was always with strangers and you didn't care. But she didn't.

On the way home, Autumn wondered again at the way she now found herself at the centre of her mother's life after spending most of her time so far neglected and unwanted at the outer edge of it.

But only because she was needed, not because she was wanted in her own right.

She leaned forward to speak to the cabbie.

'I've changed my mind — I want to go somewhere else. To Wimbledon.'

She gave him the address. Suddenly she had a strong urge to go and visit her foster parents; she wanted to be cosseted and treated as she had been during her childhood whenever her mother had made her feel insecure. She wanted to be given a mug of hot drinking chocolate and a big chunk of homemade fruitcake, and to be fussed over by the only two people who had loved her unconditionally all her life.

At that moment she didn't want to be a responsible adult with a job and a boyfriend while at the same time trying to referee Julie and Hannah and also find her baby sister; she wanted to be a little girl again herself.

Just for a couple of hours.

She knocked and waited then the front door opened.

'Autumn! Come in, my lovely.' Alec beamed with delight and shouted over his shoulder, 'Jan, it's our Autumn.'

As she stepped into the familiar large square entrance hall, a woman appeared with a baby on her hip and a toddler hanging on the hem of her vast floral skirt. 'Come through, darling. Usual chaos, but it's so good to see you. Are you okay? Nothing wrong, I hope?'

Autumn hugged and kissed each of them in turn.

'I'm fine. I just wanted to see you.'

Alec and Jan O'Leary had three adopted children and had fostered others nearly all their married life. Autumn loved them both, dearly. A well-matched couple, they were both small, round and slightly old-fashioned in appearance. Their house lacked many of the modern so-called essentials, but it was warm and welcoming and had been a homely haven for Autumn all her life. Every time there had been a trauma with Julie, Jan and Alec had scooped her up and made her feel like the most wanted child on the planet.

'Come on through and we'll have a catch up. The big ones are at school and the babies are due for a nap so I'll take them up and you and Jan can have a natter in peace.' Alec wrapped his arms around Autumn in a bear hug and laughed. 'Oh, I'm so pleased to see you looking so well!'

He took the two little ones from Jan and the two women walked through to the kitchen.

It never occurred to Autumn to do anything other than sink down into the battered leather armchair in the corner and pull her feet up underneath her.

She felt as if she was home, even though it was just for a while.

26

'Well, it's up to you what you do but I always think you should give everyone a chance. Nothing ventured, nothing gained. At best you could grab yourself a sister and brother, but if it turns out you don't get on, then so what? Don't see how you stand to lose anything.'

Neil had turned up to visit Julie just as he had said he would; he had brought a six-pack of Diet Coke, a packet of cigarettes, and several packets of different flavoured crisps, and now they were sitting side by side on the new sofa in the lounge with music playing in the background. It was the first time she had seen him out of his hospital uniform of navy slacks and white tunic and she was surprised to find how different he looked. He hadn't morphed into Brad Pitt and his hair and beard were still a little straggly but he was wearing casual tight black jeans and a loose, dark red, Ben Sherman shirt. He looked good. Smart and fashionable but not too off-puttingly aware of himself.

He seemed oblivious to her scrutiny as he carried on talking. 'I mean, I'd have thought the problem would have been if your long-lost family *didn't* want to see you. But they do so go for it, I say.'

'You don't know the background. You don't know what went on in my past . . . ' Julie hesitated, unsure whether to say anything more or not. She decided not. She didn't want to scare him off with all the gory details. Or even just some of them.

'You've just said it yourself.' He smiled at her winningly. 'It's in the past. It's gone and it'll never return but it can also never be changed. The past is written in stone, but the future is whatever you want to make it.'

He leaned forward and picked up a bag of crisps. 'Share? Or do you want a whole packet?'

Julie smiled. 'I'll have a whole packet now I'm officially a fat pig with an over-eating disorder.'

'Nonsense! You look fantastic. That haircut really suits you — the hairdresser done good.'

There was something strangely comforting about sitting side by side with Neil. He was chatty and gentle and seemed happy just to be there with her, as opposed to immediately trying to rip her clothes off and make a lunge for the unsatisfying and instant sex she had become used to with all the men in her life. They may well have enjoyed it but she certainly hadn't.

In fact, it had left Julie hating sex; she saw it as a necessary evil that women endured and could never understand how any woman would want to do it purely for pleasure. Ever since the first time she had been forced into it, with little idea either what it entailed or what the consequences might be, she had hated it. To her it had only ever meant invasion and violence at some level; men abused her body for their own satisfaction, and she herself used it as a bargaining tool.

'Are you going to see a solicitor?' Neil interrupted her thoughts as he stood up to change the CD. 'Your daughter is right, you know, that's the only way to make sure everything is legal and above board. You'll get Legal Aid. You and Seb weren't married so I think your rights take precedence but you need to check it out with someone who knows.'

'She did say she was going to try and find out where Seb was living. I could turn up on the doorstep with a couple of heavies and take Katya. Like he did.'

Neil laughed. 'Good job I know you're joking. Well, I hope you are. You're way too bright to do something that dumb. That would be a sure-fire way of upsetting the courts, wouldn't it?'

'I think I'm only half joking. Katya must be missing me . . . fuck knows what he's told her about me. I've missed her more than you can imagine.'

'Wrong.' Neil shook his head vehemently. 'I *can* imagine. Don't forget my ex has taken my kids off to Majorca to live with her Spanish toyboy in the mountains behind Benidorm. I have to take a flying cattle truck across Europe to see them!'

'Sorry.' Julie pulled a face. 'That was thoughtless of me, as usual. I do know I can be a self-centred bitch.'

'As if!' he laughed. 'Anyway, now I'm afraid I'm going to have to love you and leave you. I'm on earlies tomorrow and, unlike you, I need my beauty sleep!'

He held out both his hands and carefully helped Julie to her feet before handing her the crutches.

'Anything you need me to get you before I go? Hot drink? Sandwich?'

'No, I'm fine. I can manage. I have to get used to being independent again. Weird, huh?'

She went ahead of him down the hallway to the door. As she pulled it back, he handed her a piece of paper.

'Here's my home phone number and my mobile, just in case. The only time I don't answer is if I'm working, but if you leave a message I'll ring back.'

As she took it he leaned forward, put his hands on her shoulders and kissed her very gently on both cheeks before stepping out into the dark. 'Speak tomorrow! Be careful tonight. No tumbling down the stairs.'

Julie felt quite strangely ambivalent. She wasn't completely sure if she was pleased or disappointed that he hadn't kissed her on the lips.

She watched from the doorstep as he got into his car and pulled away then she locked and bolted the front door and went into the kitchen to have a cigarette. As she inhaled and savoured the tobacco she wondered if the wacky-baccy tin was still at the back of the drawer now that Autumn had been nosying around and tidying up. She pulled it open and slid her hand right to the back.

It was there. Warily she pulled it out and looked inside; there was still enough, carefully wrapped in tinfoil, for a skinny joint.

Putting the tin in her pocket, she prepared to make the difficult journey up the narrow staircase to her bedroom. She had thought about sleeping downstairs on the sofa but with the bathroom upstairs there was no point and she needed the exercise. It took several long, painful minutes but she got there, puffing and panting from the exertion, and went straight into the bathroom. Taking the tin out of her pocket, she opened it and, without giving herself time to think about it, peeled open the foil, shook the contents into the toilet and instantly flushed it. She just knew that if it stayed in the house she would at some point cave in.

Smiling at her reflection in the mirror, Julie felt unusually pleased with herself. It had been a long time since she had felt like that.

She could see that she looked better. Her new choppy hairstyle suited her naturally fair complexion, her sunken cheeks had filled out a little, and the dark circles that had ringed her eyes for so many years had faded.

As she studied herself every which way she wondered if she dared use the cash Autumn had left her for necessities to get some new clothes. Maybe a few things that were better suited to her new, more mature personality.

Settling down into bed, her first night anywhere completely on her own that she could remember, she thought over what Neil had said about Hannah and Ray. Although Ray meant nothing to her she did feel a certain curiosity about him; they had after all shared the same mother. She also wondered about Hannah and whether she would ever be able to rise above everything that had happened. She wasn't sure she was strong enough mentally to face up to her sister and the bitter memories, and the last thing she wanted after all her hard work was a relapse.

An added concern for her was how Neil would view her if he ever found out all the things in her past that could never be erased.

For the first few weeks, Julie had been grateful that she and Autumn were together; she had tried hard to fit into the routine at the foster home where they had been taken, but she couldn't. She was restless, just like a young bird with its wings clipped after it had already tasted freedom. And on top of it all was the looming threat that the social workers may just decide to make her go back to her aunt, her legal guardian, and then put Autumn up for adoption.

The foster parents, Alec and Jan, were kind and loving to both mother and child and promised Julie faithfully that they wouldn't let it happen. They were infinitely patient with the damaged teenager but despite their reassurances Julie felt betwixt and between; she was happy to be Autumn's mother in name but didn't want the daily graft of mothering her. Autumn had been the new toy, the baby doll for Christmas she had never had as a child, but the novelty of feeding and changing and caring for her constantly had soon worn off.

She just wanted her freedom back so Alec and Jan were left with no choice but to take over Autumn's care completely and let Julie go her own way.

That way led her back to Garth.

When she had made her spur-of-the-moment and ill-judged decision to leave Autumn with the foster parents and run off back to him and the squat, she had thought that it would be different. She had been away for just long enough to think of it nostalgically and had visions of being a totally free spirit there, unfettered now by having a demanding and time-consuming baby around. She wanted to be able to party all night and laze around all day, with the occasional 'job' in between to keep her going. Despite having already had a taste of what life in the squat was like, Julie's skewed outlook on reality meant she'd also thought it would be preferable to the claustrophobic domesticity of the foster home.

But she had underestimated the squat's key figure, the man in charge who had broken into the empty property in the first place and staked his claim on it. Garth was their self-appointed leader, pimp and dealer. By going back willingly Julie had instantly handed him the power to control her totally, and that was exactly what he proceeded to do the moment he 'allowed' her back in the door. He didn't waste any time letting her catch up with the others or settle back in, he simply put her to work straight away, 'to earn her keep' the best way she could.

Because Julie looked a lot younger than her age, Garth made her go with the men who had a preference for young girls; men who were more than willing to pay over the odds for sex with a virgin. Because she was naturally tiny and had no breasts to speak of, he made her remove all her body hair and pretend to be an innocent twelve-year-old having sex for the first time.

And it worked.

She had no idea how or where he found them all but Garth always had a steady supply of men who liked it like that. Each one different and each one believing it was Julie's first time. She despised each and every one of them, they made her skin crawl, but by switching her brain off she could act out the role, please the men and, therefore, please Garth.

And she liked to please Garth because then he slipped her extra supplies of the substances she had started to crave. Julie Grayson was intelligent and a quick learner, and Garth appreciated that in his women.

Without the ties of a baby, Julie quickly learned the hierarchy of earning. Garth's paedophiles paid the best; streetwalking in and around the West End came next, and when she was tired she would simply sit on the pavement wrapped in a filthy shawl, looking pathetic and begging. She would also shoplift and indulge in a bit of pick-pocketing if an easy opportunity presented itself.

Garth had taught her all there was to know about amorality.

But despite the deprivations of the squat and the depravity of her lifestyle, she quickly got used to being there. Garth wasn't as bad at divvying up the earnings as some of the others she'd heard about, and there was a certain camaraderie among the women there that made her feel comfortable and part of a family who looked out for each other.

It was akin to how she had felt at the hostel with Vera and Barbara.

But it all changed again for Julie the day the bailiffs turned up with a court order and the police in tow, to repossess the house forcibly.

Scared of the consequences, she didn't wait around to see what would happen to the others or where they would go, just gathered up her meagre belongings and headed back to the foster home in Wimbledon where Autumn was still living with Alec and Jan and pleaded to be allowed to stay.

She didn't tell them why but still they welcomed her back and, after several meetings and assessments, Autumn's social worker agreed she could try once, again to be a mother her daughter.

And Julie did try. She did her best at the foster home and was eventually given a flat of her own on the eleventh floor of a neglected tower block. She was thrilled to bits when she moved in and for a while happily played house there, but the feeling soon passed and she found she couldn't cope with the constraints of single parenthood. After a few months of struggling she took Autumn to Alec and Jan once more who welcomed the little girl back into their family with open arms, leaving Julie free to go off again and carry on living as if she had a death wish.

Very quickly, she managed to find Garth, the man she loved and hated in equal measure. She just couldn't seem to break away from him.

27

Hannah was restlessly prowling round the house, trying to understand exactly what had happened and at the same time work out what to do about it. There was no denying that Ben had deceived her, both over his job and also their finances, but then again, she tried to convince herself, there could be an explanation.

Aimlessly she walked over to the mantel-piece and picked up the two photos that Autumn had shown such an interest in. She held them up together; as she studied them side by side she wondered how her life could have been turned upside down so quickly.

Maybe her aunt had been right when she had always gleefully stated 'Pride comes before a fall' after hearing of any small success for either of the girls.

But despite her aunt's constant prophecies of doom and snide comments, Hannah, unlike her sister, had eventually risen above her background and been extraordinarily proud of everything she had achieved, in both her personal life and her career; now it seemed that her hard-won perfect life was not so perfect after all.

Once all the evidence of Ben's deceit and betrayal was laid out in front of her it was so damning there was no way of denying it, but still she wondered if there was an excuse for what he had done.

She was about to try ringing him again when she glanced out of the window and glimpsed the shadow of someone skulking outside by the cherry tree in the front garden. Immediately she started racing around the house, double-locking the doors and windows, scared witless at the thought of the debt-collectors and bailiffs who had already sent threatening letters demanding payment or goods. Then she hid in the downstairs cloakroom. She perched on the toilet seat, shivering and terrified, as first the front door and then the back was forcefully rattled, followed by the conservatory windows.

'Hannah?' a voice called out eventually. 'Hannah, are you in there? Hannah?' It was Ben, calling through the letter-box.

Taking deep breaths to try to stop her heart from thumping, she went to the front door and looked through one of the glass side panels.

'What are you doing? What do you want?' she asked as calmly as she could.

Frowning, he shaded his eyes from the sun with his hand and looked at her through one of the triangles of reinforced leaded glass.

'Er . . . to come into my house, if that's all right with you?' His tone was typically sarcastic and it really grated on her. For the first time ever she thought, How dare he?

'Actually it's not all right with me. You've got a nerve! After swanning off without a word.'

All too aware of what had happened the previous time she had stood up to her husband, Hannah felt a shiver pass through her despite the warmth of the day. At the same time part of her still wanted to open the door and throw her arms around him, the way she knew she would have done if she hadn't found out about the job and the debts.

'Duh, Hannah! This is my house and I want to come in. Unlock the fucking door!'

'No.' Again she kept her voice calm.

'Come on, Han, don't be so silly. You don't really want to do this, do you? Unlock the door. NOW!' he shouted through the letter-box as loudly as he could.

'No way!' she shouted back at him. 'Do you seriously think that I'll let you in after what you've done? Not a chance.'

'What? I go off to work for a week and you think you can shut me out of my own house? Open the door or I'll kick it in.'

'Just try it and I'll call the police . . . ' She paused then and felt her shoulders sag involuntarily. She wasn't used to confrontation of any sort with Ben and her first instinct was to do as she was told. As she always had done.

'Call the police?' His voice was loud and incredulous. 'Call the police because I want to get into my own home? Go for it. I'd like to hear their reaction to your hysterical crap.'

She knew he was starting to get angry and she had two choices. Let him in and say nothing or else confront him.

'Look, Ben, I know about all the debts and I know about the job you don't have. I know everything and I don't trust you any more. This is my home and now it's at risk because of your deception . . . '

Hannah saw him bend down and casually pull a brick off the top of the circular flowerbed in the middle of the drive. Then quick as a flash, he threw it towards her. It bounced off the wall of the house, just missing the glass in front of Hannah. She ducked back behind the frame as he snatched up another and then another.

'That's rubbish! You're talking rubbish . . . who's been feeding you this nonsense? It's not true . . . ' Despite the bluster, Hannah could hear the panic in his voice.

'Yes, it is. I've opened all the mail and I've spoken to your firm. You got the sack and didn't tell me . . . '

'You spoke to my firm? You fucking bitch! I didn't get the sack . . . how dare you interfere in my life like that? It's none of your business.'

The next brick actually hit the window but without enough force to smash through the double glazing.

'You wouldn't answer your phone, I was worried, and it *is* my affair. It's my money as well as yours that you've gone through,' she shouted at full volume despite the tears streaming down her face. 'Now I'm telling you, I'm not letting you in. You'll have to come back later when I've got my solicitor here. I need to know where I stand.'

'Come back later? This is *my* house, it's in *my* name! Now open the goddamned door . . . '

Peering at him, she could see that he was raging with anger and frustration. He started marching up and down, swinging his clenched fists back and forth, his face contorted. She had never seen him as angry as this before and it scared her, but she tried to stand her ground.

'No, it's not your house, it belongs to the bank and they want it back, as you well know. You haven't paid the bloody mortgage for months! You haven't paid anything to anyone. You've spent everything we had, everything we'd worked for . . . Ben, how could you do this to me?' She didn't want him to know she was crying but she couldn't help it. The sobs came hard and fast.

'Han, look, I can explain. I can explain everything. I didn't want to tell you because I didn't want you to hate me . . . please let me in. We can sort this out.'

Hannah knew that he saw her tears as a sign that she was weakening so she backed into the house and dialled Autumn's number. She hated involving her niece but couldn't think of anyone else who would be strong enough to deal with Ben.

'Oh, God, Autumn,' she blurted out when the phone was answered. 'I'm so sorry to call you again but Ben's turned up. What shall I do? He's outside lobbing bricks at the door — he's off his head, I think he's probably having a breakdown of some sort. He knows I know, I told him . . . '

'I'll be right there, depending on traffic.'

'Shall I call the police?'

'Only if he tries to break in or if you're scared he's going to do something to himself. Otherwise just hang on in there and distract him somehow. I'll be as quick as I can.'

* * *

What Hannah hadn't realised was that Autumn was actually pleased to get her call because it gave her the opportunity to get what she wanted: a face-to-face with the man called Ben Durman. She wanted to see if he was who she thought he was, and then his reaction when he recognised her.

When the phone rang she had still been in bed, having a luxuriously solitary lie-in as Leon was away on business in San Francisco. But without a second thought she jumped straight up, threw her clothes on in record time, and then called Leon's driver to see if he was free.

Within fifteen minutes they were en route for the borders of rural Essex. As the car swung into the narrow lane, Autumn dialled her aunt's number. 'I'm here. Where is he?'

'Around the back. I think he's going to try and get in through the window on the landing, but the garage is locked so he can't get to the ladder . . . he's steaming with anger.'

'Are you going to come outside and talk to him?' Autumn asked.

'Do you think I should?'

'Well, I guess it's better than letting him in. Unless you don't want to talk to him at all.'

'I want to talk to him, to find out what's going on, but I'm just a bit scared of what I'm going to find out and I would hate him to have a go at you . . . '

'No need for either of us to be scared, Marius is here with me.'

Autumn knew they were both quite safe. She had Leon's driver, a retired boxer, alongside her.

Marius had been a lightweight so was neither tall nor wide, but he was muscular and fit with a slightly battered face that looked rather handsome and deceptively unthreatening — until he lowered his head and glared.

As they both got out of the car, Autumn quickly pulled up the collar of her jacket and tucked her long hair under a bright pink knitted beanie hat. If it was who she thought, she didn't think he'd recognise her away from the club environment and without the green feathers and stage make-up, but she wanted to make sure she had the upper hand when she eventually confronted him. She didn't want to give him any time to prepare an excuse.

Suddenly he appeared from around the side of the house. 'Can I help you?' he asked, so politely that Autumn wanted to laugh.

'I'm a friend of Hannah's and this is Marius. Hannah asked us over. Said she wanted someone here with her when she spoke to you. Just in case.'

'Just in case of what?' Ben's smile seemed genuinely curious. 'What on earth . . . ?' He paused then and held up his hands. 'Oh, right. I guess you work with my wife. Has she been making up stories again?' He sighed dramatically. 'I've lost my key and she thought I was an intruder so she threw a fit. She can be a bit hysterical, my wife. But it's all under control, as you can see, so you can go now . . . '

Autumn smiled. 'I'll have a chat with Hannah first, see how she feels. She did invite us after all.'

She had looked him over carefully as he was

speaking and now knew without a doubt that Ben Durman was the man who regularly came to the club. Over the many months he had been visiting, she figured he must have tipped her thousands of pounds. Although she had had no way of knowing for sure, Autumn was mortified by the thought that much of it had probably come from Hannah's hard-earned salary.

Bastard, she thought as she smiled at him pleasantly.

'Hannah will be out in a minute and I'm going to hang around while you have a chat.'

'Actually you're not. Not on my property you won't hang around.' His smile was still in place but it was fixed and cold and certainly didn't reach his eyes. 'So now I'd like you to leave — both of you.'

The front door opened and closed quickly then and Hannah walked over to the three of them.

'Hannah, darling.' Ben reached out and took her hand, gripping it so tightly that her knuckles cracked. 'Explain to your friends that this is just a misunderstanding. You and I have things to talk about, on our own.'

'Ben, this is Autumn, my niece. I told you about her, and now I've told her all about you.'

'Ah-ha. I knew there was someone else behind all this nonsense, it's just not like you to be like this. Let's go inside,' he said. 'Alone.' He frowned as he looked at Autumn more closely then and for a second she thought he had recognised her, but he turned away and tried to pull Hannah forcibly back to the house. 'Come on. I don't want our business aired all over the neighbourhood.'

Angrily she snatched her hand away from him and stood her ground. 'There's no chance of it *not* being all over the neighbourhood when the bailiffs come to strip the house and evict us, is there? They'll all be watching then.'

'Not here,' he hissed. 'This is between you and me, sweetheart. It's our business. And I can explain everything. Really I can.'

Hannah's eyes were all over the place and Autumn could see she was wavering. A part of her wanted just to walk away and leave them to it, but the other part was furious with Ben for deceiving her aunt on every front.

'Last chance, Han. Either we go indoors now, on our own, or I'll . . . ' He stopped talking and looked at her hard. 'What's it to be?'

'I want Autumn with me when we talk. You hit me, Ben, remember that? You hit me and there's no ignoring it.'

'Oh, do stop being such a child, Hannah! It's really irritating. But then again, *you're* irritating. Have been for a long time!'

He waved his hand dismissively then smirked nastily at her before making a big show of turning his back and pulling his phone out of his pocket. He clicked away on it, sending a text message. A few moments later a silver convertible Saab with darkened windows and the hood up screeched to a halt beyond the gate; Ben walked over to it and climbed into the passenger seat.

'Ben!' Hannah called after him. 'Wait. We have

to sort this out . . . '

But he didn't look back at her and, as quickly as the car had arrived, it was gone.

But not before Marius had noted the registration number and all the car's details. He was known to be one of the few ex-boxers to have kept all his faculties intact.

28

After Ben had roared off with his companion, the two women went indoors, leaving Marius leaning against the bonnet of the Mercedes as he chatted away on his mobile phone.

Autumn was confused by the speed of events and was struggling to be neither judgemental nor irritated, but it was difficult for her. Her view of relationships was very black and white. In her eyes, Ben had lied to Hannah and been so dishonest that he deserved to be booted out for good with no further negotiations.

But instead she saw her aunt behaving in exactly the same way her mother always had; they both seemed to give the men in their lives the control and freedom to do whatever they wanted, and then they were surprised when it all went wrong. Autumn couldn't ever imagine letting a man have that much control over her or her life.

Her gut instinct was to be honest and tell her aunt about Ben's visits to the club, but she was scared of breaking the very new and still fragile bond between them. To prove to someone their husband was a financial disaster was one thing; to tell them that their husband had sat and salivated, with his mouth almost touching your crotch, and then tipped you well for it, was something else. That could well be the breaking point that would end their embryonic family relationship before it ever really began. Autumn still desperately wanted Hannah to meet up with Julie again and for them to get on. She also wanted to meet her American Uncle Ray and his family. For the first time in her life she felt as if she was part of a real family, her own family, albeit one she had yet to find out about. She could never have imagined how exciting that thought could be or how important it had quickly become to her.

'I hate to ask this, but what do you really think Ben was up to when he was pretending to be at work? He must have been somewhere, both daytime and night-time . . . '

Autumn hesitated for a moment. She wanted Hannah to think it out for herself. 'Could he have been doing something illegal? Maybe got himself into some sort of trouble? Perhaps he took some money from his employers. Sometimes these companies don't want the bad publicity so they don't call the police. That has happened at Birds before now.'

Hannah frowned and shook her head as they walked indoors together. 'A few weeks ago I would have laughed at the idea, but now I haven't a clue. The Ben you just saw is a stranger to me. I can't seem to see anything straight any more.' She paused and Autumn stayed quiet, letting her think this through. 'Ben has always been a bit of a control freak, it's his nature and I knew that from the start, but at the same time I have to admit that on the whole I've been happy with him and our life together. He seems driven to make every decision, so some of this is my own fault for sitting back and letting him have free rein over our lives. Suppose the unequal division of power suited us both.'

Still Autumn stayed quiet.

'Well, say something,' Hannah sighed. 'What do you think? I mean, you're far more worldly-wise than me despite being half my age. I've led a very sheltered personal life, going straight from the restrictions of our aunt's house to marriage to Ben. Very dull really. Your life seems so exciting by comparison.'

Autumn laughed. 'Do you mean because I work in a club and wear a skimpy costume and tons of slap? No, it's not as glamorous or exciting as it seems, but the money's good and I'm lucky because I'm at a very expensive and exclusive place so I'm well protected from the more lecherous customers.'

'What does Julie think about it?' Hannah enquired.

'She's never really mentioned it. She knows it's what I do but I don't think she really cares either way. My foster parents weren't over the moon but they know I can take care of myself. I learned that from Ma when I was just a toddler. I could make a cup of tea and cheese on toast when I was three, and roll a decent joint by the time I was eight. But I wasn't allowed to light it. Even Ma had her standards!' Autumn laughed dryly.

'And your boyfriend?'

'Leon's a businessman and one of the club's owners so no problem there, that's how we met. But I've just had a huge promotion. I'm not going to be dancing any more, I'm in charge of all the other dancers . . . ' She stopped mid-sentence as her mobile phone beeped in her bag. After she had checked her message she clicked it shut and looked at Hannah. 'That was Ma, wanting to know if I've done anything about Katya. I know you've got all this other stuff going on but . . . '

'As soon as I'm in the office, I'll have a talk with my colleague and see what we can do. But I'm going to have to meet up with Julie soon if I'm going to be able to do anything official. I need her permission. Maybe I could go and see her during the week.' Hannah looked thoughtful. 'Yes, that's what I'll do. I'll go and see her. I'll just turn up and hope for the best.'

'Do you want me there to act as referee or should I stay out of the way?'

'If you don't mind, I think this is something I have to do alone. I'll let you know how it goes, but I'd be grateful if you can find out when she's going to be there.'

'I'll try, but I can't guarantee anything where Ma is concerned.'

Autumn quickly changed the subject, actually quite relieved Hannah didn't want her there. She didn't want to be piggy-in-the-middle when Julie opened the door to find her sister on the step.

* * *

Julie was feeling exhausted and over-emotional. She had had a free day from all her various appointments so that Neil could take her to visit

Jethro at the home in Hampshire, but she hadn't realised just how weak she still was. It had been a long drive and, even with leg-stretching stops en route, she ended up in pain and barely able to move once she was home.

Her hyper-sensitive emotions had switched rapidly between relief and hurt when she had realised that Jethro was as happy as could be where he was and without her. Although he had certainly seemed pleased to see her when she arrived, within minutes he had gone off again and was playing with his new friends, seemingly oblivious to his mother and Neil watching from a distance. Seeing him so comfortable and secure had hurt Julie in a way, but it also made her wonder if maybe her son's boundless reserves of energy needed more stimulation and space than she could give him, boxed up in their small council house in London.

She didn't voice her thoughts to the staff at the home or to Neil but she wondered if now was the right time for Jethro to live away from home permanently.

As she lay full-length on the sofa, aching all over and feeling sorry for herself again, she started to think about her sister. Her blood still boiled at the unfairness of what had happened, but there was a long-suppressed part of her that realised she couldn't completely blame Hannah for something she didn't know anything about. After all, she had had no idea of the circumstances surrounding her younger sister's first pregnancy.

And then there was Ray. Was it his fault that

he had been lucky enough to be whisked off to America by his real father? Was it really fair to resent his good fortune? she wondered.

For the first time she thought that maybe she was directing her anger and resentment at the wrong person. Maybe Autumn and Neil were right. It was the Aunt who was to blame and no one else. Aunt Marian was the sole cause of so much misery, and just maybe should have been brought to book for it long ago.

Maybe it was too late.

Maybe it wasn't.

The more she thought about it, the more Julie realised that she would have to go back to the old house and find out what had happened to the Aunt and her next-door neighbour, Gerald Kelly. If she was going to move on, she had to know before it ate away at her all over again. Dragging herself up from the sofa, Julie grabbed nervously at the three-pronged walking sticks that she was now using instead of the crutches. Just that small progression had given her a sense of achievement at the time but now she could feel the familiar waves of depression washing over her again. Her life was a mess, she was a mess, and she hated herself.

She delved into the depths of a small wicker sewing basket that she kept in the cupboard and pulled out the foot of the ragdoll that she had kept all those years. The doll that Hannah had given her had been lost in the fire at the hostel but she had managed to keep hold of the foot from her own doll. She hadn't looked at it for years, but as soon as she held it all the old emotions came flooding back.

She made her way upstairs and climbed into bed, fully clothed, clutching the battered and barely recognisable piece of cloth. Snuggling down under the covers, she curled up on her side as best she could and started to suck her thumb as she always had as a child, regardless of the bright yellow mustard and burning hot chilli sauce mix the Aunt had forced into her mouth as punishment for doing so.

She knew that the time had come for her to face her demons and exorcise them from her life once and for all.

She lay in the same position all night, wide awake, just thinking and planning.

29

'Lord knows, Ray, I didn't mean for this to happen, but you do know you have to shoulder some of the blame? It takes two to make a marriage work.'

Stella was sitting in the pink quilted armchair in the bedroom, watching him gather up his belongings. Her legs were casually stretched out in front of her but her arms were crossed defensively across her chest. 'I mean, you have to admit, you are a workaholic, you're never here and I've had to spend a lot of time on my own. Something was bound to happen. I was so lonely, felt abandoned . . . '

Ray shook his head in disbelief. It was the first time he had been back to the house and seen Stella since catching her with Denny, and it felt strange; no matter how much he thought about what had happened that day, and since, he just couldn't get his head around it. He realised that she had been primed on what to say, probably by Denny, and that she was getting the blame transference in before he could say anything.

'Awww, poor Stella, having to put with a husband who works to support his family just as hard as he possibly can. Shame! It's all my fault, not yours. Such a bum rap for you, having to live in this house and not have to go out to work.' Ray ran his fingers through his hair in frustration as he looked at her. 'You're actually saying I *forced* you to screw around with a boy nearly young enough to be your son? Crap! And now you want me out of the marriage and the house? Jeez . . . he's a no-good golf bum, barely out of goddamned diapers!'

'There's no need to cuss anyone out, Ray. That's not like you. And Denny isn't a boy. You make it sound kind of dirty . . . '

Ray laughed out loud. 'Oh, yeah. That I do! 'Cos it is. Don't think I haven't checked him out. He doesn't have a pot to piss in of his own, and he lives in a rental apartment the size of your closet. He's screwing you and screwing you over at the same time.'

Ray was packing for the trip to London he had arranged on the spur of the moment. Afterwards he had wondered about his decision and briefly thought about cancelling, but he wanted to make himself do something that had no connection to Stella and the marriage he had once cherished.

Now, listening to her whining, he was pleased he hadn't cancelled. He had to get away.

'And why do you have to go to London, Ray? Why now? We have to meet with the lawyers, there's so much to resolve, the house and all . . . '

'You want it resolved right now? This very moment? Of course, Stella. Anything you want, Stella. Not! That isn't how it works.'

'Ray's tone was sarcastic. Rather than feeling sad or guilty at the sudden and dramatic ending of their marriage, Stella's main concern seemed to be the division of their belongings. She had so far demanded the house with all the contents as it stood, two of the cars, the timeshare in Orlando and a heap of alimony, based on the value of the business.

But despite her calling him almost every day and turning up randomly at the car-lot, Ray had stayed strong and steadfastly refused to discuss any of it; he simply couldn't bear the thought of Denny getting to enjoy everything he had worked hard for all his life.

Stella continued as if he hadn't spoken and he realised she was actually whining. 'We can't both live under the same roof any more, can we? And this is the family home. We have the children to consider — their base is here. Their security is here. You work all the time so the best option is for me to have the house. I've dedicated my life to you and the kids, I deserve recompense for that . . . '

He looked at her and wondered again how he could not have noticed what was going on. He could see now that his wife looked different. She was pounds slimmer, her hair was longer, lighter and casually styled, and her clothes were more flattering, maybe even designer. She certainly looked classy even if she wasn't acting it. Her whole demeanour was younger and more glamorous. She definitely looked closer in age to Denny than she did to him, and it saddened Ray. He could see now that the relaxed semi-retirement he had planned with her in their condo by the sea was just a pipe-dream that she had played along with, not relishing the prospect as he had. Somehow or other he had missed the transformation in Stella that must have happened in front of him.

Perhaps she was right and he had been neglectful, even if it had been with the best of motives.

'I'm not discussing it now,' he insisted. 'I'm going to London to see my sisters, to revisit my past and have a little fun at the same time. Meanwhile, you and your snivelling little lover-boy can just wait in line and hope I don't blow everything while I'm gone! I may come home via the scenic route of the rest of the world with a twenty-year-old Playboy bunny on my arm. Or I may not even come home. Ever.'

He carefully put the final few items in his case and pushed the lid shut.

'Now, excuse me, I have a plane to catch.'

'I'll take you to the airport then,' Stella offered.

'No, I'm taking the car.'

'But I'll need that car! The kids have got the others . . . '

'Get one of them back then. Or, better yet, get your very own super-hero, Denny the golf pro, to buy you a new one!' Ray stopped and banged his open palm against his forehead. 'Ooops, forgot! Lover-boy doesn't have any money, does he? Tell the kids I'll call them from London or wherever, or they can call my cell.'

He swung the suitcase and overnight bag off the bed and carried them downstairs and out to the car. Stella didn't follow him. There was an air of finality about this departure. Even though he wanted to turn back, he didn't. He could see in her eyes that Stella simply didn't love him any more. There was no point in dragging any of it out any longer. He could maybe have forgiven her a fling, but in her eyes at least her affair with Denny was the real thing. There was no going back from that.

Ray sped through the open gates and out of the estate without a backward glance, painfully aware that he was leaving his home, his hard-earned home that he loved, for the last time.

He wanted to let Stella stew for a while so he hadn't told her that he had already set the wheels in motion to buy a beachfront condo for himself. It wasn't as luxurious as the one they had planned to live in together but it would do while he got used to the changes in his circumstances, both emotional and financial.

He took a pill, pulled on an eye-mask and slept for most of the overnight transatlantic flight, waking only when the cabin lights went on and the crew started serving breakfast. Determined not to think about what was happening back in Long Beach, he focused on seeing his sisters again.

He could still picture them as clearly as if the accident had just happened. Two little girls being led away by an angry and frumpy-looking middle-aged woman he'd been told was their aunt and new guardian.

His father had tried his best to persuade everyone that the three siblings should all stay together, but their aunt had been adamant they should go to live with her.

Now he knew why. When he had spoken to his elderly father after Hannah had told him about Julie, Chuck told him that after the crash there was a large insurance pay out that had been divided three ways between the children — a policy that their parents had taken out to secure their upbringing, just in case.

As the girls' legal guardian, their aunt had been given control of two-thirds of it.

When they'd parted, Ray had hugged and kissed his baby sisters and reassured them he would see them again soon. At just fifteen years of age it had never occurred to him that this would be the last time he would set eyes on them for many years. He had met Hannah just the once when she was in California with Ben, but Julie he had never seen since that day.

Now he was going to see them both again, hopefully, and despite being excited at the prospect, he also felt unusually nervous.

Ray decided against calling Hannah right away. Instead he went straight to the central London hotel he had booked, checked in, dumped his suitcase on the bed and then went for a long walk up the Embankment.

As he walked he could clearly remember just a few months before the accident going on a family day out to London. His mother and step-father had taken them all to visit the Tower of London, to see the Crown Jewels and the ravens. Julie had been too young to appreciate it but Hannah had clasped her big brother's hand and loved every moment of the expedition.

Afterwards they had walked along the Embankment, eating ice-cream and watching the tourist boats chugging back and forth.

Had it been a sunny day or was that purely his imagination? He sat on a bench and looked at the impressive building that to all the visitors queuing to get in and out was a landmark of British history. To Ray it held memories that he deperately wanted to relieve every moment of.

He closed his eyes and could see Hannah slipping his hand and running ahead to get up close to the ravens; he could see Julie clapping her hands and giggling in her buggy, pushed by their mother, smiling contentedly at her husband who had an arm looped around her waist.

That day had been idyllic, as had the holiday in Cornwall shortly afterwards. Then in one crazy moment it had all changed for ever for all of them.

Big man Ray could feel his eyes prickling with tears so he flipped his sunglasses down to cover his face and walked slowly back to the hotel. He decided he would go to Cornwall alone and then catch up with his sisters afterwards. He knew it was probably because of his own recent emotional upheaval but he felt he had to go back to where they had all holidayed together; and then to the place where the accident had happened all those years ago.

He had ghosts to lay and he couldn't do that in London.

30

Hannah stared mesmerised at the ringing phone on the table as if it was a spitting cobra waiting to strike if she reached out her hand to it. She was terrified to pick it up.

'Answer it, dear,' Fliss said gently. 'You can't keep avoiding everything. It'll just get you in more trouble. You have to deal with these people. Tell them the truth about Ben . . . '

But Hannah didn't. Again she let the answer-phone pick up. Again the caller's number was unidentified and there was no message left.

'It's the bloody debt collectors!' She looked at Fliss. 'I just know it . . . they only wait for so long before they start circling like vultures.'

'I've told you, Hannah, it's not as bad as that.' Her friend gently touched her arm. 'What you have to do is phone everyone on the list Autumn wrote out for you and explain your situation to them. That's how to deal with it. Don't be intimidated.'

'I know, but they *do* intimidate me. They don't believe I don't know where Ben is. *I* can't believe I don't know where Ben is. I've even considered having him listed as a missing person.'

Hannah prowled round the ground floor of her house as she spoke, constantly checking the locks on the doors and windows and peering out.

'All this pacing and worrying will get you

nowhere. Why don't you take a walk into the village? Jimmy will be here in a minute. I can make him a cuppa and keep him company while he works. There's a cake and plant sale in the church hall you might enjoy . . . '

The two women were waiting for Fliss's son Jimmy who worked for a burglar alarm company and was going to fit a sophisticated system at cost price and reinforce the weak-spot window on the landing. Hannah was neurotically determined that no one was going to get inside the house while she wasn't there. She had seen first-hand how some of the debt collectors worked; had seen clients threatened and intimidated in their own homes by thugs who pretended that the door had been open. There was no way she was going to let that happen to her, especially as she was out at work half the time.

'No, it's okay. I'd better not buy anything, especially not cakes after Ben said I was getting too fat. An enforced starvation diet will be good for my fat arse. Maybe there's a bright side to all this. If I can't afford to eat then I'll lose weight. Logical really.'

Suddenly Hannah stopped her relentless pacing and smiled ruefully. She held up her hands in apology.

'Oh, I'm sorry, Fliss! I'm really sorry. You're such a good friend and I am such a bitch! I didn't know quite how much of a bitch I could be until recently. Now I know I'm really good at it. I could even be a professional. Look at me, I've learned how to do bitch!'

She saw Fliss's eyes fill up. 'What? I was only joking . . . '

Fliss jumped up and hugged her. 'I know — and that's what's so great! You're getting your sense of humour back. You're turned the first corner. The only way is up now.' She settled back down on her chair again. 'While we wait, tell me how it's going with your sister?'

Hannah grimaced slightly. 'It took me all my nerve and I sweated on it all day but finally I gritted my teeth and went round there . . . only to find she wasn't even in. What an anti-climax! Now I'll have to go through it all again tomorrow. I have to see her, I need her permission to trace Katya.'

Again the phone rang. After a reproachful glance from Fliss, Hannah made herself pick it up.

'Hello?' she said abruptly, but there was only silence at the other end. 'Hello?' she repeated.

'Hanny?' The voice at the other end was faint.

Hannah froze. She'd immediately recognised that voice. And besides no one had ever called her that apart from her sister.

'Julie . . . is that you?'

'Yes, it's me. I'm sorry, I'm sorry . . . It wasn't all your fault. I should have told you . . . I shouldn't have blamed you. It's not your fault, it's not your fault . . . '

Hannah had trouble understanding what she was saying, the words sounded slurred and distant as if Julie was talking from inside a tunnel.

'What's going on — are you okay? Tell me what's happened?'

'I'm sorry. I blamed you and it wasn't your fault. Now there's nothing I can do to get revenge, get some justice. Aunt Marian is mad now and Gerald is . . . '

'Gerald?' Hannah couldn't figure out what was going on so she gestured to Fliss to pass her a pen and paper. She hurriedly wrote down Autumn's phone number and told Fliss to call it on the mobile. 'Julie, listen to me. I don't understand what you're saying . . . Julie? Julie . . . Can you hear me? Where are you? Are you at home? Tell me where you are and I'll come and find you . . . Julie, I love you. Please tell me what's wrong? Tell me where you are . . . '

Julie went quiet but Hannah knew she was still there; she could hear her breathing at the other end of the line. She tried to take the mobile from Fliss. 'Autumn's not answering,' her friend whispered. 'I've left a message for her. Maybe she's at work.'

'Give it to me quickly,' hissed Hannah, and then handed the other phone to her friend. 'Keep listening to this. I think Julie may have taken something, she sounds so weird. I don't understand why she's phoning me. Autumn must have given her the number, I suppose.'

Hannah punched in her niece's number again. This time she answered. 'Look, I was going to call you back later, I'm busy right now,' she stated abruptly.

'Do you know where Julie is?' Hannah asked urgently. 'She's just phoned me. She's still on the phone, in fact, but she's not talking. She sounds sick or drugged or something . . . she sounds so strange, I can't get any sense out of her. She's in an awful state. I just know it, but I don't know where she is. Do you?'

'I haven't a clue. I'll ring round, check with Neil at the hospital, he might know . . . ' Autumn cried before the mobile went dead again.

Hannah tried to think. It was all too bizarre. Something serious must have happened to fire Julie up to phone her, but she hadn't a clue what it could be. Why bring up Aunt Marian and Gerald right then? She thought back over her sister's words. 'Aunt Marian is mad.' Did that mean Julie had seen her? And Gerald . . . what had he got to do with it? she wondered.

'Is Julie still there, do you think?' She took the phone back from Fliss.

'I think so but she's breathing really heavily and not responding to me. Maybe she's just crying . . . '

'JULIE!' Hannah shouted down the phone. 'Answer me, JULIE!'

But there was nothing but silence.

Suddenly Hannah had a moment of clarity. She snatched the mobile and called Autumn again.

'I think I know where she is! I bet she's gone to the old house to look for Aunt Marian . . . that's what she meant. She said Aunt Marian is mad. How would she know if she hadn't been to see? Oh, my God, suppose Julie's done something to her?'

She gave Autumn the address. 'I'll call a cab, get there as soon as I can,' her niece barked, 'and I'll check Ma's house on the way.'

Hannah went up to the bedroom, grabbed a pair of jeans and a jumper, threw them on and headed for the door. Then she remembered that Fliss was still waiting patiently in her kitchen.

'Are you okay to stay here? I'll be as quick as I can, but I have to go and find Julie — she's in trouble. I can't let her down again.'

'Just go, I'll deal with Jimmy and anything else. You go and help your sister. I'll take the cats with me and then it doesn't matter how long you are. My spoiled little Dolly will love that, being bullied by these two. Not!'

'You're a star, Fliss. And If Ben shows up then tell him to go screw himself.' Hannah kissed her friend on the cheek and rushed out to her car.

The familiar drive from Essex into London seemed to take for ever, as did finding somewhere to park, but eventually she clicked the car locks and walked up to the front door of the old house. Nervously she rang the bell then stepped back. She was relieved when Autumn flung it open.

'I've been to Ma's and she's not there. Thank God you've come, Hannah. I haven't got a clue about any of this. It's like some sort of horror movie . . . it's vile in here, really vile. I'm just about to chuck up . . . '

Hannah looked over her shoulder at an old lady hunched over a Zimmer frame who was peering down the hallway at them, her face screwed up in bemusement. 'Hello, dear. Have you brought me my dinner? I'm starving,' she said.

'Oh, my God,' Hannah murmured quietly in

shock. 'Oh, my God.'

She knew instantly that the bent old woman outlined in the doorway was her aunt, but she would never have recognised her anywhere else. Her hair was gun-metal grey now, thick with grease and hacked off close to her head. Ragged, dirty clothes hung off her now bony body. The whole house smelled of stale urine and rotting debris and was filthy to the point of being a health hazard. Hannah could feel her feet sticking to the carpet as she stepped into the eerie darkness of what used to be her home.

'Hello, Aunt Marian,' she said with a smile, forcing the words out of her mouth.

The Aunt looked at her curiously. 'Hello. Who are you? Where's my dinner? Have you brought my dinner? I'm starving.'

'I'm Hannah. Remember me?'

Her aunt looked at her vacantly. 'Hannah . . . Hannah. You're my mother.' She looked around. 'Where's Daddy?'

Autumn laughed humourlessly. 'What *is* going on here? There's no sign of Ma and this one has no idea what I'm talking about. Lord knows why she's living here alone in this squalor — don't your lot deal with stuff like this? It's worse than a chimp's cage in a Third World zoo.'

Despite everything, Hannah was shocked by Autumn's harshness. Whatever had gone on before, Marian Beecham was now just a shell of herself. A confused old woman barely surviving with a broken mind. She was not the Aunt Marian Hannah remembered.

'Don't be so hard, Autumn. Believe it or not,

this is Aunt Marian, the woman who brought me and your mother up and treated us so appallingly. But now she's senile and doesn't even remember who we are. She messed with our minds and now hers has gone completely. It's a sad turnaround . . . '

There was a knock on the door.

'I wondered if everything was okay?' asked the young man on the doorstep. 'I live next-door and try and keep an eye on the poor old dear. She never has any visitors other than the occasional home help, her family never bother with her, and today there've been three of you. Is she being assessed at last? I've made dozens of phone calls to Social Services, Help the Aged, and so on and so on ad infinitum. No one seems to care.'

'Three of us? Who was the first one here? Did you see her? Where did she go?' Hannah fired the questions at the man who was looking increasingly bemused.

'Er . . . she was here a couple of hours ago, I think. Small and blonde, if I remember. I heard a bit of a commotion going on out in the garden and then it all went quiet. I thought the old lady was probably being difficult with Social Services . . . ' Again he paused and looked suspiciously at Hannah and Autumn. 'She's got quite a temper when she loses it, as I well know! She even hit the woman from Meals on Wheels so now they deliver her meals to my place. Won't come inside any more.'

Hannah turned away and went back into the house, leaving Autumn to deal with the neighbour. It was so bizarre to be back here, especially as, if she ignored the filth, the layers of dust and grime everywhere and the sickening smell, it still looked the same as when she had left all those years before. All the same furniture still in the same places . . . and when she went upstairs to look for Julie she discovered that even their old bedroom was exactly the same. Nothing had been replaced anywhere inside the house in all those years.

As she looked around, all the painful, long-buried memories came flooding back, as did her hatred for her aunt. But it was for the woman she had been. Hannah simply couldn't equate the brutal, domineering bully of their childhood with this sad old lady, hobbling around looking completely bewildered.

She knew now what her sister had meant on the phone. And suddenly, with a flash of intuition, she knew where Julie was now.

Hannah pushed her way past the Aunt and Autumn, pushed the disused back door open and ran out into the wildly overgrown and neglected garden.

'Julie!' she shouted. 'It's okay, I'm coming. I'm here now . . . '

31

There was no longer a door on the outside toilet so as she reached the semi-derelict cubicle Hannah immediately saw her sister sitting almost upright on the splintered piece of old wood that straddled the brown-stained toilet bowl; her head lolled over against the wall and she seemed completely oblivious to the damp, mossy bricks pressing against the side of her face.

She looked as if she was asleep, with her thumb firmly fixed in her mouth; her other hand was clenched tightly into a fist in her lap and seemed to be holding something, but Hannah couldn't see what. Her phone lay smashed on the floor between her feet.

The smell in and around the cubicle was vile. It was obvious the cistern was broken and that the wood had been put there to cover up whatever was in the bowl. Hannah also guessed that every cat in the neighbourhood used the overgrown garden as a kitty-toilet. Smells assailed her from every direction and she wanted to gag, but instead she tried not to breathe too deeply and concentrated on shaking her sister hard, to try to get a response from her.

'Julie . . . ' she murmured through her own tears now streaming down unchecked. 'Julie . . . it's me. I've come to get you . . . Julie . . . Julie, please look at me! Come on, I'm going to take you away from here. Everything's okay.

We can go home now . . . '

As she struggled to rouse her, Hannah looked round for help and saw that Autumn, silent and scared at seeing her mother in that state, was peering over her shoulder.

'You go and call an ambulance. I don't know if she's actually taken anything but she seems to be catatonic. She's gone into meltdown, probably because too much has happened to her too quickly and her system is weak. Oh, Jeez, why on earth did she have to come back here? And, more to the point, why isn't that old woman safely tucked away in a bloody home?'

Hannah stepped back from Julie and saw her aunt hovering at the back door with the next-door neighbour close behind, obviously wondering what was happening.

'Who's that in there?' the old woman asked, peering curiously through screwed-up milky eyes. 'Who's that in my cupboard? Is she cooking my dinner? I'm starving.'

Her expression was one of puzzled incomprehension. She sucked noisily on thin lips sunk deep in her face because of her lack of dentures. She clearly had no idea who anyone was or what was going on.

'It's Julie. Remember her? And I'm Hannah. We lived here with you, remember?' Hannah tried.

'No, you're not. You're not my children.' The Aunt smiled and moved her Zimmer frame to try to get down the back step. 'My children are little girls . . . naughty little girls. They're locked in their room upstairs. You're not them, you're too big. Hannah and Julie are little! My babies . . . '

She started to laugh. Despite everything else about her being completely different, that loud, spiteful cackle was exactly the same. Hannah would have recognised the awful sound anywhere and instinctively backed away from it. Once again she was a defenceless child, and once again she was petrified of her aunt.

Then she heard another sound and looked at Julie. She sat wide-eyed and with her thumb still in her mouth, but it was obvious from her expression that she'd heard the laugh as well and it had penetrated her shocked state.

Still stunned by the sight of her mother's disintegration, Autumn spun round to face the Aunt, anger and hatred written all over her face.

'You stupid old woman! Look what you've done to my mother. You wicked old witch . . . you're disgusting, you should be dead . . . '

As Autumn moved purposefully towards the Aunt, the man from next-door stepped forward; Hannah quickly grabbed her niece and wrapped her tightly in her arms. 'Don't do it, Autumn. She doesn't have a clue what's going on, she's in her own little world now and she'll never come back. I'll do something about her later, but right now we have to concentrate on Julie. Help me get her out of here and into the house while we wait for the ambulance.'

Together they manhandled Julie to her feet and helped her to walk indoors. She yelped in pain from the pressure on her healing hip but still said nothing.

'You hold her up,' Hannah ordered. 'I'll try

and find a chair that isn't soaked in pee. I can't believe she's been allowed to live like this. It's disgraceful . . . '

The neighbour who was still hovering next to them, looking decidedly uncomfortable, shook his head. 'Look, I don't know what's going on here but I've done my best. I've tried to get her help so many times but she just won't let anyone in. There's a home help but she's useless. Stands out the front chain-smoking, does a bit of shopping and then scarpers. It's horrible but we did everything we could to help.' The young man shrugged his shoulders and Hannah felt sorry for him. He seemed genuinely to care about Marian Beecham and her dire circumstances.

'I wasn't having a go at you, I know it's not your fault. Which side of her do you live?'

He gestured towards the house that used to be Gerald's.

'Do you know anything about the man who used to live there — Gerald Kelly?'

'Not really, except that he died a few years ago. That's when we bought the house, at an executor's sale. Someone said he was a friend of Miss Beecham's and that he left everything to her, including the house. But it wasn't long after that that she started to go senile so we never really got to know her as she was — only as she is now.'

Hannah smiled sadly. 'You didn't miss anything. She wasn't a nice person at all, but she and Gerald were friends for years. He was the only person she ever cared about. Apart from herself, of course.'

The young man still looked slightly suspicious of the three strange women in the house together. He was tall and lanky, dressed top to toe in black, with spiky black hair, a strange tattoo on the side of his neck and several lip piercings, but his expression was gentle and caring. Hannah took to him instantly.

'I'm Jase, by the way. I know it's a bit late but can I ask who you are?' he continued. 'I don't want to sound nosey but I am a bit bewildered by all these visitors after so long with no one crossing her threshold.'

'Oh, we're just distant family. We haven't seen her for many years — family disputes and all that. It's a long story, but we'll try and sort something out for her.' Hannah smiled reassuringly. 'She certainly needs far more care than she's getting, I can see that. Residential, in my opinion.'

'Do you need a hand with . . . ' He looked at Julie, unsure what to call her.

'No, it's okay, you've done more than enough.' Hannah smiled in polite dismissal. 'I'll let you know what's going to happen to Miss Beecham as soon as I get something arranged. Thanks for your help, I really appreciate it.'

She saw him to the door and waved as he jumped the dividing front wall back to his own house next-door. But as she turned back inside, the Aunt clunked the walking frame noisily towards her.

'Where's my dinner, you lazy fat lummox?' she asked angrily, getting closer and closer to Hannah. 'I'm starving and no one has given me anything to eat. Get me my dinner — *now*.'

Hannah stood rooted to the spot as the old woman picked up her Zimmer frame and crashed it down as hard as she could on the floor. 'You're nasty little vermin, vermin, vermin! You should die, both of you. Unwanted little bastards. Die . . . ' The venom in her voice was horrifying as once again she used all her remaining strength to raise the frame right off the ground, but this time she lifted it up in front of her with the four legs pointing forward like a weapon and aimed it straight at Hannah.

In that second something clicked in and Julie was suddenly aware of the danger. She lurched to her feet and lunged for the frame, at the same time pushing the Aunt to the ground. Then, to Hannah's horror, she toppled over on to the old woman. Aunt Marian lay on the floor, spewing abuse and spittle, as Julie pummelled her from above and grabbed at her throat. It took the combined strength of Autumn and Hannah to get Julie off her.

'You fucking old bitch . . . you let him do it! You knew and you let him . . . I'm going to break your fucking neck and then you can rot in hell for ever!' Julie screamed as they struggled to hold her back. 'You knew, I know you knew . . . '

Autumn forced her mother back down on to the chair and stood guard over her as Hannah helped the old woman to her feet and led her towards another chair on the opposite side of the room. 'Can I have my dinner now? I'm starving,' she asked as if nothing much had happened, but when Hannah picked up the frame and handed it to her she could see that her aunt was holding her arm at a very strange angle.

'Jeez, she's broken her arm! What are we going to tell the ambulance crew about this? The catatonic woman we phoned you about is no longer off in a trance, but the old woman who lives here has mysteriously acquired a broken arm?'

Julie looked around curiously as if she had just woken up. She blinked rapidly and glanced down at her hands, turning them over as if she didn't quite recognise them as hers. Her left hand was still clenched tightly around something and the thumb on her right hand was red raw and bleeding around the nail bed from where she had chewed it. She unfurled her fist and looked down at the filthy battered doll's foot that lay in the palm of her hand, then quickly snapped her fingers shut again before looking straight ahead at Hannah and Autumn.

'What's going on? Why's everyone here?'

'Long story, Ma, but the ambulance will be coming in a minute for you to go for a check-up. You were acting crazy, we thought you'd OD'd or something.' Autumn looked at her mother closely. 'Have you taken anything? You can tell me, we just need to know before the ambulance gets here.'

Julie went quiet and carried on looking around as if she had been transported here while she was asleep. Hannah could see she was trying frantically to remember exactly what had happened.

'No, nothing. I've not taken anything. I just

knew I had to come here. I remember getting the bus but I don't remember what happened then. Must have gone a bit nuts but I'm okay — I'm not going to that hospital. I'm not going back there.'

'No, not nuts, just having a brainstorm, I think,' Hannah said.

Julie looked at her strangely. 'Hannah? What the fuck are you doing here?'

'You called me . . . '

Julie frowned. 'Did I?'

'You did. But that doesn't matter. What matters is that you're okay. Not so sure about her, though. Maybe in the end she paid a higher price than we could ever have anticipated.'

Still looking at her sister, Hannah smiled sadly and nodded towards their aunt. She wanted to reach out to Julie, her baby sister, and hug her, but something told her it would be a step too far at that moment.

There was an uncomfortable silence as they waited, all of them looking at Marian Beecham who sat rocking back and forth and humming to herself, completely oblivious to her surroundings and the three strangers in her house.

In the end, with Julie refusing treatment, the ambulance crew took only Aunt Marian to hospital to be treated for her fall. Hannah agreed to follow on after locking the house up, and Autumn took Julie home.

Once everyone had gone, Hannah looked around for her aunt's handbag and house keys, and at the same time made some quick notes so that she could tell the hospital social worker exactly what conditions in the house were like.

Instinctively she stripped the beds and put the soiled bedding into sacks to throw out, then gathered up as much of the other rubbish as she could. She could see that everything in the house would have to be thrown out. Urine had soaked through everywhere: into the beds, carpets and chairs. The whole place needed stripping completely and fumigating.

There were mouse droppings everywhere in the kitchen, even on the cooker hob and in the cutlery drawer, and the lino was swollen and cracked from where there had been a leak of some sort.

There was no getting away from the fact that the house was a health hazard and their aunt was unable to look after herself. Hannah hoped the severity of her dementia would mean she would have to go into residential care, whether she agreed to go voluntarily or not.

It was while she was looking for the bag and keys that she came across a battered old leather suitcase pushed under a bed. She pulled it out, thinking it would do to take some things to the hospital in, but it was already full. Hannah opened it and slowly took out the contents.

As she flicked through them quickly her horror increased with each new discovery. Inside was a wad of bank statements that showed the Aunt had a small fortune squirrelled away in a series of bank accounts. There was also an old biscuit tin containing several thousand pounds in assorted notes, all neatly bundled and in marked envelopes, and several shoe boxes crammed with letters and papers.

After quickly scanning some of these, Hannah learned for the first time of a trust fund set up for Julie and herself. There were stacks of letters postmarked USA from both Ray and his father, plus letters from other family members all asking after the girls and offering their help. There were also dozens of unopened birthday and Christmas cards addressed to them that went back to the date Hannah and Julie had come to live here.

They had never seen any of them.

Hannah was devastated by what she found. They were never destitute orphans with no one else to care for them; they were little girls who had been loved and cared for but had been snatched away by a money-grabbing woman who didn't even want them; just wanted the wealth that came with them.

With everything finally there in front of her, Hannah could see that their aunt was actually beyond cruel and could understand exactly how Julie had felt when she had discovered that she was senile. It meant that Marian Beecham would never be held accountable — to them, to the law or to herself — for the way she had treated them.

Knowing she had to get to the hospital as quickly as possible, Hannah pushed everything back into the suitcase and put it in the boot of her car.

She wondered about taking some night things to the hospital for her aunt but there was nothing here worth packing so instead she took some of the money from the biscuit tin. She decided she would buy everything her aunt needed new rather than rummage round in this filth any longer. She didn't want to do it, she didn't want to go to the hospital and have anything to do with the woman, but she knew she had to, for decency's sake. It was what would be expected of a family member.

Before she left the house she phoned Autumn. 'How's Julie doing?'

'Okay. Much better in fact, but she's still not telling me anything more about what happened in that house or what it was that triggered her shock. She says she wants to speak to you, though. Can you come over? She wants to speak to you without me there, apparently. Autumn is redundant as usual. But I have to get to work anyway.'

'Don't be upset. I still have to go the hospital but I'll come on after. I have to be there with the Aunt, even though I don't want to. The last thing we need is for them to patch her up and send her home.' Hannah paused. 'By the way, did your mother say any more about Katya? Will she see a solicitor?'

'I don't know, I haven't asked, but I'd guess that's what she wants to talk to you about.'

'Well, I'll do the best I can to get there tonight. But to protect Julie, I have to go to the hospital and speak with the Aunt's doctors first.'

32

Hannah walked into the hospital carrying the bag she had bought en route at the local superstore and filled with the necessities for a hospital stay. She headed straight to Accident and Emergency but they directed her over to the geriatric ward, tucked away at the far end of the sprawling old hospital.

She walked up to the desk and introduced herself. 'I've come to see Marian Beecham. I was told she's here. I've brought some nightdresses and toiletries, pretty much all she'll need in the short-term, but I also need to talk to someone urgently about her long-term care. There is no way she can go back to her home, it's not fit for human habitation . . . '

'Are you a relative?' the nurse behind the desk interrupted her.

'I'm Hannah Durman, her niece and formal next-of-kin, I guess. I'm aware she needs a full assessment of her needs,' Hannah stated assertively. 'I'm a social worker, though of course not here in that capacity . . . '

She stopped when she noticed the expression on the other woman's face.

'I'm sorry, Mrs Durman. We haven't had time to call anyone . . . in fact, we haven't got all her details yet. Sadly Miss Beecham passed away a short while ago. She was transferred up to the ward from A and E in preparation for surgery sometime overnight to pin her arm, but she suffered a massive stroke. It was instantaneous. She had no idea, suffered no pain. The stress of the accident and then hospitalisation was probably just too much for her.'

Hannah felt her knees go weak and her head start to spin. All she could see was Julie hurling herself on to Aunt Marian, pushing her to the ground and then trying to batter her.

'Come through to the family room, it's more private in there.' The nurse led her down the old-fashioned corridor ward lined with a cross-section of able and disabled elderly patients. Once inside, she poured a glass of cold water from the fountain in the corner and handed it to Hannah.

Sipping it slowly, Hannah forced herself to think clearly. She knew she had to keep a level head and say nothing. It was an accident, a plain and simple accident that could have happened to anyone who used a walking frame. Aunt Marian fell over her frame. It was an accident.

'Thanks, I wasn't expecting news like that. We weren't close and we haven't seen my aunt for many years, but it's still a shock. Just as it was to see her living conditions. Tell me again what the cause of death was?'

The nurse smiled sympathetically. Hannah could see she was only young and probably not long qualified, but she had a good attitude and Hannah was moved by her kindness.

'Well, it's for the doctor to confirm, but Miss Beecham was very malnourished to start with and her senility was very advanced, as was her osteoporosis. The broken arm, and the trauma of coming to hospital and having all the necessary procedures in A and E, was probably just too much for her system to take.' The young nurse shook her head. 'I'm sorry. I'm sure the doctor will speak to you and there will have to be a post-mortem as she died so soon after arrival.'

Hannah stood up again.

'I'm just going to make a couple of phone calls then I'll come back . . . '

'You can use the phone at the desk, if you wish.'

'Thanks, but I need some air anyway so I'll go outside,' Hannah said quickly.

She got outside as fast as she could and called Autumn.

'The Aunt has died. She had a bloody stroke or something when they got her up to a ward. They're going to do a post-mortem. What did you tell the paramedics about the accident? Did you mention Julie's part in it?'

To Hannah's surprise, Autumn's voice instantly became angry.

'Hey, you heard what I said to them. You were there for most of it. I told them the truth: that she tripped over that filthy bloody frame the old bag was attached to . . . Ma didn't cause it, if that's what you think. I was there, remember? The old woman was barking! She was going for you, Ma was protecting you, and the old woman fell over . . . '

'Oh, okay, no problem — except that then Julie tried to throttle her! Not really a good thing to do to a senile octogenarian with bloody advanced osteoporosis!'

'It's not fair, blaming Ma . . . ' Autumn started, but Hannah was on a roll.

'Maybe not, and I don't doubt I would have done the same, but trust me, if there's anything untoward they'll suss it in the post-mortem and report it to the police. You need to talk to Julie about it, just in case they want to talk to her. I'm trying to protect her.'

'No, I don't have to talk to her. *You* talk to Julie about it. *I'm* going to work.'

Autumn cut the call off, leaving Hannah feeling more upset than cross. After a few seconds' thought she could see that her niece had been burdened once again with far more than someone of her years should have to cope with. The girl was close to breaking.

Hannah went back to the ward, and the nurse she had spoken to previously led her through to a curtained cubicle. Only then did Hannah realise that her aunt was lying in the bed, covered only with a thin white sheet. The nurse quickly pulled it back, revealing her head and shoulders.

'I'll leave you alone for a while.'

'No, it's okay.'

But she had already disappeared through the faded curtains before Hannah could protest further.

She didn't want to look at Marian Beecham, her hated aunt, but a morbid curiosity made her look at, and then study, the once familiar face. She looked at it carefully and with a detachment that was devoid of any emotion; it was as if she was looking for a clue to what had made Marian the woman she had become. What it was that had turned her into the vicious person that Hannah and Julie had known so well and hated so much.

But there was nothing there to tell her and Hannah felt nothing. In the short time she had been away from the ward the staff had washed her aunt's face, brushed her hair, and laid her out in a white hospital gown that made her appear almost saintly. So many times in Hannah's childhood she had wished the woman dead and yet, now she was, she wasn't moved to any emotion, seeing her like this on the hospital bed. She felt neither sadness nor relief.

Dry-eyed, she sighed, pulled the sheet up again over her aunt's face and went back out to the desk.

'Is there anything more I need to do here? Paperwork or something?'

'Not really. We'll transfer your aunt to the mortuary and the post-mortem will be done as soon as possible. It's just standard procedure. I mean, the odds were against her in that condition. You'll need to come back to the office to collect the paperwork necessary to register the death and arrange the funeral. If you ring them tomorrow, they'll tell you when it's ready.' The nurse looked at her. 'What do you want to do about her things? You left her bag here just now; I've put it behind the desk . . . '

'Give it to someone who needs it. It's all new and I'm sure you can make use of it,' Hannah said as she turned to leave.

'I'm sorry for your loss.'

'Thank you.' Hannah smiled sadly and walked from the ward, away from her aunt for ever.

And then she cried — but not for her dead aunt; she sobbed for her own and Julie's lost childhoods, for the years the sisters had spent apart that could never be relived, and for the way it had impacted on them throughout their lives.

After several minutes and many curious looks from passers-by, she pulled herself together, wiped her eyes, blew her nose and phoned Fliss to tell her she didn't know when she would be back.

Then Hannah left the hospital car-park and drove to see her sister.

* * *

Leaning heavily on her walking sticks, Julie pulled the door open wide and, without making eye contact or saying anything, stood back to let Hannah in.

'You go in first and I'll follow,' Hannah said with a smile. She knew she would have to tread very carefully if she was going to be able to mend bridges here.

With her head down, Julie turned and slowly made her way up the narrow hallway and into the sitting room.

'So the vicious old bitch is dead at last? At least something good has come out of today.'

'I guess. It's been a strange day, one way and another. Where shall I sit?'

'Wherever you like. I'll put the kettle on.'

Hannah hesitated, unsure whether to offer to do it or not; she decided against.

'Tea? Coffee? Coke? Though not the real coke as such, I've given that up. Rots the brain apparently.'

Hannah laughed. 'Coffee would be good. I drink far too much of the stuff, but there you go.'

'Milk? Sugar?' Julie's voice was expressionless as she asked.

'Just black, thanks.'

Hannah found it sad that she and her sister were at last in the same room together yet talking as if they were strangers in the local café, but it was at least a start and she remained optimistic.

Julie disappeared into the kitchen and Hannah sat down on one of the armchairs, thinking that her sister would probably be more comfortable on the sofa.

After a few minutes Julie called through, 'I can't carry the mugs so you can come and get it yourself or we can sit in the kitchen.'

'The kitchen,' Hannah said as she quickly walked through. 'It's always more cosy. I spend more time there at home than anywhere else. Well, when I'm not at work, of course, though I do work from home a couple of days a week . . . ' She stopped talking and laughed. 'This is silly. I'm waffling on about nothing and you're making drinks when all I really want is for us to make up, be sisters again, forget about all the awful stuff that went on.'

Ignoring her comments, Julie put the mugs on the table one at a time and then sat down, indicating for Hannah to sit opposite her.

'You've been in my house before, haven't you? When I was in hospital, when you met Autumn.'

'And your other children. Katya is such a cutie and Jethro is so handsome. Oh, Julie, I really wanted to come and see you before this but Autumn didn't think it was a good idea while you were so poorly.'

'Ah, yes. The saintly Autumn who thinks she's my mother.' Julie laughed humourlessly. 'My daughter who thinks she is my personal Mother Superior. My conscience in a fucking miniscule G-string.'

Hannah didn't want to respond and break the very tenuous link between her and her sister. Instead she looked at her and smiled sadly because Julie had no idea how good a daughter Autumn was or how lucky she was to have her.

'I don't have any children. My husband never wanted them and I thought I didn't either. It's too late now, of course, I no longer have a womb and very probably don't have a husband either. Lose, lose, eh? It'll just be me and two demanding Siamese cats ad infinitum.'

For the first time, Julie looked at her sister with some of the old light in her eyes. 'Men are all fucking bastards — a complete waste of space. Who needs them?'

'Right now I think you're probably right.' Hannah held her mug across the table. 'Cheers to that.'

Julie instantly raised hers and clinked it on Hannah's. 'Cheers. Fuck 'em all.'

Then they both laughed.

'I know you know all about me and my shit

life and the drugs and all that because you're a nosey old social worker, but I don't know about you. So tell. What's your life been all about? What's happening with you now?'

And Hannah told her. Into the night they talked, about what had happened to each of them after they both left their aunt's house all those years before but carefully skirting around life in that house.

Suddenly Hannah looked at her watch. 'Oh, my God, it's three and I've got to get back to Essex and go to work tomorrow. Well, not strictly to work, I'm working from home, but . . . '

'Stay here if you want.' Julie shrugged to make light of the offer but Hannah could see it for what it was. She knew that if she rejected this invitation, Julie would see it as a rejection of herself.

'I'd like that but I will have to leave early in the morning. The cats again! My babies . . . '

Julie laughed, really laughed, and in an instant Hannah was back to the time when she and her sister were close.

'Babies my arse! I'd never have expected you to have a couple of fucking cats instead of the statutory two point four children. Though I suppose me having three levels it out a bit.' Her laughter faded and her face changed like quicksilver; she stared intently at Hannah.

'I need to know something, Hanny . . . Did you know? Did you know what was going on?'

'What do you mean? Of course I knew what was going on. I lived with it as well, you know, I was there . . . '

'Did you know about Gerald, I mean?'
'What about Gerald?'
'That the disgusting old bastard raped me. Over and over again. And made me pregnant. Did you know that he is Autumn's father?'

'You're going to have to go. I've tried to talk to her but she won't have it. She says you're faking it, that you're just trying to skive off school,' Hannah said as she came back into the bedroom. It was eight a.m. and Julie was still in bed, feeling like death warmed up.

'So do you think I'm faking it? I bet you do. You never believe me any more than she does.' Julie glared out from under the covers at her sister.

'No, of course not, I can see you're ill, you look awful. Maybe you need to have your tonsils out . . . You've had a lot of time off school and you know it sends her crazy if we're around during the day; she'll be so horrible to you if you do stay home.'

Julie wasn't faking it at all. Her throat burned and her head ached. She really couldn't face getting up and dressed and then catching two buses there and back. She often played truant but this was nothing to do with school.

'You're nothing but a lazy little tyke! I'll drag you out of that bed by your hair if you're not up by the time I come back up,' Aunt Marian had said when she'd stomped up the stairs earlier. 'I'm not having it.'

Hannah leaned over the bed and put her hand on her sister's head. 'Look, I've got to go, I've got to finish off some Maths and I can't do it here. Why don't you just get dressed and go to school and let them send you home? I'll back you up. She won't be able to do anything about that, and if you're lucky she'll be out by the time you get back.'

Julie thought for a moment. Her instant reaction was just to stay there and brave out the inevitable battle that would follow, but for once she hadn't got the energy.

'Okay, okay, I'll go . . . fucking bastard old woman! I hate her.'

'So do I but annoying her is just dumb, she always wins. Look, I'll see you at breaktime if they haven't sent you home by then.'

After Hannah had gone, Julie threw back the covers and pulled on her clothes. She didn't bother to wash or go into the kitchen, just grabbed her school bag and went straight out of the door.

If she had to go to school to get sent home and have some peace then that was what she would do; it was better than playing truant and being out and about when she felt so poorly.

As she slammed the front door, Gerald appeared from his house.

'Morning, Julie.' He screwed up his eyes and peered at her through grubby glasses. 'Oh, dear, are you feeling all right? You look a bit flushed and peaky to me.'

'No, I'm not feeling all right,' she snapped angrily. 'I'm ill but the old bat is making me go to school anyway. I hate her . . . '

'Now, Julie, that's not nice, is it? Marian does

her best for you two girls. But I tell you what, why don't you come in here? Your auntie won't know and you can have a little sleep in my spare room. We don't have to tell anyone, do we? I'll look after you.'

Julie was about to say no, her inner voice told her to say no, her distrust of Gerald told her to say no, but almost involuntarily she said yes. The thought of a day off school, in the warm, with a bed to rest in and no aunt to make her life a misery, was just too appealing.

Looking over her shoulder to check that her aunt wasn't watching, she threw her bag over the wall then quickly jumped after it and ran straight into Gerald's house. He followed behind her and quietly closed the front door.

'Come on now, let's get you tucked up in the warm. You'll feel better after a rest, I'm sure.'

With a friendly smile and a gentle hand guiding her in the small of her back, he showed her to the guest bedroom and left her alone; the bed was already made up so she ripped off her top layer of clothes and sank into it gratefully, wrapping herself in the bedclothes, which were soft and fluffy, unlike the scratchy old blankets and darned sheets on her bed next-door.

After a few minutes, Gerald knocked on the door and brought her in a mug of steaming cocoa made with hot milk, two paracetamol tablets, and a hot-water bottle tucked inside a pink quilted cover.

'There you are, my dear. Now you have a little nap and I'll look in on you later, see how you're doing.'

And he had.

But he had come into the room without his trousers and underpants on, and without a word had immediately pulled back the covers and clambered into the single bed on top of her. Before Julie could even register fear or flight he had reached down and skilfully moved her legs apart before pulling her knickers to one side and forcing himself inside her as hard as he could. The pain was almost unbearable but she didn't make a sound. Julie was in shock.

It was over in a few short minutes and as soon as Gerald had finished he got out of the bed and left the room. When he came back in he was dressed and smiling.

'This is just between you and me, Julie, remember that. You mustn't tell anyone, especially Hannah. Oh, no, not the starchy Miss Hannah.'

Silently she had stared at him with hatred in her eyes. Hot tears burned her cheeks as she realised she had been lured in here expressly for this purpose. Julie Grayson, the loud-mouthed know-it-all who thought she was streetwise and knowledgeable, had been reeled in by an old man like an unsuspecting fish on a line.

'Now, now, don't look at me like that, dear. If you do tell Hannah then I'll have to tell your aunt how you led me on. I mean, you came into bed willingly, didn't you? I didn't make you, did I? And of course Marian will never believe you.'

Gerald smiled at her almost paternally and patted her shoulder. 'Now you have another little sleep and then you can go home and pretend you've been at school all day.'

So she didn't tell. Gerald Kelly, bribed her, blackmailed her, and continued to rape her right up until the day she ran away, pregnant with his child. During that time Julie never told a soul because, apart from anything else, she knew all the time that Gerald was right. No one would ever believe her.

33

Hannah felt so sick and faint she leaned forward and put her head between her knees. She had had no idea but the moment the words were out she knew them to be true. That was why Julie had been so devastated to discover that Gerald was dead and Aunt Marian was senile. She had gone back to confront them.

'Did you know, Hannah?' She asked urgently. 'Truthfully, did you know?'

Hannah lifted her head up and looked her sister straight in the eye.

'Oh, my God, Julie, I had no idea. I swear to you, I had no idea, not an inkling. Even when I put two and two together because of Autumn's age, I just thought it must have been Josh. Why didn't you tell me? Why on *earth* didn't you tell me?'

'Because Gerald said that if I told then he would stop you from going to university. I had no choice, if we were going to escape. I hoped you'd guess . . . notice . . . realise . . . I don't know. I wanted you to find out, but I couldn't tell you or anyone.'

'Did Aunt Marian know it was going on?' Hannah asked.

'I think she must have done. That's why I went round there tonight. I'd not thought of it for so many years but suddenly it was all back in my head and it was important to confront her with it. But now the old bitch has put one over on me again. She's gone and died on me.'

Julie started to cry. 'I know it isn't Autumn's fault, but when she's being so fucking reasonable she reminds me of him. Gerald could reason his way out of a paper bag, and so can Autumn. I love her and I hate her. It's so hard . . . '

Neither of them went to bed that night. They talked through till dawn but only covered the bare bones of their years apart. But it was a start. As she was getting ready to go home to work, Hannah plucked up the courage to mention Katya.

'Julie, I want to find her for you. I don't want you to think I'm interfering but I want you to get her back. It's not right that you should lose her. Autumn gave me some details but if you can tell me everything you know about Sebastian, I'll use my resources to find her.'

Suddenly Julie looked wary again. 'I don't know . . . '

'Please let me help you, Julie? Please? I owe you so much . . . '

She shrugged. 'Give it a go, if you want, but I bet you don't find them. Seb is a master of deceit, as I've discovered.'

'Oh, I will find them. Trust me, I will, and I'll get Katya back to you, one way or another.' Hannah smiled with relief and quickly dug in her handbag for a notebook. Julie raised her eyes to the ceiling and tutted.

'Typical fucking social worker, always got a pad and pen in hand ready to write down every word!'

* * *

As soon as she was home, the first thing Hannah had to do was figure out the new burglar alarm and check if Ben was or had been there. She knew that if he had come back he would have got inside somehow.

But he wasn't there so she went back out to her car and got the suitcase.

Taking it indoors, she found an old sheet in the airing cupboard, spread it over the lounge floor and systematically took everything out of the case. Kneeling on the floor, she methodically started to sort it all out into piles. She put the unopened cards for her and Julie and the tin of cash to one side, then started sifting through the personal papers, bank statements and share certificates.

Her aunt's finances were so complex, Hannah quickly realised they would need a solicitor to deal with it all. A brief adding up of all the accounts showed a sum just short of three-quarters of a million pounds, and that was without the value of the house added in. The Aunt had a small fortune stashed away.

She thought of all the things they had been denied as children, always being told there was no money to pay for anything; they had never been able to go on school trips or holidays, they had had no toys and only ever had secondhand school uniforms scrounged by their aunt from the school 'for the orphans'. Sweets and treats were never allowed.

They had both been led to believe that Marian

Beecham had taken the two little orphaned sisters in out of the goodness of her heart, when all the time she had actually been busy amassing her own private fortune courtesy of the pay out from their parents' insurance policy.

Next, Hannah added up the cash in the envelopes. It was all in twenty-pound notes and there was fifteen thousand pounds exactly, less the hundred she had taken to buy the overnight things.

She gathered all the cards together and put them in a carrier bag. She hadn't told Julie about the suitcase, knew it was the wrong time to lay any more on her fragile sister, but when the time was right, when it wasn't likely to send Julie back into meltdown, she would and then they could read them together.

All that money and Marian had lived, and more or less died, in freezing, smelly squalor. Hannah sighed. She was no longer angry, just sad that one woman could vindictively shatter the lives of two children without anyone else noticing. Without anyone else doing anything about it.

'No, no, no, you greedy selfish vermin!' Marian Beecham lashed out furiously across the small dining table with the back of her hand and caught Hannah full force on the side of her face. 'I took you two in and gave you a home when no one else wanted you. I feed and clothe you out of the goodness of my heart, but still you want more. You are both nasty little vermin. You're no better than the

rats that scavenge outside in the dustbins.'

The next swipe nearly got Julie but she was quicker than Hannah and ducked just in time to avoid the huge hand that swooshed past, just missing her eyes.

Both girls had been given letters to take home about the school's day trip to France. It was the first year of them both being at the same secondary school; Julie was eleven and Hannah just thirteen. Hannah had tried to tell her sister that it was pointless to give the letters to the Aunt but, as always, Julie had to be confrontational and had handed them over at the tea table and asked if they could go.

Hannah's face stung from the fierce backhander and she wanted to cry but daren't.

'Well, why can't we go to France?' Julie asked defiantly, oblivious to her sister's pain. 'It's educational so that means we have to go. And we want to go. The teachers want us to, everyone else is going . . . '

'Educational? A day trip to France? I'm going to ring the school tomorrow and tell them what I think of their education. You're not going. Do you think I'm made of money? Do you think it grows on the tree out there?'

Marian bellowed at them so fiercely that spittle from her mouth flew across the table and landed just in front of Julie's plate.

'You just want to make them take us for nothing, like you always do. You want them to feel sorry for the orphans and then give us free places,' Julie carried on.

'Enough from you,' the Aunt barked. 'Now go

to your room, both of you. I don't want to see you again today. GO!'

Scared of what would follow if they disobeyed her, Hannah immediately pushed her chair back. They had only been at the table a few minutes and she was angry that Julie had once again ensured they both went to bed hungry. There was no way the Aunt was ever going to agree to them going on the trip so it was just Julie looking for another confrontation on principle.

But while Hannah stood up, Julie leaned back in her chair, crossed her arms defiantly and deliberately locked eyes with the Aunt.

'Why can't we go if we want to? It's a school trip, for God's sake, not a beano to Margate.'

In a flash the Aunt was up on her feet and had caught Julie by the hair. She wound it round her hand as tightly as she could and dragged her into the kitchen. Hannah heard the running water and knew what was coming next. But instead of doing anything, she froze in the doorway and watched silently.

As Julie kicked and tried to wriggle away, the Aunt expertly twisted her hand and pulled the child's hair so tight some of it was detached by the roots. With the other hand the woman put the plug into the old stone sink and filled it with cold water, then she pushed Julie's face down into it until her head was submerged and held it there. She then pulled her up for a couple of seconds before pushing her under again.

'Stop it!' Hannah shouted. 'You're going to drown her — let her go!'

Still holding Julie's head under, the Aunt spun

round and glared at her. 'Do you want to be next?'

Hannah was terrified. She had suffered that punishment herself when she was so small the Aunt had had to lift her up by her hair and her belt to get her face in the water, and she had no intention of ever having to go through it again.

Over and over Marian Beecham performed the same manoeuvre until Julie finally went limp.

Still holding her hair, the Aunt dragged her outside and locked her in the toilet despite its being mid-winter and Julie being soaked from top to toe in freezing water.

Hannah really had to fight the urge to grab the kitchen knife from the bread board and bury it in the Aunt's back then. She hated her so much, but she was also terrified of her.

Instead she grabbed a slice of bread and ran upstairs to wait until Julie was allowed in again an hour later.

Hannah got her frozen and shivering little sister out of her wet clothes, dried her and helped her into her nightie and dressing-gown, manoeuvred her into bed and then clambered in beside her to cuddle her and help her get warm.

'Why the fuck didn't you stick up for me? Why did you let her do it?' Julie asked.

'I couldn't stop her, you know that, no one can. Why did you push her to it? She always wins in the end.'

'One day she won't. One day I'll get my own back on her,' Julie murmured before she went to sleep in Hannah's arms.

Hannah sighed. It was too late for her sister to get her own back now but she knew that was for the best. At least Julie couldn't hurt either Marian or Gerald and then have to suffer the consequences.

Maybe instead Julie could at last find some peace in her life.

Hannah gathered everything into some sort of order, put it all back in the suitcase and then took it upstairs to hide under her own bed. The last thing she needed was for Ben to find it and think he had some sort of claim on any of it.

Hannah was always conscientious when she was working at home so she quickly showered, changed her clothes and went downstairs to work in the kitchen. It was just before nine and she was ready to start. Sleep would have to wait until she had caught up from the day before.

She filled the cafetière, opened her laptop and clicked the answer-phone to check for messages. There were several from various finance companies and debt-collection agencies demanding payment of some sort but still nothing from Ben, which concerned her. Naturally she was worried about him. She didn't know what he was doing, where he was or, of course, with whom.

Despite everything he was still her husband and she still loved him. He had been her life for so long and it wasn't as easy to turn her feelings off as Fliss and Autumn seemed to think it should be. She wanted to know what was going on but she was also scared of what he might do when he came back. When he had lashed out, she had seen a side to him that she hadn't suspected before and it had frightened her.

And, of course, if he didn't come back, she would have to deal with the aftermath of his financial meltdown.

She poured herself a strong coffee, sat down at the kitchen table, did a few neck stretches and tried to clear her mind.

Then her mobile rang.

'Just wondering if you got to see Ma yesterday?' asked Autumn.

For a moment Hannah was thrown. 'Yes, I did,' she said cautiously.

'And?'

'Slowly, slowly, I think we're getting there.'

'And Katya?'

'I've got to go to the hospital today so I'm going into the office en route — I'll see what I can do there. Look, I'm sorry to cut you short but I'm working, can I call you later?'

'Yes, of course. There's something else I need to talk to you about . . . '

'Okay, but not now, I've got someone here with me,' Hannah lied. Suddenly she felt overwhelmed by everything that was happening and wanted some thinking time alone.

34

'Yoo-hoo!'

Barry glanced up and smiled as Hannah looked round the open door to their office.

'Hello, you. What are you doing here? You're meant to be at home slaving over a hot computer and exercising your literary skills on the most boring piece of work we've ever had to do for our masters.'

'I know, I know, and I have been, but there's some last-minute research I need to collect. I left it on my desk by mistake. I'll have it all finished by tomorrow, I hope. Only three days late but who's counting? Anyway, how's it going here?'

'It's very good,' Barry replied. 'I just heard from our great leader that we can have funding for another two agency workers while they try to recruit some permanent staff. That'll put us up to quota on staff levels for a change.'

Hannah sat on the edge of his desk. 'And about time too. Maybe if there's enough staff then everyone won't be so disillusioned with the job. I've been feeling so guilty. I know you've been madly busy and I've not been pulling my weight with the clients lately. All I can say is, life's really been a bit of a bitch.'

Barry looked at her thoughtfully. 'I guessed that. No offence intended, of course, but you look dead beat. Is it anything you want to talk about? If so shut the door and pull the blind down. If not then put the kettle on and we'll talk about something else!'

Hannah gently pushed the door closed and pulled down the roller blind that told the office outside they were in a meeting and not to be disturbed.

'You're right, I am dead beat, I was up all night. I won't bore you with all the gory details right now, Barry, but I've been in touch with my sister at last. It was all a bit complex but the gist of it now is that, while she was laid up in hospital with a broken hip, her ex-partner has gone off with her daughter Katya and disappeared. I want to find the child and help get her back home with her mum. Any suggestions? I know this was your field before you came here.'

Barry leaned back in his chair, swung one leg across the other and linked his hands over his ample stomach. 'Okay, for starters, what have you in mind? You must be thinking something . . . And, next, it was not so long ago you were horrified at how dysfunctional the family was, so as devil's advocate I have to ask the question: is being with her mother in this child's best interests?'

Hannah laughed as she blushed. 'Do you know what? I can't believe how judgemental I was being then without knowing all the facts. I was actually being a snob . . . But, to answer you, yes, I do think she should be with her mother. I think the very fact that the father has snatched the child and disappeared shows a side to him that is less than reliable. He should have gone to the courts. So, this is something I have to do for my sister, and also for myself. Call it reparation for all the things I did wrong by her.'

'So what do you need to know that you don't already?'

Hannah could see the way Barry's mind was going. He thought she was looking for his approval of her involvement. And he was probably right.

'I guess I'd like to know how you think the family court would view it if it came to a custody battle? Both of them have a history of substance abuse but Julie is clean and on the wagon since being in hospital. I need some help and I'm hoping you know someone who can give it.'

'In my opinion, formal legal advice would be best. And, yes, I do know someone,' Barry answered, keeping his tone very neutral. 'But how does Ben feel about you doing this? You told me he didn't want you to have anything to do with your family and you had more or less agreed. What's changed?'

Hannah laughed. 'I realised I was being a superior bitch and that he was being an old bigot! Not that that matters as . . . wait for it . . . Ben might well have left me. He's run up a fortune in debts and disappeared. Gone! Hence my recent air of distraction.'

Looking stunned, Barry sat upright in his chair. 'No! Ben? He did that? Wow! I don't believe it. How could that have happened? I thought he was Mister Sensible?'

'Well, Barry, if I knew that I might not be warding off the bailiffs right now with a big stick!' Hannah laughed even though it wasn't really that funny. 'But with all the other distractions going on, I've discovered I'm less upset about it than I would have expected. I know I'm probably still in shock but at this immediate moment my priority is Katya because time is of the essence there. Her father is Spanish as is his fiancée — maybe even wife by now. They could be anywhere. We may have to use a private detective.' She paused and pulled a face. 'And I hate to say it but I'm going to have to take some time off. Is that okay? If the staff numbers are going to rise . . . '

Barry waved his hand dismissively. 'Not a problem. There comes a time when you have to think of yourself. This is just a job and you can keep it, lose it, get another one. You've only got one family. As I think you've discovered.'

'Oh, Barry!' Hannah felt almost tearful, she was so touched. 'That is very kind of you. Come on, I'll treat you to lunch at the greasy spoon over the road, if you've got time.'

She slid off the edge of his desk, went round to her own and clicked on her computer. 'Better check my emails, I suppose.' Out of Barry's line of vision she quickly logged on and typed in Sebastian's full name but nothing came up. It was a dead end, but one that she had thought was worth a try. She clicked on her emails and scanned through them before logging off again.

'Lunch it is,' Barry said as he reached for his battered old flying jacket and the record bag he used as a briefcase. 'Well, at least a coffee and a sarnie. I've got three-quarters of an hour before I have to head off to the nick and pretend I'm an appropriate adult for a change. Yet another drunken adolescent who thought he could take on the world and ended up battering someone half to death. Now, of course, his parents don't want to know so I'm it.'

As they both smiled at the irony, Barry started rummaging around in his desk drawer. 'Here, let me fish out some phone numbers for you . . . but do try and keep as much of a distance as possible, for your own sake, especially where private investigators are concerned. Then, if it all does go pear-shaped, you can step away from the situation.'

He quickly scribbled some information on a piece of paper and handed it to her. Hannah put it in her bag along with a file from her desk that she needed for the presentation she was working on.

'Thanks, Barry. You're a good friend and I appreciate the advice. Your wife and daughters are really lucky to have you.'

After a snatched lunch, Hannah drove on to the hospital to collect all the pieces of paper necessary to register her aunt's death. Her relief when they confirmed that it was from natural causes was overwhelming. She knew that it hadn't really been Julie's fault, Marian had been old and frail, but there was a part of her that had been convinced the postmortem would show something and then they would all end up in court.

It had been an unwanted thought but there just the same. Now all she wanted was to get the formalities over with. Much as she wanted to have no part in it, Hannah's conscience wouldn't allow her to shirk responsibility for the funeral so she went straight to a local undertaker whose card she had picked up in the hospital, to arrange a basic service and cremation, as soon as possible.

Then she went to the Aunt's house but this time took care to remain dispassionate as she went from room to room. The whole place would have to be gutted so she called in a clearance company she knew of that would deal with the disgusting job of stripping it bare from top to bottom and then cleaning it.

There was nothing worth salvaging in the whole house other than a box of photographs that Hannah found in her aunt's wardrobe. She really didn't want to look through to see if any of them were relevant so put them in a carrier bag to take home and store with the other stuff.

After she had finished, she pulled the filthy curtains across, locked the doors and went round to knock at the house next-door. The house that had been Gerald's.

'Hello, Jase.' Hannah said as he opened the door. 'I thought you should know that Marian Beecham died last night, probably from the shock of being taken to hospital. I've made the arrangements for the funeral if you'd like to attend. Also, the house is going to be cleared and fumigated next week . . . '

'Would you like to come in?' He stepped back and waved her into his hall. She was just about to step forward when she remembered what Julie had said. How Gerald had not only raped her in her own bed at Marian's, but how he had stopped her from going to school and made her come into this very house where he'd raped her the first time. While Aunt Marian had pottered around and tended to her precious roses, Gerald was in the adjoining house raping her niece.

Did she know? wondered Hannah. Would she really have accepted her friend raping a child? Her own niece? Hannah stepped back quickly.

'Thank you, but I'm really pushed for time today. I just wanted to let you know it'll all be cleared and fumigated, including the garden.'

'It'll be nice not to have to live with the smell and the fear of rats, but it's sad she had to die for it to happen. If she hadn't lived in such squalor, if someone had made her accept help . . . '

'Yes, well, there's nothing we can do about that now. And I really do hope you're not blaming us for her decline because you know nothing about her,' Hannah interrupted angrily. 'She was a wicked, wicked woman! And as for that disgusting pervert who lived *here* . . . '

'Hey, hey, hey!' Visibly shocked, the young man held up his hands to stop the verbal onslaught. 'All we did was try and be humane to a vulnerable old woman who lived completely on her own. The rest of it is irrelevant to us, especially as she's dead now anyway.'

Hannah's hand flew up to her mouth as she realised exactly what she was doing. 'Oh, God. I'm sorry! I really am. I don't know what came over me . . . I think it's just all hit me. You're a good person and I appreciate what you did.

Really. Now I have to go. Maybe I'll see you at the crematorium?'

'Yes, you will,' he said gently before turning back into his house and closing the door. Hannah could see that he thought her nearly as mad as her aunt had been.

Instead of going home to work, she then drove straight round to see Julie so that she could set wheels in motion to find Katya.

35

'Have a seat, Holly. I thought I'd take advantage of us both being here at the same time to have a chat with you, see how you think you're doing — especially as you've been working at the club for nearly a year now.'

Autumn was in her newly allocated office in the basement of the club and had called in Holly, one of the dancers, to talk to her. She could see the girl was both nervous and curious at being the first person to be summoned by Autumn in her new role, and her voice was noticeably strained.

'Okay.' Holly smiled cautiously. 'What do you want to know exactly?'

Autumn smiled back and leaned forward with her elbows on the desk and her fingers linked.

'Well, Holly, I'd like you to tell me how you think you're doing in the job and if you still enjoy it. I'd also like you to tell me about the new taxi company we've got the late contract with.'

She paused just long enough to let Holly visibly relax before continuing, 'Oh, and I also wondered how you feel about the house rules for the dancers. I know some of them are hard to keep to and we're going to review them shortly, but as they stand . . . ?' Autumn smiled encouragingly as if oblivious to the other girl's air of discomfort.

‘Oh, everything’s great. I love it here, and I think I get on with everyone who works here, though I don’t use the cabs that often. My boyfriend usually picks me up.’ The girl stopped talking and looked at Autumn defensively. ‘Why? Have there been complaints? Most of the punters seem to like me and I’ve got several who only want me to dance for them. Same as you always had. That’s good for the club as well, isn’t it?’

‘Of course it is. If they like you, they stay longer and spend more at the bar. But nonetheless you have to stay firmly within the rigid customer — dancer boundaries set by the club for the dancer’s own protection.’ Autumn’s tone changed slightly. She needed to get this point across. ‘Without those rules the dancers would be constantly groped and molested, both in and out of the club, and that wouldn’t be good for our reputation. This is a classy place, not a sleazy pick-up joint, and we want to keep it that way.’

Autumn studied the dancer who was nervously shredding a tissue and not making much eye-contact. Holly was back on edge, looking nervous and guilty, and Autumn knew why.

The silly girl was having an affair with a customer.

Everyone loved Holly Percy; she was a living breathing Barbie doll. She was petite and dainty with small, pretty features, wide blue eyes, and a mass of platinum-blond curls that bounced halfway down her back. Her breasts had been surgically enhanced, but not so overtly that it was glaringly obvious, and it was usually the younger men who hung around appreciatively beneath her cage when it was suspended over their heads. As a trained dancer and gymnast, she had such a breathtaking fluidity of movement that on the poles, and even in the confines of the cage, she managed to make Autumn feel quite gawky and graceless in comparison.

However, her cute and breathless girliness was an elaborate cover up for a very clever young woman who was both ambitious and ruthless. Autumn had recognised that immediately. Holly Percy was the one dancer that she knew she had to keep a close eye on; the only one who was snapping at her heels, both professionally and personally. She had spotted Holly on many occasions using her expansive charms to try to catch Leon's attention so she knew that this 'boyfriend' was merely a convenient stop gap en route to achieving her ambition of fame, fortune and a wealthy husband.

She was, however, an asset to the club and Autumn didn't want to lose her to one of their competitors. But she did want to keep her firmly in line.

'So, Holly, tell me how you see the customer — dancer boundaries? Do you understand the rules and why we have them?'

With her head down, Holly looked at Autumn through her eyelashes.

'Of course I do. We all know them. No touching or being touched, no favourites, and certainly no sex for money.'

'And no relationships with customers who still frequent the club and may therefore cause a problem. We just don't do jealous boyfriends or husbands on the premises. So . . . is there anything you want to tell me?'

After a pause, Holly sighed. 'Okay. I can see where you're going, Autumn, but surely it's not a problem if I see someone who no longer comes to the club?'

'Depends how long it's been going on, and how long it is since the punter concerned stopped coming here.'

'He doesn't come to the club any more, and I didn't meet him here anyway. I met him in Alessandro's one day after work. I was off-duty and he bought me a drink. He didn't even know I worked here and I didn't know he was a punter. I mean, they all look the same after a while, don't they?'

Autumn smiled slightly but didn't show her disbelief. 'And do you live with him?'

'Oh, no. I like my own space. He stays over sometimes but goes home at weekends. He's married.'

The challenge was there in Holly's words and Autumn knew exactly what she meant. Leon was married and Autumn was seeing *him*.

'Anyway,' Holly continued defensively, 'how do you know about him? I've been really careful, and when he did come here before, he stayed away from me. He would hang around . . . he would watch another dancer he used to fancy.'

Autumn laughed at the girl's audacity. 'I know that, Holly, and you know that I know! Anyway, just a word of warning. He is not allowed on the premises, and if the relationship goes belly-up then I don't want it impacting on the club. Understood?'

Holly visibly sighed with relief. 'Understood.'

'Now, off the record, tell me about him.'

'Well, he's older than me, has his own business, no children and is great fun. We're going on holiday soon.'

'And are you in love with him?'

'Oh, gosh, no.' Holly's laughter tinkled around the small office like delicate wind-chimes. Very annoying delicate wind-chimes. 'I like him, but that's it. It can be hard meeting the right men when we work the hours we do. Exchanging glances over the baked beans in Tesco doesn't do it for me so sometimes I make do. And Benjy is it right now.'

Autumn took a deep breath.

'So you won't be too bothered if I tell you that I know him and everything about him. His name is Ben Durman, he's a lying, cheating scumbag with no job and not a penny to his name that isn't borrowed. Oh, and he's a control freak to boot.'

Holly looked so dumbstruck, Autumn felt almost guilty for leading her into the trap. After the convertible Saab had spun away from Hannah's home with Ben in the passenger seat, Marius had noted its registration and wasted no time in finding out, via his contacts, who owned the car. Then he had told Autumn.

Bingo! Holly Percy.

'You didn't go out with him, did you?' the girl

was stammering. 'I know he liked to watch you dance . . . he had a bit of a thing about you actually, he told me. Before we got together, of course.' Holly smiled her well-practised vacuous pouty smile.

'Hardly! The most I can tell you is that he's a sort of relative. However . . . if you wish to continue seeing him away from the club it's absolutely your business, but bear in mind that Benjy is definitely not the one to buy you diamonds and whisk you off to a yacht in Monte Carlo. You'll end up dancing your little legs off to support *him*, if his past history is anything to go by.'

Holly shrugged and smiled. 'Oh, well. See how it goes. But I promise he won't come in here, and it won't affect my work. I love my job!'

'Good, good. Shall we go and grab a coffee now?' Autumn asked to signal that the subject was closed. 'I think the machine is on the go.'

* * *

Autumn had already been at the club for hours, making up for the time she had taken off, when Leon walked in. She jumped up and smiled to see him.

'Leon! You should have phoned, I'd have waited at home for you.'

As she went to put her arms around his neck, he moved back slightly.

'What's up? Has something happened?'

'I hope not. Apart from the fact that I've been away and I'm wondering why you've not been here. Melanie phoned me. Said you left them all in the lurch three times, leaving her to deal with the girls. That's not on.'

Autumn suddenly felt on edge. 'What? No hello? Nothing except for an instant bollocking? I had a family crisis — there was a death,' she replied defensively, angry at Melanie for snatching at this opportunity to try to drop her in it. Melanie had been at the club for several years and was rumoured to be furious over Autumn's promotion because she had anticipated something similar for herself.

For a moment, Leon looked sheepish. 'I'm sorry. Who died?'

'My mother's aunt. I'd never met her but . . . ' Autumn stopped mid-explanation. As soon as she said it out loud she wanted to kick herself, it sounded so stupid. If one of the girls had given that as a reason for not turning up for work, she'd have laughed at her and given her a warning. 'I'm sorry, Leon, I know that sounds weird but it was actually far more complex than it sounds. I'll explain later. Anyway, I've been here nonstop ever since so nothing has been missed or neglected.'

She smiled and reached out affectionately to touch his cheek. 'Tell me about your trip, I've missed you . . . '

His eyes narrowed as he pulled away from her again.

'Can you give a quick run-through of anything I should know about?' he asked abruptly. 'I've got a lot on today, there's so much going on right now, which is why I need you to be one hundred per cent reliable — especially when I'm not here. Dead or dying obscure family members just aren't on my radar. Especially after all the time you had off because your mother was in hospital.'

Autumn looked at him closely.

'Okay, point taken. It won't happen again,' she said. 'Now, do you want me to get you a coffee first or shall we get straight down to business?'

'Business first. Always. And I've already had coffee,' he said abruptly.

She decided that if Leon wanted everything to be businesslike then that was exactly how she would play it. She told him what had been going on and he briefed her on the two meetings coming up that he wanted her to attend in his place. She was relieved that by the time they'd covered everything he seemed more relaxed, more like his usual self.

'Shall we go home for a couple of hours? Have some rest and relaxation,' she asked with a smile as he sat back in his chair.

'Sorry, no can do. I have to go to Surrey for a few days. Half-term and all that.'

Usually when he arrived back from a trip they would fall straight into bed and make love for several hours before sharing a few verbal niceties and a cafetiere of coffee; Leon would then head off to his wife and children in the country. From there he would manage his other business interests for a few days and play at being Best Husband and Daddy before, duty done, returning to London to be with Autumn again.

Leon's wife Olivia knew all about his need for

a mistress but turned a blind eye because she loved the luxurious lifestyle that marriage had brought her. In fact, Olivia had been one of his mistresses herself for several years before her upgrade.

Autumn didn't mind about any of that. She had known the deal when she had first agreed to be his mistress, and it certainly suited her as much as it suited him. But at this moment in time she felt uncomfortable. She hated it when Leon had one of his distant phases with her; it made her very jittery and insecure, and Autumn Grayson hated nothing more than feeling insecure about anything.

'I think I'm missing something here, Leon,' she said slowly. 'Do you have a problem with me at the moment? If so I'd like to know what it is, whether it's personal or business?'

There were a few moments of silence. Eventually, Leon answered her. 'I suppose I'm just hoping I didn't make a mistake with your promotion . . . '

'Oh, right! Is this all because Melanie couldn't resist the urge to tell tales — about something I would have told you anyway? The only reason I didn't call and tell you myself was because it wasn't a problem, in my opinion. You know Melanie loves turning the knife, bloody bitch that she is.'

'Yes, she is a bitch and a notorious tell-tale.' For a second Leon seemed almost triumphant as he looked her in the eye. 'And you know that. So you shouldn't have made the mistake of giving her the opportunity to twist the knife in your back. Anyway, I have to get going. I'll call you later. I'm driving myself so feel free to use Marius if you need to — unless, of course, it means taking him away from something else.'

Again Autumn felt as if she had just been hauled over the coals by the headmaster. He stood up, leaned over the desk, kissed her chastely on the cheek as if she was just an acquaintance then turned and left, pulling the door firmly shut behind him.

Autumn had come across Leon's mood changes before. It often happened sudden and usually while he was brokering a deal and the pressure was building. He kept a cool head over business and could take a deal to the wire without blinking, but every so often the stress would overflow and he would be sharp and irritable with Autumn. She was angry with him for a few moments after he had left but quickly shrugged it off. It would soon blow over; Leon would come round again and everything would be back to normal.

As she was contemplating whether to go home or stay for another few hours it occurred to her that she may as well be hung for a sheep as a lamb. She picked up the phone and rang the firm of private investigators the club used.

'I have a private job for you. I need you to find someone for me. His name is Sebastian Rombar and he's disappeared with my little sister.'

She told Bill the PI everything she knew and then, after she had put the phone down, wondered if she had done the right thing.

It rang again.

'I've heard from Ray,' Hannah said excitedly. 'He's already over here and down in Cornwall of all places, doing some sight-seeing before he comes to London. Honestly, I was so cross he hadn't called the moment he arrived! But he wants us all to meet up so I said I'd try and arrange it as soon he lets me know when he's coming here.'

'Cornwall? Why Cornwall?'

'I don't know, I didn't ask, maybe for the surfing? He's a bloke, they're a law unto themselves, aren't they? I'm seeing Julie tomorrow. We're going to a local solicitor, so I can tell her about this then. She's coming here. I hope Ben doesn't turn up in the middle of it, I still haven't heard from him.'

'Hannah, there's something I need to talk to you about . . . '

'Go on.'

'Not on the phone. When can we meet up?'

'Tomorrow? Neil is bringing Julie so I'm assuming they'll go back after the appointment. Why can't you tell me now?' she asked curiously.

'I'm at work and I've got someone waiting to talk to me. I'll see you tomorrow.'

Autumn hung up the phone before Hannah could ask again.

36

'It was really strange. In one way it was as if we'd never been apart but in another way it was as if we were total strangers.' Julie frowned as she tried to find the right words to describe her meeting with Hannah. 'I suppose we *are* strangers and we've led such different lives . . . though Hannah's in a bit of bother at the moment with her old man. See? Its not just us scummy chavs who do it, even snobby social workers get involved with assholes as well!' Julie laughed but it quickly faded when she realised Neil hadn't joined in. In fact, Neil didn't say anything.

After Julie's physio appointment he had persuaded her to go out for a drive in the afternoon, to have a few hours away, and they had ended up sitting in his car on the almost deserted seafront at Southend, watching the small boats rocking about at anchor, and eating huge ice-cream cornets, despite the drizzling rain that had been niggling away persistently all day.

'Hannah has promised to find Katya for me. What do you reckon? I've tried. I've phoned all of Seb's friends — even his enemies — and no one has seen anything of the bastard. Certainly not since he took Katya. Someone did say he might have gone to Spain, but that may just have been for his honeymoon. The old bill don't give a toss because Seb's her father so we're going to see a solicitor tomorrow, near where Hannah lives, probably some classy geezer . . . '

'That's good. A solicitor will be able to tell you the right way to go about finding Katya. The legal way so you don't get yourself in bother.'

'Maybe. Or should I have the heavies out tracking him down? I know enough of them. I still think I should do the same as him and get a couple of goons to snatch her back.'

Neil shook his head. 'You've got to find her first and that could take a long time if you don't do it all properly. I really hope you get her back, Jules. It's vile being separated from your kids'. He looked at her then and smiled.

'I know. All the times I prayed for a night off from Jethro and Katya . . . I'd have killed for a night on the town with no worries . . . and now I've got all the time in the world on my own and I hate it.'

After a few minutes more of companionable silence while they finished their cornets, Neil sighed. 'Well, we'd better head for home. I've got to go back into work for the late ward round. I hate split shifts but at least we got a couple of hours away from the everyday bullshit of life!'

'And I need to have a shower and an early night. I've got Lady Hannah coming round tomorrow to take me to her stately pile. Hope she doesn't expect me to be impressed.'

'Do you want me to take you? I could wait outside. Save her having to drive all the way into London and back again.'

'Thanks, but better not. Hannah might take offence, she enjoys doing things like that. Do you know what? Her and Autumn between them could outdo the Pope for saint-like behaviour.' Julie was suddenly on her favourite whinge, talking faster and faster, to the point of gabbling. 'They're both so good and kind and caring they make me sick! They actually make me feel like shit on their shoes when they tippy-toe around and speak all slowly and carefully, as if I'm subnormal.' She put two fingers up to her mouth and pretended to gag. 'Stupid cows! I know more about fucking life than both of them put together with knobs on. I might be a fucking junkie but I've still got a working brain.'

'Unfair, Jules. Unfair and ungrateful, in my opinion. I don't know Hannah but she's offered to help you get Katya back, and I think you're dead lucky to have a daughter like Autumn. If my kids grow up like her, I'll be well happy.'

Julie looked at him sideways. She could feel the frustration bubbling away inside her. She knew she should pull back but she couldn't. 'And you know nothing either! You know fuck all about the real me and my life, and you know even less about Hannah and Autumn, so don't tell me I'm unfair and ungrateful! That's total bollocks.' She tossed the last little bit of her cornet out of the window and clicked her seatbelt angrily. 'Let's go, shall we?'

As they drove back to London in silence apart from the music Neil had put on, Julie was well aware that she had done exactly the opposite of what she had intended to do. She had managed to drive a wedge between Neil and herself and was deliberately pushing him further and further away when all she really wanted was to get closer to him.

Just the night before, while her ever-present insomnia had once again kept her awake, she had lain alone in bed and fantasised about her and Neil being together. She had imagined them being a proper couple, the way she had never been with anyone in her life. She could picture them together and Katya with them; she knew with certainty that Neil would be a good step-father, and imagined his children coming to stay, and then them even maybe having a baby of their own. They would all be one big happy family.

She had savoured the fantasy and wrapped herself in it warmly, yet now she was trashing it all by pushing him away as if he meant nothing, to her. She hated herself for doing it but she didn't know how to stop herself.

'Would you be able to take me to Hannah's tomorrow then?' was the best she could come up with to ease the tension. 'Just drop me off?'

'Only if you really want me to, and if you check that Hannah doesn't mind. Oh, and if you also stop treating me like I'm some sort of conniving scumbag trying to put one over on you by wanting us to spend time together! You know I just want to be with you. I don't understand why you lump me together with all the losers in your past.'

Julie noted the note of subdued anger in his voice and felt bad but still couldn't bring herself actually to apologise to him.

Instead she dug in her bag and pulled out her phone.

'Hannah says that's fine.' Julie snapped as she put it away again. 'What time are you free?'

'Day off, I told you. I'll pick you up at ten?'

'Okay.'

Neil pulled up and double parked outside her house. He went round and opened her door and then passed her the two sticks she still needed for support.

'Thanks.' Julie looked up at him and sighed. 'I'm sorry, Neil.'

'I know you are. Now chill. I'll see you tomorrow.' He kissed her gently on the mouth and then got in his car.

Julie turned back as she reached the front door but he had already pulled away.

37

The television was flickering in the corner of the room with the sound turned down. Hannah sat on the sofa with her feet up on the coffee table in almost unconscious defiance of Ben's rules and regulations; automatically she gently stroked the two purring cats curled up on her lap.

She was thinking about the way recent events had so quickly overtaken her previously calm and quiet life and turned it on its head. If she hadn't walked out into the reception office at work at that particular moment then everything could still be the same. Her life would still be with Ben and Ben alone.

Would she turn back the clock? she asked herself.

Her thoughts flitted back and forth over recent events. As she thought about her brother Ray and his phone call, she suddenly realised why he might have gone to Cornwall.

It had been on the way home from a camping holiday there that the fatal accident had occurred. Ray had been that much older than his little sisters and would, of course, have remembered everything about the crash and its aftermath. Once this idea was in her head, Hannah knew instinctively that was why he had gone there.

'Bugger, bugger, bugger!' she muttered out loud when she phoned him back on the number he had given her and got the messaging service.

'Ray, I'm sorry. I didn't realise straight away but I think I know why you're in Cornwall. Call me back as soon as you get this. Please.'

She herself had no recollection of the accident; she had tried many times to pull something out from the depths of her memory but there was nothing. She could remember Julie and herself being collected from somewhere and taken to meet Aunt Marian. The two girls had clung together like young monkeys as their aunt had been introduced; she also remembered them being pulled firmly apart by the strange woman and told not to be cry-babies.

Or rather, she thought she remembered. When she tried to analyse it, she wasn't sure if it was a real memory or a constructed one because of what had come after. She could see why Ray would want to go back, and although she was hurt he had chosen to go alone, she could understand it. The incident must have affected him deeply.

Hannah mentally shook herself back to the present. She didn't want to think about any of that at that moment; it was too much on top of everything else that was happening. She reached across the sleeping cats for her handbag and pulled out her notebook and pen to make a list of the things she would have to ask the solicitor, both about Katya and about Aunt Marian.

After much thought she had taken the decision to use the solicitor Fliss had recommended rather than the one Barry had given her the details of. It had been Fliss who had suggested it was best to keep work-life and home-life apart, to avoid unnecessary complications, and it had also been Fliss who had asked about the existence of a Will in her aunt's writing.

Although she hadn't been looking for it at the time, Hannah had gone through all her aunt's papers before authorising the house clearance and there definitely was not one, nor a copy, nor any paperwork relating to one. According to Fliss, no Will meant that Marian Beecham had died intestate and there was a strong likelihood that Hannah and Julie, as her closest living relatives, were joint beneficiaries — which meant that there was a possibility of their getting back all the money their aunt had embezzled from their trust fund.

Hannah had smiled wryly when Fliss had said this. They may never be able to right the wrong done to them in childhood but there was no denying that money would help both of them, especially Julie, who had suffered most at their aunt's, and Gerald's, hands.

Her phone beeped in her handbag and she pulled it out and checked the messages.

I'm sorry, Hannah, I've been a fool. I want to talk to you and sort things out. Can I come home? Ben.

She nearly dropped the phone and then re-read the message several times, looking for a hidden meaning. Ben had never said sorry to her for anything and yet now he was texting her like this? She didn't want to soften, didn't want to forgive him, but she also felt excited in a way.

Maybe there was a possibility they could

resolve things and start over.

Maybe Ben would change.

She texted him back.

We can talk. When?

Tomorrow?

Tomorrow 4 p.m. at home.

See you then. I really am sorry. xx

* * *

When Neil and Julie pulled up before the house the next morning, Hannah was in the front garden, sitting on the wall, nervously waiting for them. She had been out there for half an hour, listening for a car in the quiet lane; her nerves were ragged. She was scared that Julie might revert back to her old self and either not turn up or else come looking for a fight, but today her sister was all smiles as she was helped out of the car by Neil who then politely introduced himself.

'I'm not here to get in the way. I'll stay out here in the car or go for a walk so you two can talk.'

'No, that's okay, come in.' Hannah smiled, instantly taking to this man who was gently and unobtrusively giving Julie a helping hand to walk without using sticks.

She had intended to take them through into the conservatory but, scared of being seen as too formal, stopped halfway. She wanted to ask Julie which would be more comfortable, but aware that she could be risking a sharp retort just waved her hand at the dining table and chairs.

'Do you like living here?' Neil asked after he

and Julie had sat down. 'It's so peaceful. I'm used to roaring traffic and fights on the doorstep.'

'I know what you mean,' Hannah replied as she fidgeted nervously in the kitchen, juggling cups; she knew that Neil was only making small talk to defuse the awkwardness.

'I like the quiet after so many years in and around London, but it took a while to get used to. The lane is unmade further along from here so we don't get passing traffic. Good for my cats.'

'Hannah told me her cats are her babies.' There was an edge of sarcasm in Julie's voice but Neil ignored it.

'Oh, I love cats. If I didn't live alone I'd have a couple, but it's not fair with the hours I work and living in a flat. One day maybe. A house in the country, roses round the door, and a couple of cats.'

'I used to say that,' Hannah laughed.

'I used to have a dog until I went into hospital,' Julie said, 'but he lives next-door now. Disloyal mutt is happy there. Bit like Jethro . . . he's happier where he is than with me. I don't know about Katya. Knowing my luck . . . '

'Well, Katya we can deal with. We'll get her back somehow. Now shall we have a quick run-through of what we're going to say to the solicitor? Actually we've got to see two of them but they're both in the same office. One's regarding Katya, and another is a probate lawyer, regarding Aunt Marian's estate.'

'Oh, fuck off. I don't want anything to do with that.'

'That's okay, I thought you'd say that. You just have to sign something authorising me to deal with it all. You and I are the next-of-kin. There's a lot to sort out at the house, with the clearance to oversee and the funeral to pay for.'

'Just dig a pit in the back garden and chuck her in it! Let the bitch rot and the house fester away.' Julie glared at her sister, leaned back in her chair and folded her arms defiantly. Hannah had seen that sign of protest many times before.

'I know how you feel but I've got to do this properly.' She shrugged, knowing that Julie would not be shifted from her stance. Hannah didn't blame her. 'I've arranged a quick service and basic cremation but it's still going to cost. I want to do it right, want to be there and see it through, then I want us to be free to get on with our lives. They're both dead now, Aunt Marian and Gerald, and our best revenge is to be happy and forget about them.'

Julie shot her a warning look then but it was unnecessary. Hannah would never breathe a word of what her sister had told her to anyone.

She had intended to broach the subject of the suitcase's contents with her sister but she decided that would have to wait. Julie clearly wasn't ready for it today.

One step at a time.

'Is coffee okay?' she asked.

'Can we take it outside?' Julie replied. 'Me and Neil are gasping for a fag, aren't we? And I bet you don't have smelly old fags in here.'

Hannah saw Neil nudge her in rebuke and it made her smile to herself. He would be good for Julie, she just knew it.

Hannah handed them their drinks and they all went to sit outside in the sun. Hannah could see Julie getting more and more wound up as she lit one cigarette from the end of another. Her hands and feet were shifting about nervously.

'Look, all you have to do is sign two documents authorising me to act on your behalf,' Hannah said carefully, trying to calm her down. 'There's no point in getting stressed about it. It's not worth it. I can deal with it all. I want to . . . '

'I just hate all this formal shit. I'll end up telling them to fuck off and that'll upset them.'

Neil took her hand. 'This is different, it's not like in court. I'll come with you. I'll sit in the waiting room and we can go straight home afterwards, if that's what you want.'

But when they got to the solicitor's, Julie got as far as the reception area then refused to go in and see anyone; Hannah took the papers out to her and, as the lawyers watched from a distance, Julie quickly signed them. She handed them back to Hannah and then, like a scalded cat, jumped straight out of her seat and grabbed on to Neil's arm, nearly pulling him over. 'We're going now, I've had enough, and I don't want to fight with Hannah, which I will if I stay. Why should that disgusting old woman have even a half-decent funeral? Why? She deserves nothing.'

Tears welled up in her eyes and Hannah's also.

'I know, but it's the right thing to do for us.

But I'll handle it. Don't you worry about it. Please? Let it go now.'

Hannah held her arms out and, after a moment's hesitation, Julie stepped forward into them and started sobbing. The small waiting room was empty bar the receptionist who tactfully looked down at her keyboard as Neil stepped back from the two sisters.

'It'll all be okay, Julie, I promise you, I promise you, I promise you . . . ' Hannah sobbed too as Julie clung to her. 'I promise.'

* * *

By the time Autumn arrived, Hannah had pulled herself together and was feeling upbeat despite everything. For the first time she believed there was a chance that she and Julie would be okay. She gave Autumn a brief summary of what had happened at the solicitor's office and reassured her that she would be acting in Julie's best interests. Hannah was paranoid about being seen as anything other than completely honest.

'I know that, Hannah.' Autumn smiled at her. 'And I'm so pleased there's finally a light at the end of the tunnel for you and Ma. She so needs someone like you in her life.'

'Thank you, Autumn. That is so nice to hear. And I will do my best to find Katya. Now I have Julie's permission, I can take it up at the office formally.'

'That's good. Between us both we may get somewhere. I've got a ruthless investigator who sometimes does work for the club out looking for

Seb. Fingers crossed, eh? Hopefully we can do it legally. If not, then so what, eh?'

'Was that what you wanted to talk about?' Hannah smiled at her niece who was suddenly looking decidedly uncomfortable.

'No, it wasn't. I want to talk to you about Ben . . . '

'Oh, right,' Hannah laughed. 'Well, that's weird because I heard from him last night. He's coming round later and we're going to talk. I don't know what will happen but he apologised, which is a first . . . '

'Hannah, stop right there! I have to tell you something. You won't like it but you need to know.'

38

'I don't believe you,' Hannah said after Autumn had told her about Ben and the club and, of course, Holly. 'That just isn't Ben. He wouldn't go to a club like that, and he wouldn't have an affair. He's not like that . . . '

'I'm sorry, Hannah, but you said that about his job and the money and he was like that then. But at least this explains it. He was spending all the money in the club and then going home with his girlfriend.'

Hannah couldn't take in what her niece was saying. She looked at her and tried to work out what ulterior motive Autumn could have for saying the things she just had. Ben spending all his money . . . *their* money . . . at a lap-dancing club? On a girlfriend he then spent half the week with?

'Nope. I'm not having it. Sorry, Autumn, but you have the wrong person. You've never met Ben so how would you know? And it's just too much of a coincidence that he would go to the club you work in. There are hundreds of them.'

'Not really. Ours is one of the top places in London. I'd bet a month's salary that he first visited with a group of drunken jack the lads from work. All 'Wah-hey!' and 'Get 'em off!' That's often how it starts. Most of them only ever visit under those circumstances, but there's always one or two who get addicted to it. It's like gambling . . . ' She stopped and looked at Hannah who was trying hard to hold herself together. 'I saw the photo of him. That one.' Autumn pointed through to the sitting room. 'It is him. I'm sorry. I thought you should know.'

'I need some space,' Hannah said and walked out into the garden, leaving Autumn inside.

Not Ben, she thought as she walked as far away from the house as she could. But then she thought, Why not Ben? He had lied to and deceived her about his job and their money. Why not take the extra step and have an affair as well?

After she had calmed down, she walked back into the house and saw that Autumn was sitting in exactly the same position.

'I tell you what, Autumn, Ben's coming round at four and I want you to be here, too. I want to see what happens. Will you do that, and stay out of sight while I ask him about this? If you're sure it's him and he's not telling the truth then we can confront him. If it isn't him then you'll admit it. Deal?'

Hannah pulled her phone out and clicked on to messages. 'Look. This is what he sent me. Why bother if he'd sooner be with someone else?'

Autumn stayed silent.

'Come on. Why would he want to come home if he's doing what you said he's doing?'

'Let's wait and see,' Autumn said sadly. 'Maybe you're right and I'm wrong.'

* * *

As soon as they heard the car pull up, Autumn ducked into the utility room that linked the house to the garage while Hannah opened the front door.

Ben leaned forward to kiss her but she quickly backed off. Instead of making a comment, he just walked through to the kitchen and sat down.

'Well?' Hannah asked, trying not to sound too angry. She wanted to sort this out properly. 'I can't be bothered to go all round the houses so are you going to tell me what's been going on? I've been off my head with worry about you, about our finances, our marriage . . . '

'I know.'

'No, you don't, Ben. So much has happened and you weren't here to support me. Isn't that what marriage is about? Supporting each other?'

He shrugged and pulled at his mouth nervously, which really bemused Hannah. This wasn't the man she had been married to for so long. All the usual brashness was gone and he looked decidedly unhappy.

'Tell me then,' she suggested.

'I got into a hole I couldn't get out of. I had to leave the firm because I did something really stupid and didn't want to tell you, so I pretended everything was fine. That was the start of it. It just snowballed.'

'Where did you stay when you weren't here?' she asked curiously.

'With one of the blokes I used to work with. He understood what had happened and what I was doing. He told me I was a twat but I didn't know how to stop it once I'd started.'

‘Why did you have to leave work? Did you embezzle some money or something?’ Hannah took a shot in the dark.

‘No, I didn’t embezzle anything, I wouldn’t do that.’ He looked hurt as he said it. ‘A group of us took some clients to a club in London, a smart club. I got drunk, behaved idiotically and got thrown out. The clients were horrified, the boss was furious, and I had to leave. That was it.’

Hannah knew that the bare bones of the story were true, but she also knew that he was being very economical with the details. She could feel herself shrinking inside as she realised that Autumn had been telling the truth.

‘Not that long ago you were saying you wanted shot of me. What’s changed?’

‘I’ve realised that I still want to be with you,’ he answered, without once looking at her. Instead he feigned interest in one of the tablemats in front of him.

‘Why? Why do you want to be with me? You said I was fat and useless and doing a crap job . . . you said you didn’t even like me. Not that I didn’t know that already.’

She noticed that he had the good grace to look guilty even though he was still trying to bluff it out.

‘Look, what is it with all the questions? I’ve told you what happened and I’ve said I’m sorry. Is that worth wrecking our marriage for? One little mistake?’

Hannah couldn’t help it. She laughed.

‘One little mistake? More like a bloody great line of them! I’m sure you are sorry, Ben, but not because of me. You're sorry for yourself because Holly dumped you and you've got nowhere else to go. Did you think that a pretty young girl like that, a girl young enough to be your daughter, wanted you as a permanent fixture in her life? You're such an idiot, do you know that?'

The look of horror on his face told her that it was all true.

'How . . . ?'

'Autumn, you can come out now,' she shouted.

The door to the utility room opened and Ben looked like a cornered animal as Autumn stood in the doorway. 'Well, well, if it isn't one of our best customers. Hello, Ben.'

'What are you doing here?' he demanded as soon as he realised exactly who she was.

Hannah smiled. 'Let me introduce you to my niece, Autumn — the one you referred to as 'Slappers R Us' not long ago. Well, such a slapper you couldn't stay away from her and her friends and actually shagged one of them . . . '

To her amazement Hannah saw that Ben's eyes were wide open and damp and his chin was quivering. She thought he was going to cry, and suddenly she couldn't bear it. Despite everything, she just couldn't bear the fact that he was hurting so much even though she knew it wasn't to do with her. Ben was besotted with Holly. He had been sucked into the whole thing and was devastated that she had dumped him.

'Autumn, can you leave us alone for a bit?' she asked her niece quietly.

'Of course. I have to go anyway, I have to get

back to work, so I'll call a cab and wait outside. Phone me later, eh?'

'I will, Autumn. Thanks.' Hannah smiled at her appreciatively and waited till the front door shut.

'Oh, Ben, how could you be such a fool?' As she looked at him and saw his sheer misery she wanted to hug him and make everything better.

'They say there's no fool like an old fool.' He tried to smile but it wasn't in him. Hannah could see how deflated he was. She knew their marriage was over, but she also knew she couldn't just chuck out her husband with nowhere to go and no money.

'Can we make it right? Can I come back?' he asked her.

'I doubt we can make it right, in fact I know we can't, but you can come back for the time being. In the spare room. We have to try and make sense of our finances and there's other stuff going on right now for me. I'll explain it all when I'm not so angry with you.' Again she stared at him.

'How could you do that to me? Wasn't I good enough?'

Ben said nothing, just looked at her.

'Go and get your stuff out of the car and I'll see what's in the freezer for dinner. Then I want to know everything. Not about you and Holly, or Autumn for that matter, I can already imagine far more than I want to about that. But about our finances.' She touched his arm. 'And I'm sorry about Holly. Really I am.'

She saw a tear start to form in the corner of his eye and looked away.

39

The day of the funeral had dawned warm and sunny. Hannah was horrified. She had wanted it to be pouring with rain. She had wanted it to be as miserable and cold as Marian Beecham herself had been.

She stood with Autumn under the canopy at the entrance to the building and waited for the hearse to arrive. On the opposite side of the entrance stood her aunt's neighbour Jase with a pretty young girl beside him. They acknowledged each other but that was it. There were a few other locals Hannah vaguely recognised, maybe neighbours, maybe professional mourners, but she had no intention of getting involved in the usual funeral commiserations. To her mind that really would be hypocritical.

Autumn had offered to support Hannah at the funeral and she had accepted gratefully, knowing that the young woman was strong enough to weather it whereas Julie was not.

After what seemed like hours but was only a few minutes the hearse finally arrived straight from the funeral home and they all watched as the undertakers lifted the coffin out and carried it inside towards the plinth. Just one small spray of white lilies lay on top. Hannah guessed they were from Jase. She appreciated the gesture even though she hadn't been able to do the same herself.

Hannah obeyed the rules of mourning. She and Autumn walked slowly behind and the others followed. As they took their seats the undertakers moved back and the vicar stepped forward.

Hannah had agreed with a local vicar that there would be no eulogy, no praise for a wonderful woman sadly missed, and no service as such. There were just the formal words and an accompanying prayer as the coffin slid out of sight and the dark red velvet drapes fell silently across. The whole ceremony from start to finish took barely ten minutes.

As the curtains closed, Hannah sat for a moment, imagining the flames licking around Marian Beecham and turning her into a pile of ash. Once again, as when she had seen her in the hospital, Hannah felt no emotion, just a sense of overpowering relief.

The Aunt was completely gone from their lives.

Hannah and Autumn sat silently side by side for a few moments more before both standing up at the same time and walking outside. Politely they shook hands with those they didn't know and then Hannah kissed Jase affectionately.

'You're a good person, Jase. Thank you. I'll pop in for a coffee next time I'm near, if that's all right with you.'

Autumn had arranged with Leon that they could use Marius. As soon as the car pulled up they climbed in and left.

'Well, that's it. Maybe Julie can start to mend now,' Hannah said.

'I hope so. Why did she hate the man next-door so much as well?' Autumn asked curiously, nearly catching Hannah off guard. Quickly she worked out a neutral reply.

'Julie linked them together. He was a weak old man who, after his wife died, let himself be sucked in and ruled by a conniving old spinster who saw pound signs on his forehead. Of course Marian achieved what she wanted when she got everything he owned after he died.' She took Autumn's hand and held it tightly.

'I wonder how Julie is? She had a check-up today with the consultant.'

'I know. How's Ben?'

'Heartbroken. I know you think I'm a daft old woman but I feel sorry for him. We have to sort out a peaceful break-up. In the meantime he's taken to his bed like a lovesick teenager, poor man.'

'He'll get over it.' Autumn's tone was very matter-of-fact. She leaned forward. 'Marius, have you remembered we have to pick something up?'

'We do?' Hannah looked at her.

'We do, and then we're going to Ma's.'

A few minutes later, Marius stopped the car outside a big old house and Autumn jumped out. Hannah watched intently as the front door opened and a young woman came out, carrying a small suitcase in one hand and holding a child with the other.

Katya.

The child jumped straight into Autumn's arms and she whisked her up in the air and kissed her several times all over her face and neck before carrying her to the car.

'Wave bye-bye to Ciara,' Autumn said. 'Blow her a big kiss and then we're going to take you home to Mummy who's all better.' Again she leaned forward and told Marius where to go.

'Okay,' Hannah said, 'are you going to explain?'

'Briefly because of little ears. My men found them, and once Seb realised that it wasn't such a good idea after all, he arranged for this handover. Apparently, Ciara had never been happy about it. Now she's pregnant herself and they're going back to Spain with his mummy and daddy to where her mummy and daddy live. Happy families all round.'

'Where was Seb just then?' Hannah asked, trying to disguise her irritation at being upstaged by Autumn.

'Inside. Pissed off and suffering from hurt pride, but that's about it. However,' she leaned over and whispered, 'I really don't want Ma to know this was anything to do with me. I mean, it was you who found out the information about the right way to go about it . . . '

'But then you went and did it the wrong way.'

'No, I didn't,' Autumn snapped. 'What I did wasn't illegal. Seb agreed to her going back to Ma. This was all you, you, you! I'm so tired of being in trouble with Ma for everything, you can take the blame this time!'

Hannah looked at the little girl who was strapped in between them but clutching at Autumn and felt more choked than she could have imagined.

'Now you stay at the gate with Aunty Hannah, we're going to surprise Mummy,' Autumn said to the child as they got out of the car and she ran to the front door and banged on it loudly.

A few seconds later, Julie flung the door back. 'What the f — '

'Surprise!' Autumn cried as Hannah let go of the child's hand and she ran straight to Julie.

'Mummy, Mummy!'

Autumn smiled as it all went on. 'I'm going to have to get back now but I'll be round tomorrow to see how everyone is. 'Bye, Katya. 'Bye, Ma. 'Bye, Hannah. Give me a call when you're ready to go home and Marius will collect you.'

Hannah shook her head in disbelief as she followed Julie and Katya into the house, unsure whether to be angry with Autumn or grateful to her.

Once inside Julie looked at Hannah over the top of Katya's head.

'Thank you.'

'It wasn't just me,' Hannah replied guiltily.

'It doesn't matter. You promised I'd get her back and I have.'

'Julie, please don't forget about Autumn. You are so lucky to have her, she's a wonderful daughter and she adores you . . . '

'I know. I'll be nice to her, I promise.'

She grinned and Hannah could see the old Julie then. The mischievous little sister she had adored all her life despite everything.

'Oh, I'm so glad we got it all sorted. Everything,' Hannah said. 'I've missed you so much'.

'Me too, Hanny. Me too.'

* * *

A few days later they were all together again en route to Cornwall to meet up with Ray.

The sun was shining, there wasn't too much traffic and everyone was in a good mood, even Julie who was sitting in the back with Hannah and Katya. Autumn was in the front with Marius.

After several stops and a full day on the road, they pulled up into the grounds of a large luxury hotel set on a hill looking out over the beach near Newquay. As the car stopped they saw Ray sitting on a bench by the sweeping stone steps, waiting.

Hannah ran straight to him and hugged him. Julie followed, albeit less enthusiastically. Ray was a stranger to her.

'Well, hello there, my little baby sisters. Long time no see, huh? And this must be Autumn and little Katya . . . hey, aren't you two just gorgeous? Must take after your mummy.'

The ice was broken.

They all spent the night at the hotel catching up on as much as they could in an evening and then, the following day, after lunch at the hotel, they all left to head for home.

A third of the way back, Ray leaned forward. 'This is it.'

Marius pulled the car over into the next layby and Ray, Hannah and Julie got out. 'I've checked it all out,' Ray said, 'and it was just over there. See that break in the railings? Near there . . . '

There was no way to get over to the centre of the road safely so they walked to the end of the layby and stopped.

'This will do. Just here. It's parallel.'

Ray had a small trowel in one hand and a beautifully crafted wooden cross in the other that he had had made in Cornwall.

'Better late than never,' he said as he bent over and dug a small hole. He pushed the cross into the ground and made sure it was stable.

Carved on it in plain script were the words: 'Mum and Dad. Always to be remembered by your children Raymond, Hannah and Julie. RIP'.

Standing together, the three looked down at the wooden cross standing upright by the side of the road, aware that it wasn't just a memorial to their parents but also recognition of the bond between the three siblings that had been stretched to its limits but never severed.

They still had a long way to go and they all had to go back to their own lives and resolve their own problems, but at that moment nothing mattered more to them all than each other.

For several minutes they stood silently, each wrapped in their own thoughts and oblivious to the noise of the traffic rushing by, until Ray reached out and wrapped an arm around both his sisters. 'I feel so happy right now. Bitter-sweet happy maybe, but happy nonetheless. How's about we spend some time now really getting to know each other? It's taken long enough already.'

Unable to speak, Hannah and Julie nodded and together they walked back the car.

They all looked back as Marius pulled out into the busy stream of traffic; a new and different life was beckoning each of them and they were ready for it.

Other titles published by
The House of Ulverscroft:

PAST CHANCES

Bernardine Kennedy

Abandoned by her mother, Eleanor spent her childhood in constant fear of her father's erratic behaviour. She's desperate to leave home and live independently like so many other girls in the seventies. When her best friend Marty, who works with her in a London hotel, invites her to share a house with him and the glamorous Megan and Venita, it's her chance to break free. But when Eleanor confronts her father with the news his reaction is catastrophic. And despite the support and guidance of her new friends, Eleanor cannot cope. Her rush into a love affair takes her down an ever more destructive path. Will Eleanor find the strength to take charge of her life or is it destined to spiral out of control?